D1173818

The Advocate

The Advocate

A NOVEL

LARRY AXELROOD

Cumberland House
Nashville, Tennessee

Published by Cumberland House Publishing, Inc., 431 Harding Industrial Drive, Nashville, TN 37211

Cover design: Unlikely Suburban Design
Text design: Mary Sanford

Library of Congress Cataloging-in-Publication Data is available.

ISBN 1-58182-137-9

Printed in the United States of America
1 2 3 4 5 6 7—05 04 03 02 01 00

To my mom and dad, Helen and Jack Axelrood,
who gave me life, love, and direction.

To my wife, Anne Sherman, my daughter Claire,
and my son Jack, who give my life meaning,
purpose, and joy.

Acknowledgments

My appreciation to Joel Greenberg, Nancy Sidote Salyers, James Linn, Rick Mottweiler, and Mark Rakoczy for teaching me how to try a case. A special thank you to the late Joan Corboy, who was always there for me.

Thanks to Stephen Connolly, Sheila Klee, Mary Sanford, Julia Jayne, Jennifer Martin, and Stacie Kutzbach for their help. My love to Anne Sherman, my toughest editor.

And deepest gratitude to Ron Pitkin for sharing my vision.

ONE

Some lawyers believe you can predict a verdict by the way the jurors file back into the courtroom. If they look at the defendant on the way in, they've acquitted him. If they look down at their feet and refuse to make eye contact, they've found him guilty. After over thirty years of trying cases, Darcy Cole didn't buy into that theory. As he stood watching the jury walk back into the courtroom, he felt a familiar surge of adrenaline coursing through his body. This was the moment of anticipation he lived for, and he wondered if the people in the first few rows of the spectator's gallery could hear his heart beating.

He glanced across the aisle at the prosecutors. Maureen Conroy, the lead prosecutor, was about forty, give or take a few years. Experienced and talented, she had given a great closing argument. She made a case filled with common sense and righteous indignation, pointing out why Lynne Tobias was a cold-hearted, calculating black widow who should be convicted of conspiracy to murder her older, wealthier husband.

The trial had been an old-fashioned slugfest. Darcy had gone toe to toe with Conroy and her partner, Michael Silverman, with Brian Ashman, the judge, stepping in as a referee to separate them in the clinches.

Darcy had hammered the jury with a few key points, the first being that the real killer, Mark Thomas, had been seen riding his bike from the scene of the shooting. A witness followed in his car as Thomas rode to an alley, where he dumped the bike and got into a car. The witness then used a cell phone to call the police. As the witness watched from his own car a safe distance away, the police converged on the car Thomas was driving.

After his arrest, Thomas was questioned for close to twenty-seven hours before he confessed to killing Charles Tobias. During that time, he failed to mention Lynne Tobias once. Nine weeks after his arrest, after consulting with his lawyer, Thomas cut a deal for a significantly reduced sentence in exchange for his testimony against Lynne.

There were other inconsistencies Darcy used to cast doubt on the state's case. He picked apart their theory about motive, working from the start of Charles and Lynne's relationship. Charles had been the pursuer and was used to getting whatever he wanted. In the beginning, he had wanted Lynne. Darcy tried to prove to the jury that moneywise, Charles' death would have been the worst thing possible for Lynne. He cast Lynne as a young woman who gave up a lot to marry Charles. A vasectomy years ago meant they would not have children. She hadn't even been able to finish law school because of the demands of being Mrs. Tobias.

Charles Tobias had been a founding partner of Tobias, Ryan, and Vanek, one of Chicago's more powerful and politically connected firms. It handled class action litigation as well as plaintiff's personal injury and medical malpractice. All were huge moneymakers.

Social events were viewed as obligations for the busy couple. Everything they did revolved around clients or work. Lynne was a dutiful wife who loved her husband and worked hard at meeting all of his needs.

Darcy had built a gentle rapport with the jury. He knew they looked to him for guidance and he gave it to them. He had the ability to ask the questions the jury wanted to hear. Explain the legal details without being condescending; speak to the jury in a conversational manner. He had an air of credibility about him. Tall and lean, he was handsome but not pretty; his black hair had mostly given way to gray. Most important, his deep voice filled the courtroom without effort. The jury leaned into him when he spoke and gave him their full attention. Whenever he made an important point, many of the jurors took notes. He liked his chances for an acquittal.

Still, the prosecution had savagely attacked Lynne's character, portraying her as a manipulative opportunist. She had allegedly destroyed a happy marriage so she could live the life of a wealthy woman. After a brief courtship, Charles Tobias had moved out of his Winnetka home and into the arms of Lynne in a luxury Gold Coast condominium overlooking Lake Michigan. Their impending marriage was problematic, though: The groom to be was still married and had children who were slightly older than his fiancée. But after a long and angry divorce, Charles married Lynne in a small ceremony at the Union League Club, officiated by a state supreme court judge. According to the prosecutors, Lynne quit law school because it was no longer necessary. As Mrs. Charles Tobias, she had wealth, status, and freedom.

Their brief married life was dominated by social activities. Lynne networked furiously and climbed through Chicago's elite circles, using every opportunity provided by her marriage.

James Ryan and Peter Vanek, Charles's partners and his friends since law school, suddenly became unavailable for social activities and weekend events. Clearly their first wives—to whom they were still married—had no desire to spend time with the trophy wife of their friend Charles.

Lynne took this as a direct threat. Charles's partners were trying to break up the marriage. If they were able to convince Charles that the relationship was a mistake, Lynne was on her way to being cut off.

But the prosecution also asserted that Charles had figured out Lynne's game. After a short marriage, without children, Lynne would not get much from a divorce settlement. The only way to cash in would be if Charles died while they were still married. Lynne would get the life insurance proceeds and access to the joint assets.

Eighteen months after their wedding, tragedy struck. Charles was behind the wheel of his Mercedes at a stoplight when a young man on a bicycle rode up next to him and fired six shots into the car, striking Charles four times and killing him instantly. This was the only thing both sides agreed on.

Peter Vanek, a longtime friend of Charles, had been a high-ranking justice department official during the Nixon and Ford years. He stepped in and pressured the authorities to find a link between Lynne Tobias and Mark Thomas.

Mark Thomas seemed an unremarkable person. He had grown up in the city and attended public schools. He did a short stint in the military, then spent civilian life working as a plumber's assistant. He did, however, have a remarkable story to tell: He said he had been paid by Lynne Tobias to kill her husband.

Darcy had done his best to disprove Thomas' story, reminding the jury that, most important, Thomas' testimony was purchased with promises of leniency. Now he waited to see if he had been successful.

The jury had finished filing back into the box, each juror standing attentively. Judge Ashman asked them to sit down, except for the foreperson, who stood holding a few pieces of folded paper.

Darcy hadn't bothered to look at the jurors as they

returned with their verdict. He knew it had been close, and he didn't know whether he had been able to persuade them. Lynne Tobias and the rest of her life was in their hands.

Judge Ashman spoke up. "Madame Foreperson, has the jury reached a verdict?"

"It has, Your Honor," came the reply.

"Could you hand the verdict forms to the sheriff's deputy, please?"

A blue-uniformed deputy retrieved the forms and walked them back to the judge.

Darcy looked at his client. Lynne was in her early thirties, with short dark hair, light blue eyes, and a cold smile. She wore a conservative blue suit and a white blouse. Her fresh manicure gave her a clean, efficient look. Her gaze was fixed on the verdict forms as they traveled from the deputy to the judge. Darcy could not detect any emotion on her part. In fact, the only emotion she ever seemed to show was annoyance. She was contemptuous not of the threat to her freedom, but of being judged by those she deemed beneath her.

Judge Ashman unfolded the verdict forms, looked them over, and counted the signatures, his face revealing no emotion of its own. He then handed them to the clerk and said, "Madame Clerk, would you publish the verdict?" Then the judge turned to the crowded courtroom and said, "Ladies and gentleman, there will be three verdicts read, and I want no outburst of any kind. Any outburst will result in your being removed and possibly held in contempt of this court."

The clerk was an elegant black woman who Darcy had known for years. She was in her early sixties. Her white hair was immaculately coifed in a style from years past. She moved in a deliberate, graceful manner, as if she had once attended a finishing school. She placed her bifocals on the bridge of her nose and in a loud, clear voice began to read the verdicts. "We, the jury, in the case of *People of the State of Illinois v. Lynne Tobias,* find the defendant, Lynne Tobias, not guilty of solicitation to commit first-degree murder."

The intensity heightened as everyone waited for the other two verdict forms to be read.

"We, the jury, in the case of the *People of the State of Illinois v. Lynne Tobias,* find the defendant not guilty of first degree murder."

Finally she read the last verdict form. "We, the jury, in the case of the *People of the State of Illinois v. Lynne Tobias,* find the defendant not guilty of conspiracy to commit first-degree murder."

There was a rush of movement as reporters shot out of the courtroom to get to the telephone or to pull out their cell-phones. A faint smile moved over Lynne's face as she grasped Darcy's hand and gave it a little squeeze. Michael Silverman sat back in his chair, clearly deflated, while Maureen Conroy stared straight ahead with her teeth clenched.

Judge Ashman slammed his gavel on to the bench and said, "Court adjourned. Defendant discharged." He glanced at Darcy, and gave him a look that said, "You may have fooled the twelve in the box, but you didn't fool me."

Darcy turned to his client. "Let's go, Lynne. It's time to leave."

She actually looked shaken at this point, and Darcy helped her to her feet. As they moved toward the aisle, Maureen Conroy rose and took a step toward Darcy, stretching her hand out. "Congratulations, Darcy. Thanks for the education."

Darcy shook her hand. "Regardless of the verdict, Ms. Conroy, you and your partner did an excellent job."

"That's nice of you to say, Darcy. Too bad there's no prize for second place."

Michael Silverman just sat there stunned.

As Darcy and Lynne left the courtroom, reporters just out-side the doors began screaming questions at them. Darcy had Lynne by the arm, and he walked her toward the elevator bank where they waited, holding off all questions; in deference to the court and opposing counsel, as a general rule, all post-trial interviews were done away from the courtroom. In the forty seconds it took for the elevator to get to the first floor the reporters peppered Darcy with questions, none of which he acknowledged. When the elevator doors opened, he stepped out with Lynne, and they walked down the corridor with the reporters in tow, their questions becoming louder, their pleas more desperate.

As they reached the breezeway, the television lights popped on and reporters with microphones encircled Darcy, blocking his exit from the building. He stopped with Lynne on his arm and stepped up to a bank of microphones. Waiting a moment for the reporters to quiet down, he fired his first salvo. "I hope those of you in the news media who were gathered here to watch the trial will report on the acquittal of Ms. Tobias with as much energy as you did when the lurid charges were made by the state."

The shouting began. The first question that stuck came from a reporter from Channel 9 News. "Do you expect the federal government to prosecute Ms. Tobias?"

Darcy looked the reporter in the eye. "You can always expect Owen Dempsey to jump into anything that would give his run for governor more publicity. If he chooses to try to get around my client's double jeopardy rights under the United States Constitution in order to pontificate and strut in front of the cameras before the primary, then I recommend he come prepared for battle. We will defeat these charges in any forum, in any courtroom in the country."

The focus of the news conference suddenly shifted from Lynne Tobias's acquittal to the personal animosity between Darcy Cole and Owen Dempsey, the United States attorney for the Northern District of Illinois. Darcy was off and running.

"Dempsey has made it clear that he wants to be the next governor of the state of Illinois. He is going to use his office to gain exposure among the voters—exposure he doesn't have to pay for. I find that abhorrent.

"As I said before," he continued, "if he chooses to indict Ms. Tobias for the same crimes of which she's just been acquitted, I'll meet him any place, any time. But I don't want him to send his lackeys. I want him to try the case head to head. That is, if he knows how to try a case."

The reporters ate it up, but Darcy always knew when to quit. He ended the press conference abruptly and led Lynne away by the arm. This time, though, she pulled away, and they walked side by side through the plaza to a waiting van.

"Nice, Darcy," Lynne said sarcastically. "Is this the firm's limo?"

"Oh, cheer up, Lynne," Darcy replied. "He had it washed for you."

Darcy opened the rear door, and Lynne stepped into the van and sat in a captain's chair. Darcy shut the door and popped into the front passenger seat. "Let's get out of here," he said to the driver.

The van began to move. "You remember Collata, don't you?" Lynne nodded. The driver looked in the rearview mirror to catch her eye. "Congratulations, ma'am," he said, nodding once. Collata was a retired Chicago cop who now worked as a private investigator, almost exclusively for Darcy. He was a big man with a thick neck, broad shoulders, and an ample gut. His shaved head and goatee made him even more intimidating.

A news radio car followed directly behind them. The stoplight at the corner was green, but Collata stopped, waiting until the light turned yellow, then red. Then he ran the red light, leaving the news radio car behind. They cruised along without anyone following them, down the boulevard, through the park, and onto the expressway. Collata stomped on the gas pedal, and the van shot down the entrance ramp onto the expressway headed into downtown. He cracked his window, pushed in the lighter, and pulled a cigarette from behind his ear, offering it to Lynne. She shook her head in disgust and pulled her own pack from her purse. She did accept Collata's lighter, though.

They rode in silence and smoke until they got to the condo building that had once been the marital home of Lynne and

Charles Tobias. A uniformed doorman approached the van with curiosity, and Darcy stepped out and opened the rear door. The doorman looked shocked as Ms. Tobias stepped out. She ignored him and instead stared bashfully at Darcy, as if they were at the end of some strange, long date. The only thing she said was "I'll call you."

Darcy watched her until she was out of sight, slammed the rear door and hopped back in. "Where to, boss?" Collata asked.

"Any place I can get single-malt Scotch, my friend," he said, ripping off his tie.

Collata reached across and opened the glove box, in which rested a bottle of single malt; he handed it to Darcy. Darcy chuckled and put the bottle back into the glove box. "I'll tell you what," he said, laughing, "I need someplace a little bit more upscale."

Collata took one last, deep pull on his cigarette, burning it down to his fingers, and threw the filterless butt out the window. "No problem," he said. "I know just the place."

"Just make sure this one has a bathroom."

TWO

The gym at the club did not technically open until 6:30 in the morning, but Darcy was always in the pool by 6:15. He had a strong, compact stroke, and he breathed on alternating sides every third pull. He still did the flip turns he had perfected years earlier.

Every morning he did his laps, his angular body cutting through the silence of the otherwise empty pool. This was his time. It wasn't so much about the exercise as it was about the solitude. There were no phone calls to take, no pagers going off. He was out of reach of everyone, and he used this time to decompress.

He sliced through the water quickly, pushing himself as hard as he could for a full thirty minutes, until the waterproof watch on his wrist beeped. At this point he threw his arms over the rope and pulled off his goggles. Darcy was seven months short of his fifty-eighth birthday, but at times like this he felt much younger. That's why he did it.

He floated on his back a minute, letting his heart rate slow. He then heard the slap of feet on the pool deck and looked up to see a bankruptcy judge waddling toward him, his ample frame spilling out over his swimming trunks. They had exchanged pleasantries in the past but had never had an actual conversation. This time the judge had a broad smile on his face. "Mr. Cole, congratulations on your case. But, more important, I loved what you said about Owen Dempsey."

As the judge climbed down the ladder and into the water, an air bubble formed in his swimming trunks, and he appeared to float there like some hairy buoy. He adjusted his goggles and looked down at Darcy. "Yes, sir. I wish I had the guts to say those things."

Darcy pulled himself out of the pool. "Thank you, Your Honor," he said, stifling a chuckle. He proceeded to the locker room and yanked his suit off. Throwing on a bathrobe, he went down to the steam room, where he picked up a *Sun-Times* and a *Tribune*. The headline in the *Tribune* said "Tobias Widow Acquitted." The *Sun-Times* was a bit flashier with "Black Widow Beats the Rap." The *Tribune* described Darcy's trial tactics as "aggressive, insightful, and well argued." The *Sun-Times* found him "lean and ruggedly handsome, with a baritone voice that seduced the entire courtroom." Both descriptions were fine with Darcy.

He continued to read. There were sidebars on the major participants and a complimentary bit on Judge Ashman, as well as an article on the two prosecutors, Conroy and Silverman. Darcy's article had virtually no personal information; it spoke only of the battles won and lost over the years. The sidebar on Lynne Tobias was a scathing summary that referred to her as an "opportunistic young woman who had destroyed a family."

Darcy leaned his head back against the warm, wet tile wall. His eyes were closed, and sweat was pouring from him as he listened to the silence, broken only by the sound of the steam escaping from the valve. He let the steam purge his body of the previous night's Scotch. It was rare that Darcy went out. Most of his life was spent in court, in his office, or at the club. The Union League Club was directly across the street from his office, not more than a hundred feet away. Across the street on the diagonal was the federal courthouse. Darcy's condo was three miles north of the office. He was almost always in one of these three buildings. While there was a certain amount of comfort to the routine, it did little to stimulate him emotionally.

His thoughts were broken when he heard the door open. "Darcy, are you in there?"

It was Darcy's associate, Patrick O'Hagin. He was wearing gray slacks, a blue-button down shirt with a tie, no jacket. Darcy was annoyed. "Patrick, why are you here?"

"Darcy, you aren't going to believe this."

"Tell it to me slowly and use few words."

"Lynne Tobias just got arrested."

"What?" Darcy asked, frowning more at the interruption than the news itself.

"The U.S. marshals, FBI, a collection of Fed boys," O'Hagin answered.

"I didn't think they would move so fast. What's the status of the case?" Darcy asked.

"Detention hearing at two o'clock before Magistrate Wilfredo Martinez," O'Hagin replied excitedly.

"Not a bad draw," Darcy commented.

"Boss, there's one more thing," Patrick said, as if he were about burst. "Owen Dempsey and Anna Minkoff are having a press conference about the case at ten o'clock."

Darcy toweled off his face, then rubbed the sweat out of his short gray-and-black hair. "Well," he said, "I think we ought to get a positive spin on this before they pollute the jury pool."

Patrick nodded. "I called your media buddies—Jim Parker

at the *Tribune* and Sandy Campos at Channel 2. I gave them my beeper number, so I should be hearing back soon."

"Good," Darcy said reassuringly. "How about that reporter at the *Sun-Times*?"

Patrick shook his head. "He's gone. I think he went to the West Coast."

"Don't we have anyone at the *Sun-Times*?"

Patrick shook his head. "No, but maybe I can get to someone at Channel 7."

Darcy carefully stepped out of the steamroom and threw the wet copies of the *Sun-Times* and *Tribune* onto a table next to a plastic chair. He sat down and looked up at Patrick. "As soon as I stop sweating, I'll take a shower and we'll go over to help the Black Widow," he said, smiling. "I'll meet you in the lobby."

Patrick nodded. "There's a rumor that Owen Dempsey, the cocksucker himself, is going to try this case."

"Is that right?" Darcy answered. "Where did you get that scoop from?"

"I still have friends over in the U.S. Attorney's Office."

"I didn't know that," Darcy replied. "I thought you burned all your bridges when you left."

"I didn't leave. I was pushed. There's no place for a gay prosecutor in Owen Dempsey's office."

"There's no place for humanity in Dempsey's office. Fuck him."

"Hey, Boss," Patrick said before he walked away. "I was wondering if maybe I could try this with you."

Darcy looked him up and down. "Well, I'm going to need you and Kathy to help me work it up, but the two of you have to figure out who's going to try it with me. I have no problem if it's you."

"Well, damn me with faint praise," Patrick said dejectedly.

Darcy just looked at him and smiled, then motioned for him to get out of the locker room.

• • •

Wilfredo Martinez was a federal magistrate in the Northern District of Illinois. He would handle the bond hearing, known in federal court as a detention hearing.

Anna Minkoff was generally regarded as the best trial lawyer in the U.S. Attorney's Office. She was tall and thin, with black hair, blue eyes, and perfect teeth. She had a strong voice and a commanding presence and she walked through the federal building as if she owned it.

At this moment Anna burst into the courtroom carrying an armload of books and note pads. After dropping the contents of her arms on counsel table, she walked over to Darcy Cole, leaving two FBI agents behind. Extending her arm, she shook Darcy's hand. "I've been looking forward to a rematch with you ever since the *Espinoza* debacle," she said confidently.

Darcy laughed. "Well, you have your rematch, but you're clearly at a disadvantage."

"How's that?" she asked.

"I understand you're being saddled with that albatross, the Honorable Governor Dempsey."

"Oh? Where did you hear that from?" she asked.

"I have my sources."

"I will be trying this with the U.S. attorney," Anna said matter-of-factly. "I don't know if I'm lead counsel or not yet. I'm sure Owen will tell me at the proper time."

"Well, then, I assume that you have no objection to Ms. Tobias getting an OR bond," said Darcy. An OR bond, or Own Recognizance bond, releases the defendant on his or her promise to return.

"Don't assume, counsel. I do have an objection. She's a danger to the community and a flight risk."

Darcy was incredulous. "What do you base that on?"

Just then the door to chambers opened and the judge's clerk came out. She noted the presence of the attorneys, then pushed a button. Within seconds a side door opened, and the marshals brought a confused Lynne Tobias from the hallway into the courtroom. Just the day before, she had thought her problems were over.

A marshal took her handcuffs off, then motioned for her to sit next to her attorney at counsel table.

For a second the clerk looked up. "Everybody ready?"

Everybody nodded.

She pushed another button and out strode Wilfredo Martinez.

"Sit down," he said, as he stepped up onto the bench. "Okay, Government, what do you have?"

Anna Minkoff stood up and began her delivery.

"The defendant conspired with others to commit insurance fraud in that she forged her husband's signature on a life insurance policy. She was the beneficiary of this policy. Furthermore, she conspired with others to have her husband killed."

Darcy jumped to his feet. "Objection. The defendant was exonerated of all charges."

"Relax, Mr. Cole," Martinez said. "I can read the papers. I believe the government is laying out its case. These are only allegations at this point, and I will keep in mind that she was found not guilty in conjunction with the murder." Martinez gave Darcy a look that conveyed a slight annoyance with the government. Anna continued without objection.

Afterwards Martinez looked at her and said, "What do you propose for bond?"

"We ask that she be detained," Anna replied.

"On what grounds?" asked Martinez.

"We believe she's a danger to the community and a flight risk."

Martinez leaned forward. "Are you telling me you don't believe there are any conditions that would allow us to safely put this woman out on bond?"

"That's correct, Judge. That's what I'm telling you."

"How about you, Mr. Cole? What say you for your client?"

Darcy strode dramatically to the podium but made a relatively simple statement.

"You know, Judge, they call it a fraud case to get around the double jeopardy issue, then they ask you to treat it as a murder case for purposes of bond. If it's a murder case, then they're prohibited from proceeding, because she's been acquitted of murder. They know that, so they're calling it a fraud case. Let's take them at their word—a fraud case in this jurisdiction would mandate that she be released on bond.

"Your Honor, this case is also full of perjured testimony by professional criminals whose testimony was purchased by the government."

Martinez interrupted him. "Mr. Cole, save the dog-and-pony show for the jury. We're not trying the case now. We all understand what your client is charged with. Let's talk about her bond status."

Darcy suggested an OR bond.

Martinez sighed. "Look, I'm not going to detain your client, Mr. Cole, and normally in a situation like this I'd be tempted to use an OR bond. But she clearly has substantial assets, so why don't we cut to the chase. A person with her education and financial means should post property as surety for her appearance in court. I wouldn't want her to walk out of custody without understanding the seriousness of these charges. Have her quit claim the deed to her house to the government and throw in her passport. We'll hold it just to make things a bit more difficult for her should she decide to leave the country."

Anna Minkoff shot to her feet, but before she could say anything the judge turned to her. "I'll note it's over the government's objections. If you have a problem with that, counsel, why don't you and your office take me up to the district court judge?"

"Thank you, Your Honor. We'll do that."

"Fine. Good day." The judge marched off the bench into chambers.

Minkoff stepped over to Darcy. "Well, we're going up now,

so why don't you just hang out here and I'll find out who's assigned to this case."

Darcy shrugged. "Okay," he said. "Just don't go forum shopping on me."

"What happened?" asked Lynne. "Am I going home?"

"Probably," said Darcy, "but it's not a sure thing yet. The case will now be assigned to the district court judge, and he'll decide."

Fifteen minutes later Anna Minkoff approached Darcy. "You're not going to believe this," she said. "We got assigned to Vernon Peters." They headed off to Peters's courtroom.

Peters had been the trial judge in the *Espinoza* case. Darcy was glad to have him again. Vernon Peters was a breath of fresh air among the stodgy and conservative judges on the federal bench. He always spoke his mind, and lawyers generally adored and feared him at the same time. He and Darcy had butted heads many times before he'd become a judge. Although they had often been adversaries, they respected each other.

Vernon Peters was one of four children. His father had come from Mississippi to Chicago's south side, where he was fortunate enough to get a job in the steel mills—a well-paying job, especially for a black man back then. Vernon's mother raised her own family and did the laundry and cooking for other families on the side.

Peters went to the neighborhood Catholic schools, and when he finished he went to the University of Illinois at Navy Pier. He worked his way through school. He did time in the army and went to law school on the GI Bill.

By the time Harold Washington became Chicago's first black mayor, Vernon Peters had established himself as a pre-eminent trial lawyer in Chicago. In the contentious time surrounding Mayor Washington's election, Peters was the beneficiary of a lot of high-profile litigation. The years that followed were very prosperous for him. Then he got the appointment by the Democratic president and became the one federal district court judge who would speak his mind, loud and clear.

• • •

Peters entered, strode to the bench, and glanced around the courtroom, acknowledging both Darcy and Anna. In his courtroom, he had a portrait of Martin Luther King Jr., and another of John F. Kennedy. This was in defiance of the chief judge's wishes, but then again, Vernon Peters knew that he had been appointed for life. He would do what he damn well pleased with his courtroom. He had that attitude toward everything in life.

He looked to Anna Minkoff and began. "Ms. Government, I have read your application for detention. Explain to me why I should detain this woman."

Minkoff began to lay it out for him. Peters listened, allowing her to finish. He then said, "Your application to overturn the Honorable Judge Wilfredo Martinez's recommendation that she be allowed to be released on bond is denied. You can take me up to the Seventh Circuit. I will also modify Wilfredo Martinez's order, with all due respect to that learned jurist. I will release her on an OR bond. Is that clear, counsel?"

"Judge, that would be over the government's objection."

"Of course it's over the government's objection," he responded. "Everything I do is over somebody's objection. I'm the judge. Now draft the order. Marshals are to release this woman. Now where do we stand with this case? Are you ready for arraignment?"

"No, Your Honor. It's the initial appearance. This is an appeal of the magistrate's bond motion," replied Minkoff.

"Let me get this straight," the judge said. "You wanted me to detain her, and you don't even have the indictment ready?"

"Well, that's not quite accurate, Judge. We do have an indictment. It's sealed."

"Well, why don't we unseal it," he said, "and move this case along. This woman's name is at stake. You've made accusations, and you haven't done anything to demonstrate how you've come to that conclusion. I'd like you to unseal it."

"Your Honor, there are witnesses who need to be protected—"

Minkoff barely had the words out when the judge slammed his hand down. "The Sixth Amendment guarantees this defendant the opportunity to cross-examine her accusers, does it not?" he asked.

Minkoff was holding her ground. "It does, Judge, but there are considerations about—"

"Damn the considerations. This woman is entitled to know. This attorney is entitled to prepare his defense. I will not tolerate this gamesmanship. Now are you the lead attorney on this case, Ms. Minkoff?"

"Well, Your Honor, I believe that I may become the second chair on this case."

"Oh, Ms. Minkoff, do tell. Who will be the first chair on this case?"

"I believe the United States attorney himself is going to prosecute this case."

"Then get him here."

"I believe he's busy with other matters right now."

"Yes, I'm sure he is," the judge continued. "Like holding press conferences to try to pollute the minds of prospective jurors. I'll tell you what I'm going to do, Ms. Second Chair. I'm going to pass this case for a twenty-minute recess. At that time, I want the lead attorney here so we can go through scheduling. Is that understood?" Peters stretched out the last syllable endlessly.

"Yes, Your Honor, that's understood. I will let him know."

"Don't let him know. Get him here!" The judge slammed the gavel on the bench and strode off.

Darcy hadn't said a word. As he left the courtroom, a number of reporters followed him. He waved them off. "Christ, I'm just going to use the bathroom."

He walked into the men's room and washed his hands,

splashing a little cool water on his face. As he toweled it off, the door opened and Collata walked in, cupping a cigarette in his hand. "How's it looking?" he asked.

Darcy smiled. "We got Vernon Peters. I haven't had to say anything. He's been berating the government, but my turn is next."

"That's all right. He'll kick your ass, too," Collata said before taking a long drag off his smoke. "Darcy, I know this isn't a great time, but we got to have a little talk."

"What's up?" Darcy said, running his fingers through his hair.

"Well, we got a problem with Benvenuti."

"We always have a problem with that little shit," Darcy said.

"No, no," Collata corrected. "It's the old man. He wants to see you."

Darcy stopped and looked at Collata in the mirror. "What's he want? Do you know?"

"I have no idea, but he says he wants an eyeball with you. I think it has something to do with the kid."

"That can't be good," Darcy said. "He usually sends one of his minions to see me. Should I be worried?"

"I don't think so," said Collata. "If he wanted to whack you, he would have done it. He doesn't need to talk to you about it. He's not going to meet with you, then have you dusted in front of him. So I think you're okay."

"You're one sensitive guy," Darcy said.

"Handsome, too," said Collata, studying his profile.

"Okay, why don't you look at yourself for a while, and when I'm done, we'll go see Benvenuti," Darcy replied. He tossed the crumpled paper towel into the wastebasket and went out the door.

Lynne Tobias was seated at counsel table with two marshals directly behind her. Darcy sat down and began to explain the situation to her. Several moments later he was tapped on the shoulder by Owen Dempsey.

"Counsel, can I speak to you for a moment?"

Darcy looked at him and reluctantly followed him to the back of the courtroom. "What can I do for you, Owen?" he said.

Dempsey had dark curly hair, which he kept short. He had dark eyes and a dark olive complexion. For a man in his mid-forties, he had a conspicuous lack of gray hair. He was a few inches shorter and wider than Darcy, and he smelled—a combination of coffee breath and cheap aftershave.

"Look, I know you have taken shots at me in the past, but I'd like us to try this case cleanly, without any personal antagonism." Even as they spoke, Dempsey's eyes darted around the courtroom in the hope that someone was watching him.

Darcy stared at him without saying anything. He detested Owen's swagger and posturing.

Owen continued. "So I guess what I'm saying is, can we let bygones be bygones?" He reached out to shake Darcy's hand.

"First of all, I don't shake hands in court," Darcy said, "because I don't want people thinking I'm making some sort of deal that no one else is aware of. And second, you want to have a civil relationship with me, prove it. Act right. And by the way, I'm still waiting for that indictment against me you promised after you blew the *Espinoza* case."

The conversation was interrupted by the return of Judge Peters. "Well, looks like the whole cast of characters is here now," he said before sitting down. "Be seated."

Before Dempsey's butt could hit the chair, Peters started in on him. "Mr. Dempsey, step up to the podium, please. I understand you're going to try this case. Is that correct?"

"Yes, it is, Your Honor. I am going to represent the People of the United States of America."

"Mr. Dempsey, no speechifying. Just answer my questions. Now, I denied the government's request to overturn Magistrate Martinez's order that this woman be released. Do you have a problem with that?"

"Yes, Your Honor, I do."

"Okay, then educate me on the error of my ways."

"Your Honor, this woman is charged with a conspiracy to defraud."

"So you're saying that this is a financial crime. Is that right?"

"No, Judge. It goes beyond that because the related conduct includes a murder."

"So you want to bring in a murder that she's been acquitted of as related conduct?"

"Yes, Your Honor, we do."

"So if I understand what you're saying, we have a woman here charged with a financial crime, which means that I could conceivably give her probation. Is that right?"

"No, Your Honor. Under the guidelines you could not give her probation because the amount of money in controversy leads to a guideline range of—"

Judge Peters jumped in. "Let me get this straight. You're saying that she defrauded someone out of a lot of money. Is that right?"

"That's correct," Dempsey said hesitantly.

"So I suppose you're saying she's a danger to the community because she stole a lot of money and she's been acquitted of killing her husband?"

"Your Honor, we believe we that we are going to be able to present evidence that she was clearly culpable in the murder of her husband."

"Well, why don't you lay it out for us right now, Mr. Dempsey?"

"Your Honor, I'm not prepared to do that. That would give the defense an unfair advantage in terms of discovery."

"Well, that's your choice. But I've heard nothing of an evidentiary value that would lead me to the conclusion that Judge Martinez was wrong when he granted conditions of bond for this defendant." He again smacked the gavel onto the bench, mostly for effect. "Is there any further business today, Mr. Dempsey?"

Dempsey stood stunned, but all eyes were on him—the performance had to continue.

"I was told you had already denied detention and I was appearing for scheduling purposes. If that is the case, then it appears our preceding discussions were nothing more than the court's own attempt to speechify. If this court is biased against the government, then it should recuse itself from this matter."

Even Darcy was impressed at Dempsey's recovery. Peters was furious.

"I can fairly preside over these proceedings, counsel. If there is a change, I'll let you know." He stormed off the bench.

Darcy turned to Lynne. "You're going to be processed, which means they are going to fingerprint and photograph you. Then you are going to sign a recognizance bond, and you'll be released. Collata will be waiting for you. He will walk you over to my office. I'll get you home. Okay?"

"Thank you again, Darcy," she said, coolly.

With her freedom on the line a second time, she still refused to break.

THREE

Anthony "Tony the Babe" Benvenuti got his nickname while climbing through the ranks of the Chicago mob. It stemmed from his ability to get the information he needed with a baseball bat. He had been an artist when it came to cracking kneecaps, crushing fingers, breaking arms—whatever it took to get whatever he needed—then he'd kill the guy. He had made his mark as a hitter, but that was long ago. Now he was an old man. He took his place as the head of the mob as others went to prison or died.

He went to great lengths to layer himself in legitimate businesses; he was untouchable by the government. He had three sons. Two of them were completely legitimate; one worked for a large union and the other one was a plumbing contractor. He also had a son, Anthony Jr., who was currently doing forty years in Terre Haute Federal Pen for narcotics distribution. Darcy had represented him.

Collata had offered to drive Darcy to meet with Benvenuti, and he picked him up in the van. The restaurant was off the expressway in a western suburb. Patrons sat at two other tables; otherwise the place was empty. An elderly, elegant waiter escorted Darcy and Collata to their table.

Darcy had a single malt on the rocks. Collata took his neat. Collata cupped a cigarette in his hand, and he was smoking it discreetly. *No Smoking* signs were prominently displayed in the lobby.

Benvenuti walked into the restaurant wearing a navy blue business suit with gray pinstripes. Two of his associates were with him, and they stopped in the bar while Benvenuti proceeded to Darcy's table.

Benvenuti was a respectable and robust man in his mid-sixties. He extended a hand to Darcy. "Darcy, thank you for meeting me here."

"Mr. Benvenuti, my pleasure."

"Darcy, please, we've been over this. Call me Tony. Collata, you're looking good."

"Thank you, Mr. Benvenuti."

"Would you excuse us, Collata? I'd like to talk to your friend here."

"By all means, Mr. Benvenuti." Collata picked up his drink and walked over to the bar to talk to Benvenuti's associates.

"Have you ordered, Darcy?"

"No, I waited for you."

Benvenuti raised his arm and motioned to a waiter, who promptly came over. He pointed to Darcy's drink. "Get him another. I'll have a Dewar's. Also, we'll each have a porterhouse medium, and bring us some calamari first."

The waiter looked at Darcy. "What type of salad dressing would you like?" Before Darcy could reply, the old man shot back, "Italian on both." The waiter nodded and left quickly.

Benvenuti fixed his gaze on Darcy. "Darcy, I like you. When my boy got pinched, I wanted no one but you. You're a straight-up guy. I appreciate that. Junior's always been an embarrassment to me, and this last fiasco was unbearable. I listened to his stupid fuckin' mouth blabbering all over the government's tapes. I wanted to puke. And yet this is my son, my oldest, named after me. What the fuck did I do to deserve him?"

Darcy said nothing.

The old man continued, "I'm embarrassed, but I have to tell you about a problem that's come up."

Darcy said, "With his case?"

"No, I wish it were. The problem is with you."

"What's the problem?" Darcy asked, glancing around the room.

"I hate to tell you this, but I believe my son is trying to arrange a contract on you."

The waiter dropped off two drinks and asked if they needed anything else. Losing patience, Benvenuti looked at him and snapped, "No. Get the hell out of here." The waiter made a speedy retreat.

Darcy looked at Benvenuti. "Your son put a hit out on me?"

Benvenuti looked uncomfortable. "He hasn't yet. He's trying. I put the word out on the street that if anyone picks up the contract, they're through. Darcy, I deeply regret this."

"I appreciate you telling me this," said Darcy. "But what am I supposed to do now?"

Benvenuti leaned into Darcy. "I would take it as a personal favor if you let me handle this. You could go to the police, but we both know they couldn't do much for you. It could cause problems for me. It could embarrass my wife. Let me handle it. The word is out that I will not sanction this hit, and if something were to go down there would be retribution. Everyone understands this, but you know I can't control the renegades. He's got two friends who are in the wind. They're knuckle-heads. There's this kid Battaglia, the one they call Joey Bag O'Donuts, and the other kid is Mangano. I can't find 'em. I don't know if they're underground. I don't know if they got the message. But when I find 'em, your problem will be over."

"What am I supposed to do in the meantime—hide?"

Mr. Benvenuti smiled. "I would like you to accept a favor from me. The gentlemen you see at the bar talking to Collata, I'd like to have them keep you company for a while. Just in case. Mangano and Battaglia wouldn't touch you with my boys there."

"This is insane," Darcy exclaimed. Then, catching himself, he said, "I mean no disrespect to you, Mr. Benvenuti."

"None taken," said Benvenuti. "I'm embarrassed by my son. I wish he weren't mine, but he is and it's my shame to carry. I sent an envoy to explain to him that I will not tolerate this. But until that's done, I think you should accept my offer of some protection."

The waiter dropped off the calamari and set down two small dishes. He virtually ran away without asking any questions.

Darcy ran his hands through his hair and sat back in his chair. "Why is your son doing this, Mr. Benvenuti?" he asked.

Tony shook his head. "After I heard the tapes, I told Junior to cop out. Keep his mouth shut, do his bit, and get out. But no, he wanted the whole show. So he went to trial. He opened up our business to people. Yappin' his big fuckin' mouth, saying stupid things on tape so everyone could hear him.

"Darcy, every father wants things to be better for his children than they were for him. I didn't want my kids in this business. My other boys understood this. They're good boys. They're married, raising their own kids, paying taxes, going to work. Junior is a fool. He wants to be a tough guy. He thinks he's Robert De Niro."

Darcy downed half his drink.

Benvenuti continued. "He's an immature, spoiled child. I failed him as a father. He blames you for his predicament. Nothing is his fault; he thinks he's in jail because you did a lousy job defending him."

"I did the best I could," Darcy said.

Benvenuti waved him off. "I told him to take the deal. I listened to the tapes. Nobody was going to beat that case. You did the best you could, but you had a fool for a client."

"I will always give you my best effort," said Darcy.

"I know that, Darcy," Benvenuti said, reaching over and patting his hand. "My confidence in you has not been shaken, but until I find Bag O'Donuts and the other yahoo, I want you to keep your head down. Capiche?"

"Of course, Mr. Benvenuti."

Benvenuti drank his Dewar's in one motion, dropped the glass, and then with his finger waved his boys over. They walked up with Collata. "Collata, enjoy the steak," he said as he got up to leave. He pointed to his men. "These two guys are going to provide Mr. Cole with some added protection for a while. This is John Doe, and that's Jim Doe."

John pulled up a chair and sat down. Jim looked at Darcy and said, "I'll be in the bar watching your backs."

Benvenuti began to walk away, stopped, and turned back toward Darcy. "If you need to get in touch with me, ask John to call me."

"Thank you, Mr. Benvenuti," said Darcy.

Darcy, Collata, and John Doe looked at each other without saying anything. Then Darcy broke the ice. "John, are you hungry?"

"No, thank you," he said. "Just pretend I'm not here." He turned his back to Darcy and began looking around the room, carefully eyeing all the other diners at the restaurant.

Collata looked at Darcy. "What's with the muscle?"

Darcy took a deep breath. "Seems Junior's unhappy with me. He's sent a kite out to put a hit on me."

"No shit," said Collata, almost gleefully. Darcy glared at him.

"Yeah, and the old man told everyone that they can't pick it up, but he can't get ahold of two of Junior's numb-nuts associates, Battaglia and Mangano. You know either of them?"

Collata grimaced. "Oh, yeah. That's Joey Bag O'Donuts."

"Okay, I've heard that twice now," Darcy said. "What the fuck does that mean?"

"It means he eats, and he's an imbecile. Unfortunately, he's also a stone killer."

"That's not good," said Darcy. "Sounds like he's stupid enough to go against the old man."

Collata nodded. "Yeah, he is. But that's why the old man gave you two of his primates as guards." John Doe turned and looked at Collata. "Sorry," Collata said. "It's just an expression." John grunted and turned away.

"I don't know Mangano," Collata continued. "But I think I can round up Bag O'Donuts."

"Let me guess," Darcy said, "you're going to check the bakeries?"

"No, no. I think I know the kid's uncle. I think he's got a joint over in Melrose Park. Don't worry, I'll find him. When I do I'll let John here know where he is."

John turned back around. "You find him and let me know. We'll take care of things."

The calamari went untouched, but the steaks were devoured. They finished dinner and motioned for the check.

The waiter shuffled over. "Gentlemen, you have been comped and the gratuity has been taken care of. I hope you enjoyed your dinner." He shuffled away. It had been an exhausting shift.

"Hey, John," Darcy said. "This isn't my last meal, is it?"

John Doe looked around. "If it's *your* last meal, it's *my* last meal."

FOUR

After his morning swim, Darcy stepped out of the club to find the Doe brothers waiting for him. They were in the same spot Darcy had left them at 6 A.M. He wondered if they had even moved.

They greeted him and walked him to his office, riding the elevator up in silence. Darcy went to open the door to his office and had his hand pulled back by Jim, who stepped in front of him, opened the door, and walked in.

Irma Rosales, Darcy's longtime secretary, was reading the *Sun-Times* and drinking a cup of coffee behind her desk. She looked up at Jim Doe and watched as Darcy stepped in behind. "Good morning, Boss."

"Good morning, Irma. How are you today?"

"Good. Who's your friend?"

John stepped in. "These are the Doe brothers," Darcy said. "They're going to be hanging around for a few days."

Irma smiled. "Hello," she said cheerfully.

Darcy grabbed a handful of messages from a plastic slotted holder. "When you get a chance, I want to talk to you about a case," Irma said.

Darcy nodded, "Now's good."

Irma followed Darcy into his office and sat down as he pulled his coat off and hung it on a hook behind the door. He then sat back in his chair, looking through his messages as Irma began to speak.

"There was a woman who came to see you yesterday. Her name is Willie Mae Watkins. She's a sweetheart of a lady and her son just got charged with murder. She doesn't have two nickels to rub together, but she said she'd make payments and I believe her."

Darcy raised an eyebrow. "You know we don't do pro bono, Irma."

"Darcy, I've never asked you to do a pro bono case. I'm not asking you now, but please talk to this woman. There's something special about her."

"Oh, yeah, what's that?" asked Darcy. "She's got a kid charged with murder. That makes her special?"

Darcy immediately regretted saying it. He knew better than to question Irma's judgment. She looked at him. "Meet with her, Darcy. For some reason this woman has touched me. She's working two jobs. Her son's never been in trouble before, and she said the only thing they have on him is an oral confession the police said he made. Frankly, the whole thing stinks.

"Darcy, you know, the system isn't fair. Just because someone has the money and can get a lawyer who knows what he's doing, he has a shot at beating a case whether he did it or not. This kid's going to get railroaded because there is no one who's going to step up for him. Would you talk to his mother?"

Darcy looked at her and said, "After all these years, you still have a heart. Yeah, schedule a meeting so I can talk to her, but make sure she knows she has to pay me."

Irma nodded. "Well, just be open-minded. That's all I ask."

Darcy looked at her. "You're too nice to be in this business."

Irma smiled, "You don't want me to change, do you, Darcy? Then I'd be cold and heartless like the rest of you."

There was a knock on the door. Kathy Haddon stepped into the office, carrying transcripts. "Good morning, Boss. How are you?"

"Hey, kiddo, what's happening?"

"I knocked out a double jeopardy motion in the Tobias case, but I know we're not going anywhere with it."

Darcy nodded. "Yeah, I know, but thanks for doing it," he said.

"Good job on the detention hearing," she continued.

"Patrick says he wants to try that case with me. You have any strong feelings one way or the other?"

"If it's all the same to you, I'd like to have Pat do it. I was so jammed up during *Espinoza* and doing the pretrial motions on the state case on *Tobias* that I haven't seen my kids in a while. It would be a welcome break."

"Okay, consider it done. Patrick will do it with me. Anything else?"

She was hesitant. "Well, there is one more thing. Has Irma talked to you about the Watkins case?"

He looked at her. "What Watkins case?"

"A woman came to see you, Willie Mae Watkins. I did the initial intake, because Irma asked me to talk to her. Darcy, there is something about this case."

"Not you, too," Darcy groaned. "We're not the public defender's office. Did you talk to her about fees?"

"I did. She can put some money down, and she can make payments. She's working two jobs. Anyway, what's your problem? You can go short money on this. I'll do all the pretrial prep on my own after hours."

Darcy looked at her. "What about your kids? What is it that's so special about this woman?"

"Darcy, you've taught me a lot about going with my gut

feeling on cases. Well, my gut tells me this kid has been set up. I think you should take it—and if you don't, people around here might begin to think you care more about money than law."

Darcy sighed. "Well, for your information, I already told Irma I would meet her. If you want to sit in on the meeting, fine. Find out when Irma is scheduling it. Okay?"

She smiled. "You're the best, Boss." She gave Darcy a kiss on the cheek.

"Yeah, I'm the best," he said. "I got a collection of lunatics working for me. Now get out of here," he said.

Kathy walked out smiling.

Darcy was reading and making notes when Patrick came in without knocking. "Hey, Boss, I got a little news for you," he said as he sat down. "I was talking to a couple of people, and it seems there's going to be a star witness in the G's case."

"Oh yeah? Someone different from the state case?"

"Yup," he said, leaning back and putting his hands behind his head. "Apparently, they flipped an insurance agent named Martin Thiel. He wrote a life insurance policy on the late, great Charles Tobias. The beneficiary was none other than Lynne Tobias. He's going to say that Lynne signed Charles's name on the policy in his presence. He certified that Charles was the signatory, and Lynne paid him twenty thousand in cash for his certification."

"You hear anything else?" Darcy asked.

Patrick shook his head. "Not yet. But sooner or later I'll get it all."

"You know where this insurance agent is? I'll send Collata to go talk to him."

Patrick shook his head. "I don't think he'll talk to us. The G's got him screwed in real hard. Apparently, he's going to get a pretrial diversion if he testifies, and if he messes up they're going to yank the offer. They're going to do a fraud case on him and do the related conduct of the insurance policy, which was two million."

"Oh, let me guess. That leaves him doing time?"

"Yeah, about sixty months."

"That's a lot for an insurance salesman."

"Okay, what else do they have?" Darcy asked.

"They got Mark Thomas, the flipper from the state trial, the insurance agent flipper, and probably other flippers to be named later. Plus, they'll have a handwriting expert from the insurance application who will probably match it up to our little angel."

"What about the money trail?" Darcy asked. "Have they found the money?"

Patrick shook his head. "They got bubkis on that. They've been humping dry wells left and right. They know the money went offshore, but they have no idea where."

"What's left in the estate?" asked Darcy.

"They got the marital home, a condo in Florida, a condo in Colorado, property in Montana, retirement accounts, some stocks and miscellaneous cash accounts, about two to two and a half million accounted for. But you know, Darcy, they said Tobias was worth ten or eleven million."

"Who's they? And how do they prove it?"

"They'll grab some IRS guys and show liquidation of assets with the proceeds going to companies offshore. They'll total it and come up with a big number."

"I can live with that," Darcy replied. "How are they going to prove she did it? Hell, she didn't even finish law school. She wasn't the big-time lawyer with all the connections. She wasn't handling the marital estate. Come on, he's the one dumping the assets because he knows he's got a problem with someone who's out to get him. He's looking to split. He's looking to take off in a hurry. We can turn this thing on them in a heartbeat." Darcy was up and pacing at this point.

"Well, that's a plan," said Patrick. "We're just going to have to clean her up a little. She took a lot of hits during that state trial.

"That's your job," Darcy said.

"Does this mean I get to try it with you?" asked Patrick.

"You got it," said Darcy. "But let's get through it before you thank Kathy."

Collata came into the office and pulled out a cigarette, then sat in a chair and threw his cowboy boots up onto Darcy's desk. "Well, I see you're still alive."

"Get that shit off my desk," Darcy shot back. "What have you come up with?"

"Well, I may have a line on where Mangano is, but Bag O'Donuts is in the wind. No one knows where he is."

"Great. I've been a lawyer for over thirty fucking years, and I'm gonna get whacked by a guy named Bag O'Donuts."

"Relax," said Collata. "I been shot three times, and I ain't dead. Soon we'll be able to piss on their graves."

"Well, assuming I live long enough to do this trial, I'm going to need you. Seems there's an insurance agent who's going to be a flipper in this case. He's going to say that our client signed her husband's name to a two-million-dollar insurance policy and paid him twenty large to attest that the husband signed it."

Collata finished his cigarette and put it out on one of Darcy's business cards. "All right, who is he? I'll find him."

"All I got is a name, no current address." Darcy wrote on a piece of paper and handed it to him. Collata folded it and put it in his pocket.

"No problem. What else?"

"Actually, I'd rather have you find Mangano and Donuts before you talk to the insurance agent. If you don't find those two, we really don't need the insurance agent, do we?"

Collata brushed him off. "Don't worry. I've called in a few markers on this. I got people at Chicago, Melrose Park, and the FBI helping me find these guys."

"FBI?" asked Darcy, surprised. "I hope it's not one of the agents who was investigating you."

"Hey, I was on the job thirty years. I got a few contacts left. I'll do everything I can to make sure these pricks don't get near you."

Darcy watched Collata as he walked out of the office. He was another lunatic—along with Irma, Patrick, and Kathy—but they were as close to family as Darcy had these days.

FIVE

Willie Mae Watkins was in her early fifties. A nurse at Northwestern Memorial Hospital from 7:00 A.M. to 3:30 P.M., she also worked from 5:30 P.M. to 11:00 P.M. at a nursing home near her house. She was determined and assertive, but her eyes revealed a sadness as she looked across the desk at Darcy. She was nervously adjusting the top of her blue nurse's uniform.

"He could not and would not commit murder, Mr. Cole. I know my son. I've raised him. He believes in the Good Book and Jesus. The police have one boy who's a gangster. He runs with the Disciples. He said he saw my son in the area around the time there were gunshots. The police came to my house, kicked in the door, and dragged him out of bed while I was there. They held him for four days before they charged him. When they came to court, they said he made an oral admission but would not sign anything."

Darcy leaned back in his chair. He was skeptical and wondered if she really knew what her kid was up to.

Willie Mae continued. "They don't have a weapon. They don't have any physical evidence. They set a $250,000 bond. I can't post that much money. I don't have it."

"Ms. Watkins, I don't mean to be crass, but how do you plan to pay for his representation?"

"How much would you charge, Mr. Cole?"

"Well, to be honest with you, I wouldn't touch this for less than fifty thousand dollars."

Willie Mae put her head in her hands. The sadness in her eyes spread across her face. She looked defeated. "Mr. Cole, I can't pay anywhere near that much. I can give you five thousand. I can pay you maybe as much as five hundred a month, and I'll pay that until your fee is paid. But can't you take this case for less money?"

"Ms. Watkins, have you considered going to another lawyer?"

"Mr. Cole, do you have children of your own?"

"Yes, I have a grown daughter."

"Mr. Cole, I need you to help my son. I know you're the best. I read the papers and watch the news. You just won that rich lady's murder case. You won that Alderman's corruption trial last year, and you've represented mafia men. You also won that case for that rich Cuban man. You see, Mr. Cole, I've done my homework, and I can't afford a lawyer who can't help my son. I need him home with me."

"Even if I represent your son, there's no guarantee that we'll win."

She interrupted him. "Mr. Cole, I believe in you, and I believe in God. I believe that the truth will come out, but I need someone who's going to be a messenger of God. I believe you're God's vessel here on earth for me."

Darcy laughed. "I've been called a lot of things, but never a vessel for God." He paused. "Kathy Haddon is the lawyer in my office you met with before. Would you be willing to let Kathy do your case?"

Willie Mae began wringing her hands. She looked sideways, then turned back. "Mr. Cole, Miss Haddon may be a very fine lawyer, but I still want you to do this case. I'll do whatever is necessary to have you do my case."

They were getting nowhere. Darcy didn't want to do the case without getting the money up front or some assurances that there were assets available. Willie Mae had nothing to give other than her word.

"Look," said Darcy, "let me think about it. I'll call you tomorrow afternoon and let you know."

Willie Mae looked down. "It's easier to say no over the phone. I'll be back tomorrow, and I'll be back every day until you tell me you're going to take this case."

Darcy reached for his appointment book. Ms. Watkins stopped him. "Mr. Cole, I can only be here between my two jobs. Right now I'm not working on the weekends, but if you take my son's case, I will get a job on the weekends. I will start paying you as much as I can as often as I can."

"I'll give it serious thought, Ms. Watkins," Darcy said, extending his hand.

She took it and held on to it. "Thank you, sir. I'll see you tomorrow."

"Yes, ma'am, I suspect you will."

The instant she left, Irma and Kathy were in Darcy's office.

"You are taking that case, aren't you, Boss?" Kathy insisted.

"How is she going to pay us?" asked Darcy.

Irma cut in. "Darcy, I've never said this to you before, but you make a lot of money, and you should take this case because it's the right thing to do."

Darcy was taken aback. "Irma, how are we going to justify taking this case and having to do a one-week trial for chump change? Kathy doesn't bring in any money. Patrick doesn't bring in any money. You don't bring in any money. So the four of us are dependent on me to bring in all the funds."

"Darcy, I told you I'll work up this file for free," Kathy said.

"How can you be so sure that, just because the mother is a decent woman, the kid is a decent guy?"

Irma and Kathy looked at each other. "I already met him," Kathy answered. "I did a jail visit."

"Do you have any idea how many cases I've taken where the parents mortgaged their homes or used their life savings to rescue their kid, only to have the kid bite them in the ass the next chance he gets? This nice old woman is going to end up broke and miserable, and I don't want to be a part of it."

"So let's get this straight, Darcy," Kathy said. "You'd want to be a part of her misery if she had a lot of cash?"

He sighed, but what could he say? He'd trained her.

"Okay, look, you two. There's just too much going on right now for me to pick up a murder case. Let me get through *Tobias,* and a month from now we'll revisit this."

They know they had pushed it as far as they could. "Okay, a month from now," Kathy agreed, "we'll talk. By that time you'll have all the discovery in *Tobias,* and you'll be getting ready for trial. We can start kicking around the *Watkins* case."

"I didn't say yes," Darcy warned. "I said we'll revisit it in a month. Let's see how we're doing."

• • •

Lynne Tobias was wearing a peach Chanel suit and reading *Town and Country* when Darcy stepped into the waiting room to retrieve her. As she rose from the chair, she set the magazine on the table and extended her hand to him. He put his hand on her shoulder and led her into his office, shutting the door behind him. She sat in a chair directly across from him and immediately lit up a cigarette.

"So where do we stand, Darcy?" she asked before exhaling.

"Well, we're going to file a double jeopardy motion that'll go nowhere. We'll file a motion asking for discovery. We know they're going to flip some people. I want to try to find out who the flippers are. The judge will set up a period of time for us to go through discovery. I'll set up a 2.04 conference with the prosecution."

"What's that?" she said, annoyed.

"That's where we sit down and go through all the discovery they have. They're going to hold back some, because we're not entitled to everything. The parameters of what we can get are set forth in the Local Court Rules—in rule 2.04. What I really want to know is who the flippers are."

She took a drag of her cigarette and exhaled. "Flippers?"

"Yeah, you know. People who could have been in cahoots with you, but now they've cut a deal and become witnesses against you."

"You mean Mark Thomas?"

"Exactly. And he's going to testify against you in this case, too. He took forty under the new law for the murder. That means he'd have to do all forty years. Under the old law, forty would have meant twenty because he got day-for-day good time. So now the only thing he can do is testify against you in this case so the government can go back and get his sentence reduced in the state case. They can put him in a federal institution to do his time. That's a pretty good incentive to go after you."

She crushed out her cigarette in the ashtray on Darcy's desk, then emptied it into the wastebasket. "But you discredited him in the state case. Why would they use him again?"

"I discredited him on a number of points, but let's face it. They're going to flip some people who are going to be used to corroborate his testimony. They are going to try to make this case stronger."

"I don't get all this flipping crap, Darcy," she said.

Darcy looked her straight in the eye. "Is that so? Well, one flipper is an insurance agent who's going to testify. The guy says you signed the application in front of him using your husband's name."

"Oh, that must be Marty," she said dismissively. "He's a liar. They'll never be able to prove anything."

"What's Marty's last name?"

"Thiel. Everyone knows Marty Thiel's a liar," she said.

"Okay, let me ask you this," Darcy asked curiously. "If they do a handwriting exemplar from you, and they compare it to the signature on the application, is it going to match?"

She walked to the window and looked out at the lake, watching the boats in the distance. "I suppose it will, because I did, in fact, sign it."

"Well, then, how's he lying?" he said.

"Oh, I didn't say he's lying. I said he's a liar."

Darcy was clearly annoyed. "Okay, Lynne, why don't you start from the beginning and tell me everything about your relationship with Marty Thiel."

Lynne sighed, opened her purse, and pulled out her cigarettes. She took one out of the pack and started tapping it against the desk, then put it in her mouth and fumbled through her purse for a lighter. Darcy had one on his desk, but he just stared at her. Finally, she reached over and grabbed it, then lit her own cigarette. She took a long deep drag.

"Where to begin with Marty. Let me see. . . ."

SIX

Patrick, Kathy, and Irma had all left. It was close to seven when Collata came in. "How you doing, Darcy?"

"Oh, just fine. Seems our client, Lynne Tobias, is an inveterate liar."

"She's a few other things, too," said Collata.

Darcy smiled. "That she is."

"Hey, Jim was reading *Cosmopolitan* when I walked in. Funny, I wouldn't have pegged a huge guy like him for a *Cosmo* reader. Do you think he's learning how to give a man what he really wants?"

"As long as he doesn't try it out around here," said Darcy, smiling.

Collata went to the drawer in the credenza that contained the bottle of Scotch. He pulled it out, poured himself three fingers, and left it out as he settled down into a chair with the glass in his hand. "Hey, that bottle's getting a little low. Why don't you send Tinkerbell down to get more booze."

"Tinkerbell," said Darcy. "You mean Patrick?"

"Yeah. Send her down to get more booze."

"Why are all you cops homophobic?" Darcy asked.

"Homophobic?" Collata answered. "I don't hate fags—I just like to fuck with 'em."

"Whatever," Darcy said.

"Hey, I'm just joking. I like the kid. He got fucked by the G. They tried to fuck me, too. But he's the new kid here, so I'm going to bust his balls."

Darcy leaned back in his chair. "C'mon, go easy on him. He's a good kid and a great lawyer."

Collata nodded. "Maybe, but he was a fed boy, and you know how I feel about the feds."

Darcy changed the subject. "Did you find Junior's two knuckleheads yet?"

"Darcy, let me tell you the problem with these guys. They're not even smart enough to realize who the old man is. They work for Junior. These guys are invisible. Their beepers, cell phones, and cars are in other people's names, all paid for with cash. For all I know they sleep hanging upside down from a tree branch. But don't worry, boss. I'll find the tree."

• • •

Darcy finished his morning swim, skipped a steam, and had breakfast by the pool. He ordered oatmeal, rye toast, grapefruit juice, and black coffee. After he finished eating, he got dressed and picked up his briefcase from the coat check. As he stepped through the revolving doors, he saw the Doe boys waiting where they had left him earlier.

"Good morning," Darcy said.

John said hello. Jim just looked around and nodded.

They took a short walk to the office building and up the elevator to the office. Darcy followed Jim through the open front door. Irma had not arrived. John went into the office and looked around. Patrick was the only one there. The Doe brothers took their place in the waiting room.

"Hey, Boss," Patrick said when he saw Darcy. "Junior Tony Benvenuti called you earlier."

"What did you tell him?"

"I told him to call back in twenty minutes."

He pointed toward the kitchen area. "I made some coffee."

"I had some at the club," Darcy said. He turned to the Does. "How about you guys? You want coffee?"

"No, thank you," John replied. Jim was already perusing a magazine and didn't look up.

Patrick followed Darcy back to his office. "Jeez, Darcy, how long are you going to have these guys around?" he asked.

"Oh, I don't know. They're starting to grow on me. They're not much trouble, and they're housebroken. It was only supposed to be a day or two, but they're still here."

"Well, the longer they're around, the more nervous I get."

"Apparently, Junior's been complaining about me. The old man wants to make sure he doesn't do anything stupid."

"Stupid is what he does best," said Patrick.

"The old man wants to protect me, and I'm going to let him. Anyway, what are you doing down here so early?"

"Dan and I went to breakfast."

"Yeah, what's the occasion?"

"Well, it's kind of an anniversary for us. We've been together for a year."

"Wow, that's dangerously close to monogamy for you."

"Who said anything about monogamy?" he smiled slyly. "Just kidding."

"You know, we ought to go out to dinner and celebrate. Maybe we could bring Collata. I think he'd love going out to dinner with the two of you."

Patrick laughed. "Yeah, right. There isn't enough Scotch in the city to get him through that evening."

"Now, don't tell him I told you this, but he has a high opinion of you. He doesn't care that you're gay. He's just busting your balls. When he gets to know you better, he'll bust your balls about something else."

Patrick grimaced. "Hey, would you leave my balls out of it?"

Darcy hesitated, then chose his words carefully. "Did you know the feds investigated him?"

"No shit. What for?" asked Patrick.

"It's a long story, but apparently he stood up for a friend and told the truth. That didn't sit well with some feds with a God complex, and they went up his ass with a flashlight and a magnifying glass. Nobody at Chicago Police stepped up for him, so when he hit his 30, he pulled the pin."

"Why are you telling me this?" Patrick asked.

"Because he feels you guys have something in common. They forced you out of your job, and they forced him to retire under a cloud. You guys have a bond."

"Well, Kathy likes him, so I'm sure there's something beneath that disgusting facade."

Darcy chuckled.

Patrick decided to shift gears. "Anyway, we got a problem, Darcy."

"What's that?"

"There's a rumor that Owen Dempsey is going to try to get you conflicted off the *Tobias* case."

"On what grounds?" Darcy asked.

"Well, I think he's going to allege that you and Lynne Tobias have a relationship that is unduly close."

Darcy seemed amused. "Is that right? Well, I'll tell you what. Vernon Peters is going to chew him a new asshole. Unless, of course, he's got evidence that I've been poking the ice block."

"Okay, then, I'll write the response," Patrick said. "I assume we deny the allegations?" He gave Darcy a look, and Darcy returned it.

There was a knock at the door, and Irma popped her head in. "I see our friends are still with us. Do they need anything? Do you guys need anything?"

"No, everyone's fine."

"I'm taking off," said Patrick, grabbing his briefcase.

"Hey, Irma," said Darcy, "did you know that Patrick and Dan have been together have been together for a year?"

"A whole year?" she said. "I'll make a cake!"

The phone rang, and Irma ran over to Darcy's desk, punched down a button, and answered it. "Law office of Darcy Cole. May I help you? Just a moment, please." She crushed the phone to her chest—Irma never used the hold button. "Do you want a collect call from Benvenuti from Terre Haute Federal Penitentiary?"

"Yes, I do."

"Yes, operator, we will accept."

After a brief pause, Irma said, "Mr. Benvenuti, please hold for Mr. Cole." She handed the phone to Darcy. "Here you go, Boss."

"Tony, what can I do for you?"

"Fuck you. It's Mr. Benvenuti, not Tony."

"Listen, Tony. Your father came to see me."

"Yeah, I know all abut that. He sent some fuckin' lackey down here to talk to me."

"I'd like to resolve our differences," said Darcy.

"Oh, is that what the fuck you're talkin' about? Well, you know what I want to resolve? I want to resolve your fuckin' breathing problem. That's what I want to do. I want your fuckin' head on a fuckin' stick."

"Look, Tony," said Darcy. "I don't need to take this macho bullshit. I'll hang up."

"Fuck you. You can't hang up on me."

"Hold on," Darcy said. "Hang on one second."

"Don't you fuckin' put me on hold."

Darcy put him on hold and scrambled through his desk for a tape recorder with a wire and a suction cup. He popped it on to the phone receiver and started the recorder, then got back on the line. "Sorry, I had another call. Now, what were you saying?"

"Look, you motherfucker, I don't give a rat's ass what my father says—he's fuckin' senile. It's your fuckin' fault. I'm not going to let you run me like I'm a movie. You fuckin' sold me out. Now, I'm in the joint, and I'm gonna have you fuckin' ripped to pieces. Then I'm gonna shit on your lifeless body."

"On every piece?" Darcy asked, causing Junior to explode.

"Look, fuck you! You think that I can't reach out and take care of this? You better fuckin' believe I can."

"Calm down, Junior."

"You call me Mr. Benvenuti, motherfucker."

"Tony, why don't you get someone else to handle your appeal."

"Fuck my appeal. My appeal's for shit. Seventh Circuit's a bunch of fuckin' nazis. You think they're going to let some crime boss' kid out on some fuckin' technicality?

"Let me tell you something, Darcy. I'm going to get out, and I'm not counting on your fuckin' ass to get me out. You can suck my dad's dick. You set me up. The only thing I haven't figured out about you is how you're gonna die."

"Junior, you're a genius. You know they record all the phone calls coming out of the penitentiary."

"Fuck you. Record that."

He slammed the phone down. Darcy pulled the phone away from his ear and hung it up. He rewound the tape and then hit play. After listening to it for a few seconds to make sure it was clear, he rewound it, pulled out the tape, put it in its case, and wrapped a piece of tape around it.

"Irma, would you ask John to come in please."

He sat back and waited.

Irma appeared in his doorway. "Uh, Darcy?" she said, "John's in the washroom. Will Jim do?"

"Sure," Darcy said, amused. "He'll be back to *Mademoiselle* before he knows it."

Jim came in a few seconds later.

"Yes, sir?" he said.

"Jim, I need to see Mr. Benvenuti. Can you arrange it?"

"Consider it done, sir. I'll get back to you."

• • •

Collata pulled his raggedy van into the circular driveway of the country club. It was about fifteen years old with a faded brown exterior punctuated by patches of Bondo. It had a large dent in the left front corner panel, and one headlight was held in place by black electrical tape.

Still, a valet came to the driver's side and opened the door for him. Collata stared at the pimply-faced kid in the red vest.

"Hey, kid, don't take it for no joy ride," he said, handing over the keys.

Darcy climbed out and waited for the Doe brothers in the Cadillac behind them. They all walked into the lobby, where a gray-haired man in a blue blazer with the country club's crest on it asked, "Are you here to see Mr. Benvenuti?"

"Yes."

"And you might be?"

"I'm Darcy Cole."

"And you, sir?"

"Collata."

"Your first name?"

"Yes."

The man looked confused. He hesitated, then walked away. He was back within seconds. "Mr. Cole and Mr. Collata, Mr. Benvenuti will see you in the East Room."

Benvenuti was at a table, drinking a cup of coffee, when they walked in. He motioned for Darcy to join him.

"Sit down." He looked at Collata. "Do you need to be here?"

"No, I don't."

"Well, why don't you walk around and look at the scenery."

Collata got up and walked away.

"Darcy, how can I help you?"

"Well, Mr. Benvenuti, I hate to hand this over, but I have a tape of a conversation I had with your son."

"You mean the tape where he calls me senile?"

Darcy raised his eyebrows. "That's the one." He knew better than to ask him how he'd heard the conversation. Clearly, someone at the pen was on his payroll.

"I'm concerned about it, as you can imagine," said Darcy.

"Don't be. They just seem to be more cunning than I gave them credit for. But, remember, they're Junior's guys—they'll fuck up."

He eyed Darcy. "How long have we known each other, Darcy?" he asked.

Darcy thought briefly. "I think about twelve years now."

"That's right, and you know this kid's been trouble from birth. You got him out of plenty of scrapes, and he never learned. I could have put him into a nice soft job, but he thinks he's the next Al Capone.

"You've always been a man of your word," he continued. "You've always carried yourself with dignity. You've always done exactly what you've said you would do for us. You've kept your mouth shut. You've been a true lawyer, a professional in every sense. I'm deeply ashamed by my son and his actions."

"You have three boys all raised in the same home," said Darcy. "Two of them have given you no problems. It's not your fault that Tony turned out like he did. You did the best you could."

Benvenuti shrugged, then stood up and began to gather himself. "This problem will be over soon, I promise you," he said. He began to walk away, then stopped and turned back to Darcy. "Are the Doe boys giving you any trouble?" he asked.

"No, they're great," Darcy answered. "They're—well—they're always there."

"Good. Don't get too attached. You won't need them soon."

Benvenuti handed Darcy a business card for a trucking company on the south side.

"If you need to reach me, call this number and ask for Uncle Moe. Leave your name and phone number because he won't be there. You understand?"

"I understand."

"But don't use that unless it's important."

Darcy wondered what Benvenuti considered important.

• • •

Darcy's solitary morning ritual now included the Doe brothers, who would pick him up in the morning and drive him to the pool. They stood along the wall outside the club scanning the street for God knows what. Once he was finished at the club, they escorted him to his office with a quick stop at the bagel shop on the ground floor.

Irma knocked softly, then entered the room. She was carrying a Justice Department envelope addressed to Darcy.

"Good morning," she said. "Coffee?"

"No, thank you," he replied, as usual. "What is that?"

"Oh, just something that will make you mad."

"Let me guess. They're saying that I have a conflict, and they want me disqualified as counsel for Lynne Tobias."

Irma narrowed her eyes. "Boss," she said, "there's no way you could have read this yet. How do you know what the allegations are? Is there something you want to share?"

"No, Irma. Patrick gave me a heads up. He got it from one of his sources over there. Let's read it and see what it says."

Irma pulled it out and began to read, summarizing as she went along. "It says that you have a sexual relationship with Ms. Tobias, that there's a great deal of money missing, and that you may have a financial interest in the outcome of the case."

"Uh-huh," Darcy said. "So, they have any evidence?"

"Of course not. It's an Owen Dempsey special," she answered.

"Let's see what Vernon Peters has to say about this. When is the hearing?"

"That's the good part. It's this afternoon at two. Kathy's drafting the response for you, because Patrick is covering her at Twenty-sixth Street."

"Jeez, I'm damn near unnecessary around here," he said.

Just then, Kathy walked in. "Well, if it isn't, Lance Romance," she said mockingly. "I've decided to respond to the preposterous nature of this allegation by pointing out—and I think everyone will agree—that you're just not that attractive, Darcy."

"Or rich," he added.

• • •

At 1:45 sharp, Darcy, Kathy, and Lynne Tobias were in the courtroom of Vernon Peters. Anna Minkoff was seated across the aisle at the opposing counsel table, but Owen Dempsey was nowhere to be seen.

Kathy leaned over to Anna and caught her attention. "I know you didn't write this."

"How could you tell?" she asked.

"First, you wouldn't, and second, you would have done it better."

Darcy joined in the conversation. "So that bastard hung you out to dry, did he? You're going to have to argue this in front of the Honorable Judge Peters."

"Hell, no, I'm not arguing this," she answered. "He'll be here. He's waiting to make an entrance."

"I'd ask what a nice girl like you is doing working for him," Darcy said, smiling. "But I just remembered you're not all that nice yourself."

"Thank you, Darcy," she said, smiling. "You'll like me even less after I kick your ass."

The clerk and the court reporter had come out. They stood at the front of the courtroom watching the clock.

At precisely two o'clock, out strode Vernon Peters, his black robe slightly open as he worked the zipper on it. He climbed up onto the bench and slammed his gavel down. The court was called to order, and Peters dropped his paperwork on the desk in front of him.

"Government, you have a motion to disqualify Mr. Cole. Is that right?"

A voice from the back of the courtroom thundered, "That's correct, Judge." As Owen Dempsey walked down the aisle, all heads turned toward him. He wouldn't have it any other way.

"Mr. Dempsey, this court proceeding began at two o'clock. You're late."

"Well, actually, Your Honor, by my watch I'm right on time."

He loves to dig his grave, Darcy thought.

"I read the motion that you filed with the court, Mr. Dempsey—first, in the newspapers and finally in the court file. Now, Mr. Dempsey, the allegations must be proved, and I'm sure you're prepared to do that. Is that right?"

"Your Honor, we are ready to proceed by way of proffer."

"No, no, no, Mr. Dempsey. I don't want to hear what you believe someone will say. I want witnesses."

"Your Honor, I'm not prepared to go forward with witnesses."

"Mr. Dempsey, these are scurrilous accusations you have thrown at Mr. Cole. I want evidence, and I want it now. Let me explain something to you. You, sir, have no power whatsoever. You are just a man who happens to be a lawyer, who holds the position of the U.S. Attorney for the Northern District of Illinois. Your position has power. I, on the other hand, as judge for the United States District Court, happen to have quite a bit of power. I'm going to compel you to prove these allegations. If you can't, I'm going to dismiss this petition. That's power."

"Your Honor, I will prove these allegations."

"Go ahead, Mr. Dempsey. I'm listening."

"Your Honor, I am prepared to go by way of proffer."

"Mr. Dempsey, a proffer is nothing more than what you believe somebody will say. Do you at least have affidavits for me?"

"No sir, I don't."

"Do you have sworn statements of any kind? Under oath, court reported—something?"

"No, sir, I don't."

"Mr. Dempsey, I'm going to indulge you for just a moment. Tell me what you have to substantiate these allegations."

"I have three separate witnesses who will testify before

this court, under oath, that they have seen Mr. Cole visit the defendant at her home and stay for three, four, three, and two and a half hours on four separate occasions. I have James Ryan and Peter Vanek, law partners of the late Charles Tobias, who will indicate that Mr. Tobias had a net worth of close to twelve million dollars, approximately eight million of which is unaccounted for. I have a travel agent who will indicate that someone named Darcy Cole made reservations to fly from Chicago on a charter to Grand Cayman Island and return two days later on a different charter flight. The same travel agent will say that three weeks later a man named Darcy Cole made reservations to fly to the Bahamas for two days."

"So this travel agent is going to testify that Darcy Cole, the man seated in court, made these trips?"

"Well, no, Your Honor. The trips were never used, but the reservations were made."

"And you have witnesses who will testify that on four separate occasions they saw or they know that Mr. Cole had sex with his client? I mean, let's cut the crap, Mr. Dempsey. Isn't that what you're alleging?"

"No, Judge. The witnesses will say only that he was with her for that period of time."

"Let me ask you this, sir. What law prevents Mr. Cole and Ms. Tobias from having sexual relations, if they choose to do so?"

"Well, we believe that would be an unduly close relationship between an attorney and his client."

"Yes, sir, perhaps it would be. However, my question to you is, can you point to a rule that says that a client and a lawyer cannot engage in consensual sexual encounters?"

"No, Your Honor, there is no rule, per se."

"Per se, nothing. There is no rule," Peters thundered. "Now, about this money. How does the fact that eight million dollars is missing from the estate of Charles Tobias have anything to do with attorney and counselor Darcy Cole?"

"Well, Your Honor, we believe Mr. Cole made those reservations."

"Reservations that were not used," interrupted the judge.

"In any event, we believe he was prepared to do some offshore banking."

"Well, there you go, Mr. Dempsey. You have sunk to a new low. You have no evidence. Did it occur to you that Mr. Cole could have made those reservations in an attempt to get some R and R during a heated and contentious trial? Probably not, since you haven't tried anything in the four years that you've been the U.S. attorney here."

Dempsey should have known better. He was sinking fast, and he was angry. He could feel the eyes of the press on his back, and it wasn't the kind of attention he wanted.

"Your Honor, I'm prepared to go forward with an evidentiary hearing on any date you say. Just give me a week to bring these witnesses in."

"Mr. Dempsey, even if you could prove all that you have said, there is nothing there to disqualify Mr. Cole. I will tell you this, there is nothing in your presentation so far which would indicate that you have evidence of anything other than a runaway ego and a fear of getting your butt kicked at trial. If you can come up with some evidence of some wrongdoing or some improprieties between Mr. Cole and his client, that's fine. But let me ask one last question. Under the scenario you've laid out, couldn't Ms. Tobias step up and waive any potential conflict?"

Sweat was beading up on Owen Dempsey's head, and he felt drops dripping down his back.

"Well, Your Honor, I suppose that under certain circumstances, she could."

"Why don't we ask her?" the judge suggested. "Ms. Tobias, I assume that you have paid Darcy Cole quite a bit of money to represent you."

"Yes, sir, I have," she said.

"And I assume that's because you want him to be your lawyer."

"Yes, sir, I do."

"Now without going into whether any of these allegations have merit, do you still want Darcy Cole to be your lawyer?"

"Yes, sir, I do."

"Thank you, Ms. Tobias. Mr. Dempsey, don't waste the court's time with this nonsense. You may end up being the governor one day, but first you have to get through this case. So, try it like a lawyer."

Peters turned his gaze toward Darcy. "Mr. Cole, please don't take this ruling lightly. If evidence of wrongdoing by any lawyer is presented to this court and it is proven, there will be dire consequences."

He smacked the gavel on the bench, then stood. He stared Dempsey down before stepping off the bench.

As Darcy and Kathy packed up their briefcases, Sandy Campos, the reporter from Channel 2, approached them. "Darcy, will you go on camera today?"

"What for? Don't you have enough right there?"

"I'd like to hear your side."

"My side is that I categorically deny everything. If you want that on video, fine. But you really don't need it, do you?"

"I'd rather have you on video than an artist's sketch," she replied.

"Anyway, why not get Owen to go on camera?"

"Gee," Sandy said, "and where's the challenge in that?"

"Okay, I'll give you two minutes in my office. But I need about fifteen minutes first. Deal?"

Sandy smiled. "How about five minutes at your office in ten minutes?"

Darcy extended his hand, "Deal."

Kathy tapped Darcy on the shoulder. "I'm going to run upstairs and file a few things," she said. "I'll meet you back at the office."

While he walked to the elevator with the Doe boys on either side of him, Darcy gathered his thoughts about what had just happened. He wanted the right spin for Sandy

Campos. They left the courthouse building and crossed the street. As they reached Darcy's building the bagel shop window shattered into little pieces. John jumped on top of Darcy, forcing him to the ground, while Jim scanned the situation as he pulled a large pistol out of his pocket. John quickly ushered Darcy into the lobby of his building and onto an elevator.

"What the hell?" Darcy exclaimed. "Was that a shot? I didn't hear a shot."

John Doe looked at him. "That's why they call them silencers, sir," he said, breathing heavily. "Fuck. Everybody knew you had this hearing. It was in the fucking paper, for Christ's sake. You were a sitting duck."

Darcy wasn't exactly reassured.

The law office was on the sixteenth floor, but they took the elevator to fourteen, where they got off and walked to a stairwell. John had Darcy sit on the stairs while he pulled a cellular phone out of his pocket. He dialed a number and waited for a response.

"Yeah, I'm here," he said. "He's fine. What's up?"

There was a pause, then he said, "Okay, I'll take him to his office. Meet me there." He hung up.

"Okay, Mr. Cole, we're going to walk two flights."

As they climbed the two flights of stairs and reached sixteen, John poked his head up, gun in his right hand. He looked up and down the hall, saw nothing, and waved for Darcy to come up. He then held Darcy by the back of the jacket and walked behind him, looking around.

They entered his office, where Irma was at her desk. John Doe looked at her. "Any visitors or clients that you don't know?"

She shook her head. "No, just us."

They went in, and John Doe locked the door behind them. "Don't go to your office," he ordered. "Stay near your secretary, away from the windows."

Darcy complied.

"What happened?" Irma asked.

Darcy looked at her. "I don't want you getting nervous, but someone may have taken a shot at me."

"Oh, my God," she said. "What's going on? Will we be killed?"

"No, ma'am. Everything's safe here," John said. "You can count on that."

Darcy turned to Irma. "Page Sandy Campos from Channel 2. Tell her I can't meet her today. Oh, and call Lynne Tobias, too. Let her know that I'll call her when I figure out what's going on here."

It was nearly thirty minutes later that three men wearing suits walked in the front door and nodded to John Doe. John motioned them over to him with a tip of his head. He looked at Darcy. "I think you'll need to take the rest of the day off, Mr. Cole."

"Where are we going?" Darcy asked.

"You can't go home. We'll take you someplace where you'll be safe for a while."

"Let me gather a few things," he said. "I need my briefcase, a few files, and my reading glasses."

"Don't go into your office. Just tell me where they are," said John. "I'll get them for you."

There was a knock at the front door. Irma opened it, and Willie Mae Watkins walked in and sat on one of the chairs in the waiting area.

"Who's that?" John asked.

"That's a prospective client's mother," Darcy replied.

John turned to one of his three friends. "Search her," he said.

Darcy intervened, "No, please don't do that. I know who she is. She's not involved in the shooting."

"I'm sorry. We have to search her," John insisted.

One of his friends approached her and said, "Ma'am, can I see your purse and that bag please?"

She handed both of them over. He searched them and then gave them back.

"She's clean," they said.

Darcy looked at her. "I'm sorry, Ms. Watkins. Something happened, and they're just investigating it. I won't be able to meet with you today."

"That's okay, Mr. Cole," she replied. "Tomorrow, perhaps." And as she had done every afternoon since the first day she met with Darcy, she reached into her bag and pulled out a well-worn Bible, then opened it to a bookmark. She put the bookmark into her purse and began to read.

Darcy got up to leave. "Call Collata. Tell him to page me from wherever he is," he said. "I don't know where I'm going, so just tell him to page me."

"Okay, Boss."

"Tell Patrick and Kathy to be careful. Have them page me later, too. Close the office and go home. Someone will escort you."

"Maybe we would be safer here," said Irma.

John Doe interrupted. "We'll take care of everyone here, Mr. Cole. But we have to leave now."

Once they made it out of the building, they ran through the loading dock into a waiting vehicle. Darcy could see police cars with their lights flashing on the street in front of the building. They went in the opposite direction, toward an Embassy Suites hotel in Deerfield, a suburb north of Chicago. John Doe went in and returned with a room key. They went upstairs.

Darcy had the bedroom. John and two of his men had the living room area.

"I'm going out for food," he told Darcy. "So just tell me what you want. You're just going to sit tight for a while."

"What's a while?" Darcy asked.

"I'm not sure yet," John answered. "Just try to relax."

John had Darcy write down his pants size, shirt size, and underwear size. Then he sent one of his guys out to buy Darcy clothes and toiletries.

He came back with a big bag from Marshall Field's; in it

were a pair of khaki Dockers, a couple of golf shirts, boxers, socks, and T-shirts. In another bag from Walgreen's were disposable razors, shaving cream, toothbrush, toothpaste, hair brush, a few magazines, and a couple of newspapers. He also brought back a cell phone with the number taped on the back of it.

"If someone pages you, use this to call them back," John said.

• • •

Darcy talked to Kathy, Patrick, and Irma a couple of times a day for the next three days. Other than that he watched TV and did countless sets of sit-ups and pushups. By his fourth night of captivity, he was starting to go nuts. He managed to persuade the boys to at least take the next room over, promising them that he'd leave the door between open at all times. That way he didn't have to share a bathroom with three monstrous men.

And Darcy began to crave his routine. He wanted to get back to the club for his morning swim, to eat his breakfast by the pool. Most of all, he wanted to be back at work.

Over those few days, Darcy had a lot of time to think. He realized that he wasn't afraid of dying—though he'd prefer to put it off for a while. But he isolated his real fear. The worst fate that Darcy could think of was to be idle. No retirement village in Florida for him. He wanted to be plugged into the action. He liked defending criminals in a big city. He liked the reputation he had built for himself. How many more years could he stay on top of the game? That was his true fear, growing old and useless.

John Doe interrupted his thoughts. "Good news, Mr. Cole. You might be going back to work in the morning." He handed Darcy a handful of movies from Blockbuster. "Relax and watch a flick. You'll be home before you know it."

Darcy looked through the videos but never bothered to put one in the VCR. Instead, he nodded off while watching

CNN. He awoke when his pager began to vibrate. Picking up the cell phone, he called the office.

"Yeah, it's Darcy," he said sleepily.

Irma asked him to hold for Patrick. "Hey, Darcy," he said, "I did the 2.04 conference with Anna Minkoff. I have all the discovery."

"Any surprises?"

"Well, they got a few more flippers."

"No kidding!"

"Yeah, and we got some tapes, too."

"Audio or video?"

"Just audio, but they were nice enough to provide transcripts of the tapes, too. I'll compare them to make sure they're accurate."

"Send them out to be authenticated and duplicated," Darcy said. "I want to be sure they're not putting together more of a case than they truly have."

"I'm way ahead of you," Patrick said. "I had Collata deliver them to the audio guy. When are you going to be in, Boss?"

"Soon, they tell me. I may be in tomorrow. I'm losing my mind here."

"Well, hopefully, this will just be a good story," Patrick said.

"Yeah, someday, maybe. Call me when you need me," Darcy said.

Darcy's pager went off again, and he looked down to see a government number. He dialed it, and after four rings, someone answered. "Anna Minkoff, can I help you?"

"Yeah, Anna, Darcy Cole returning your page."

"Mr. Cole, hi. Now that you have all the discovery, I wanted to discuss with you whether your client might be interested in working out a plea agreement."

"Well, Ms. Minkoff, I haven't seen all the discovery yet. I've been out of the office for a few days."

"Yes, I heard someone took a shot at you."

"That's the same rumor I heard," said Darcy. "Do you have any confirmation that it's true?"

"Let's see, you have represented murderers, drug dealers, money launderers, pedophiles, sexual offenders, and mobsters. Who could possibly be angry with you?"

"Probably some cop or federal agent who holds a grudge."

"Darcy, I want you to know that I sincerely want you alive and healthy. After all, what pleasure could I derive from convicting Lynne Tobias if you're not in top form?"

"I'm touched by your concern, but aren't you second chair in the Tobias case?" Darcy asked.

"Ah, make no mistake about it. I view this as an opportunity to go head to head with you. No kudos to you, but to be the best you have to beat the best."

Darcy dropped his facade. "Look, Anna, I think you're a great lawyer and I look forward to trying this against you. Drop Owen, and we can go one on one."

"Right. Easier said than done. In any event, if you're willing to discuss a plea agreement, we should do it soon because I understand that Judge Peters is going to set a trial date for the twenty-eighth of next month."

"Bless his heart," said Darcy.

"He doesn't let his docket get crowded."

"As you know, Anna, if you tender an offer of a plea agreement to me, I'll run it by my client as I'm obligated to do. But if I were you, I'd be prepared to tee it up."

"You might have gotten away with a little flimflam in *Espinoza*," Anna countered, "but this isn't a money laundering case. This is a murder case, and I'm going to nail your ass to the wall."

"Ms. Minkoff, this is a fraud case. The murder you're talking about is merely related conduct. After all, if it were a murder case, we'd have a double jeopardy issue, wouldn't we?"

"Just be ready, Darcy. I don't want to hear any more excuses."

"I'll see you on the fourteenth at the final pretrial, Ms. Minkoff."

Anna's voice softened. "I'm serious, Darcy, and really, take care of yourself."

"I will, Anna, I promise."

• • •

At 6:30 the next morning, there was a knock on Darcy's door. It was John Doe.

"What's up, John?"

"You can get dressed, sir. We're going to drive you back downtown."

"Well, good. What happened?"

"I've been told everything is okay now. I don't know the particulars. I'll drive you downtown. If you want to stop at your place, I'll take you by there first."

The trip on the expressway into the city started off sluggishly with moderately heavy traffic. Darcy watched the horizon beyond the road change from large homes to a mix of businesses and strip malls and back again to homes as they passed some of the near north suburbs. Fifty minutes later they reached the front of his building.

Darcy ran up to his apartment and grabbed some work clothes. He had John drop him at the club. He had missed three workouts while hiding out in Deerfield, but his stroke was actually a little stronger because of it. It occurred to him that a couple of days off now and then would probably help his routine.

Afterwards, he grabbed a *Sun-Times* and sat in the steam room, trying to get up enough steam for a nice clean shave. On page three of the *Sun-Times* a headline caught his eye: "First Mob Hit in Years." He read the story and found the victim to be Joseph Battaglia, known on the streets as Joey Bag O'Donuts. The article discussed how Battaglia had been found with his kneecaps broken and his testicles crushed. The body was recovered in a real estate office in Melrose Park, a suburb west of Chicago. It quoted a Melrose Park detective as saying,

"It looks as if the victim was tortured prior to his death." No shit, Darcy thought. It made him queasy, the fact that this gruesome act had been committed because of him. No, that wasn't right, he decided. It was because of Junior.

At least one of the monsters hunting Darcy was gone. Now they had to find Mangano. Although if word got out about how Bag O'Donuts met his end, Mangano might just go ahead and kill himself. That'd be okay, too, Darcy thought.

Darcy headed across the street and got on the elevator. After he reached the sixteenth floor, he burst into his office. "What do you have for me, Irma?"

"Well, welcome back, Boss," she greeted him. She handed him a stack of phone messages. "There's mail on your desk. It's been piling up."

"Any of it worthwhile?"

"Not really. You need to pay some bills."

"Oh, good. Get Patrick and Kathy in my office as soon as they get in," he said.

"They're in. I'll round them up."

"We'll meet in the conference room."

Darcy walked into his office and threw his coat on the hook behind the door. He grabbed a legal pad and reading glasses and walked into the conference room while thumbing through some mail.

"Okay, all this crap is over," he declared, throwing everything onto the table. "We've got a trial starting next month on the twenty-eighth. Let's get busy."

"But you've got Morales on the twenty-eighth," said Kathy.

"Bump it," Darcy said, peering over his bifocals.

"Judge Reynolds is going to hit the roof," she said.

"Don't worry about it. He used to be in private practice. He knows these federal judges are a bunch of cocksuckers. To them, no other courts exist. The state courts probably have three or four stacked up for trial that same day. What else do we have?"

"Nothing that we can't take care of," said Patrick. "I listened to the tapes and I ran them against the transcripts. The transcripts are accurate. They haven't added anything to help their cause."

"Good job, Patrick," said Darcy. "What else?"

"I have a list of their witnesses."

"Is that the final list?" he asked.

"Well, they may sneak in a couple more, but I think it's pretty close to final."

"Damn, Patrick. Good job. It's as if you never left there."

"Collata has some interesting things on the insurance agent."

"Is that right?"

"Oh, yeah. Look at this," Patrick said as he slid a folder to Darcy. As Darcy begain to look over the materials from Collata, Patrick continued, "Also, I went over all the discovery materials in the file and divided up tasks to be done to prepare for trial."

Darcy was about to adjourn their meeting when Kathy spoke up. "Wait, Darcy. Have you talked to Irma? Ms. Watkins has $10,000, and she can pay $500 a month till the balance is paid."

"That would mean that after ten months we'd have $15,000. Is that right?"

"Yes, that's right," she said.

"We don't do murder cases for $15,000. Do we?"

"Well, I think we should this time."

"Who's representing her son now?" he asked.

"The public defender."

"Which public defender?"

"I'm not sure. Someone in the murder task force."

"Well, they're experienced. I'm sure they'll do a good job. Anyway, I thought we were going to let it go until after the *Tobias* trial. In the meantime, the public defender can begin the investigation. Anything else?"

No one spoke up.

"Good, get to work."

Darcy walked into his office to find Collata smoking a cigarette with his feet on his desk. "Darn, you're still alive."

"That's a rumor started by people who don't like me," Darcy answered. "What, no Scotch today?"

"Hell, I've only been up for two hours."

"Really? That long?" said Darcy. "I saw your work on the insurance agent. It looks good."

"It was easy," Collata said. "There are a lot of people who want to see him fall."

"Good. Let's give him a push in front of a jury."

Suddenly they heard shouts coming from the waiting room. Collata reached down to an ankle holster and pulled out a gun.

Owen Dempsey walked into Darcy's office without knocking, followed by two guys who Darcy knew were FBI agents. They were his usual entourage.

Dempsey pointed to Collata. "Put that away or I'll have my men shoot you."

"Shut the fuck up or I'll shoot them, then I'll shoot your balls off," Collata said as he holstered it.

"Do you know about the murder of Joseph Battaglia?" Dempsey asked.

"Just what I read in the paper. Why? You want to accuse me of it?" asked Darcy.

"I want to question you about it," he said.

"Good, send me a subpoena for the grand jury. In the meantime, I don't want to see your face around here."

"Remember, Darcy, I gave you your chance to talk about this," he said. "I'm holding a news conference at 4:00. You're welcome to be there." And just as abruptly as they had entered, Dempsey and his entourage left.

• • •

A United States flag hung to his left, and the seal of the United States Attorney's Office was on the podium before him as

Owen Dempsey stood in front of a packed press conference. Several assistant U.S. attorneys stood behind him.

"Joseph Battaglia, known on the streets as Joey Bag O'Donuts, was a renegade crew member of Anthony Benvenuti Jr., a made member of the Chicago mob. He was found brutally murdered this morning in a Melrose Park office building. We have reason to believe that the murder had something to do with defense attorney Darcy Cole, in that an alleged contract was put out on Mr. Cole by Anthony Benvenuti Jr. I will now take questions."

Several reporters shouted at the same time. He selected the question he liked.

"No, I don't know why Mr. Benvenuti, a disgruntled former client of Mr. Cole's, would allegedly put a contract out on his life. But as you know, Mr. Cole has represented many notorious people over the years, and it's hard to speculate as to exactly what went wrong in this particular case. I will say that Mr. Benvenuti was convicted on all counts and received a lengthy prison term, which may have resulted in a de facto life sentence."

He was in his glory, throwing accusations without any proof or evidence and relying on the fact that he couldn't comment on an ongoing investigation. Then Sandy Campos from Channel 2 dropped a bomb.

"Mr. Dempsey, could you tell us about your relationship with Karen Fowler and whether or not you used public funds to have a tryst with her?"

A hush fell over the room, and Dempsey looked as if he had just been kicked in the stomach. "Is that a question or an accusation?" he asked.

"Could you tell us, sir, what your relationship is with Karen Fowler, and whether or not on two separate occasions you used taxpayer money to have a tryst with her?"

"Madam, I am happily married and the father of two children. This is nothing more than political dirty tricks because of my involvement in the governor's race. If you have any evidence, bring it forward, but I dare say you have nothing."

Jim Parker from the *Tribune* stood up, "Sir, are you denying that you had an extramarital affair with Karen Fowler?"

He looked at him. "Yes, sir, I certainly am. Ms. Fowler is merely a friend of mine and someone whose judgment I trust."

Parker took another shot. "Well, sir, wouldn't it be unusual to take a paralegal to a conference in Denver?"

"This news conference is over," Dempsey barked, and he stormed off.

Parker continued to scream questions at him. "Sir, would it be unusual to have a paralegal at a conference in Miami, considering that conference in Miami was on prosecutorial ethics?"

The press agent for the U.S. Attorney's Office stepped up to the podium. "Ladies and gentlemen, this conference is over. Please show yourselves out."

• • •

Patrick and his significant other, Dan Arvin, joined Darcy and Collata at Gibson's for dinner. After Scotch and red meat, they drifted into the bar to drink some more and wait for the news. On camera Owen Dempsey looked like a deer in the headlights as he was pummeled with questions. What had started as an attack on Darcy had him backpedaling madly. After the aborted news conference, he issued a press statement in which he categorically denied any untoward involvement with his paralegal, Karen Fowler. What's more, he reiterated what a good family man he was.

Then Sandy Campos began her report, showing the videotape that would be the end of Owen Dempsey. It was a tape of Dempsey dancing on the deck at a Miami Beach hotel between the pool and the ocean, his hand squeezing the backside of Karen Fowler. Later there was footage of him embracing her during a long passionate kiss on the beach. There was no mistaking the identity of either one.

Collata's cigar glowed red as he puffed the smoke into the air and sipped back another Glenlivet. "Goddamn, that was funny," he said.

"Not to Mrs. Dempsey," Darcy said.

"Not much of a point to Ms. Fowler finishing her legal education," said Patrick.

"Must be nice to have such good friends in the press," Collata said.

"It is," Darcy replied, "and they couldn't have performed better if I'd fed them the questions."

SEVEN

Vernon Peters's chambers were down the hall from his court-room, on the twenty-fifth floor looking east out over Lake Michigan, Soldier Field, and McCormick Place. Not bad for a guy who'd come from modest beginnings.

Around him were reminders of where he had started and how he'd gotten where he was now. His diplomas, elegantly framed, were displayed with photos of him with President Clinton, Mayor Harold Washington, Jesse Jackson, Rosa Parks, and Justice Thurgood Marshall, among others. The photos illustrated his successful career, each showing him at a different age. There were also framed photos of his family, showing his children from their childhoods to their adult years.

Minkoff and Darcy were seated across from his desk.

"Judge, I'm asking that you kick this for two months and exclude the time so that I can prepare the case with another prosecutor," she began.

Judge Peters exploded into laughter. "You've got to be kidding! Your boss gets his dick caught in a mousetrap, and you want us to help you out on this? Please, Ms. Minkoff! The trial date stays. Unless Mr. Cole has a problem with that."

"No, Judge, we'll be ready."

Peters reached into his humidor and pulled out a cigar. He rolled the end around in his mouth, then took out his cutters, snipped, and lit up without asking if anyone minded.

"You know, Ms. Minkoff, you guys are turning into the gang that couldn't shoot straight. Your office loses the key piece of evidence in the *Espinoza* trial, one of the biggest cases you've had here in years. Now, on the eve of a trial he's hoping will push him into the governor's mansion, Dempsey gets caught having sex with his paralegal, and at the taxpayers' expense. You know, Ms. Minkoff, some people would say that's theft, perhaps fraud. Certainly it's official misconduct, all of which are felony offenses in the state of Illinois."

"I'm well aware of what the allegations are against Mr. Dempsey. However, the interests of justice will not be—"

He stopped. "Ms. Minkoff, cut the bullshit. You're on trial on the twenty-eighth. We all know you were going to try this case, and he was sitting there for the cameras. The three of us know exactly what's going on. So on the twenty-eighth we are going to pick your jury, ma'am."

He puffed on the cigar. "Darcy, you son of a bitch, you sit there like the cat that ate the canary. I wonder how the press got a hold of this story. Isn't it interesting that Sandy Campos and Jim Parker are the two reporters who seem to have everything. And I could have sworn they were friends of yours."

"Again, Judge, you give me too much credit," answered Darcy. "Owen Dempsey made his own bed."

"Let me tell you a story about this man, Ms. Minkoff. As you may know, Darcy Cole was a prosecutor over at Twenty-sixth and California. You know, state court—it's not this white-collar bullshit you have over here. Anyway, there was this mob-connected jewel thief, a second-floor man, and he had gone up on the Gold Coast and climbed into an Astor Street brownstone. My theory was that it was supposed to be empty and it was supposed to be all for insurance—but, lo and behold, the homeowner didn't want to have to pay his wife a divorce settlement. So she was laid up in there dead. Darcy was prosecuting this jewel thief for murder. I was representing the thief, and I believed he hadn't killed anybody. He was just a thief. He got set up by the husband, who whacked his wife and then waited until the thief got up there, then had the police catch him there.

"You may not know this about Mr. Cole, but he was married at one point and had a little girl, the apple of his eye. She was about ten when we did this trial, and the only two things he did were try cases and go around with his daughter. She meant everything to him. Well, a week before this trial was supposed to start, Darcy's wife up and left him for some doctor. Ran off to New York and took his daughter with her.

"Now, in those days, wasn't much you could do. Little girl was gone. Well, a week to go to trial and Darcy was crushed. His whole world was in New York. Nothing was holding him in Chicago, but he had to try this case. He walked into court, just like you did, and asked the judge for a continuance. Judge said, 'I don't give a rat's ass about your personal life. I care about this case. It's set for trial. Try it, or pass it off to one of your partners.' But Darcy wouldn't. So he came in. He tried it straight up. We went head to head, two-week trial, forty-five minute guilty. I deserved the verdict, but he seduced that jury like an English gentleman with a handful of hundreds in a New Orleans whore house."

He puffed on the cigar a bit more and the room was silent.

"That was the worst time of my life, Vernon, and you know it."

Peters looked at him. "Yup, and that's when I knew you were a better trial lawyer than me, because I couldn't have tried that case."

He turned back to Anna. "I was so impressed with his argument that I confronted my client in the lockup. He gave it up. He had killed the woman. I had believed him. Remember, I was no young innocent at the time, but I had bought my guy's story. That was the first and last time I ever asked a client if he did it. Darcy left the courthouse, walked to his car, and drove through the night to New York."

Anna Minkoff cleared her throat. "Well, that sure is some story about two old war horses. But you know what, Mr. Cole? Now it's my turn. I'm going to beat you. Judge Peters, you can be the belligerent old shit that you are, but there aren't going to be any missing tapes in this case."

Peters had a smile on his face. "You see, Ms. Minkoff, I knew all along you were the trial lawyer in this case. So all you did was lose 190 pounds of baggage."

Anna looked at both of them, then stood up. "Well, I am the trial lawyer in this case now, and you two don't intimidate me. I'll see you in court."

Peters continued to puff on his cigar. He looked at Darcy. "You ever talk to your ex-wife anymore?"

"She died. Cancer. When my daughter was in her third year of college."

"And how's your daughter?" he asked.

"You know, she's turned out real well. Thank you for asking."

Peters opened up his humidor and pushed the box over. "Cigar?"

"Don't mind if I do." Darcy reached in and pulled one out.

The judge leaned over and cut the end of it, then slid the lighter over to Darcy.

"You know, Vernon, we're a lot alike. We really don't have shit except for this job."

"You got that right," Vernon said. "My kids went away to college and never came back. I miss them. Sometimes I wish they weren't so goddamn independent. They all call me on Father's Day, though."

Darcy lit up his cigar. "Yeah, Father's Day. That's the day that reminds me of what a failure I am."

EIGHT

Darcy was drinking wine out of a juice glass—no need for formality when he was just trying to get back to sleep. Outside his window, he watched the few cars on Lake Shore Drive. The lake was dark and still, the sun hours from rising. He found himself more and more often waking at three or four o'clock in the morning, unable to sleep. The emptiness of his life pulled him from his sleep—nothing to dream, perhaps. In the predawn darkness, he imagined the drivers below with lives fuller and richer than his.

He lived in a huge two-bedroom condominium with a living room, a small dining room, a kitchen, a den, and two bathrooms. It had a nice view looking northeast along the lake, down Lake Shore Drive toward the golf course. He had taken it years earlier as a fee in a federal case from a defendant charged with bank fraud.

He had a television in his den that was seldom on. The few

hours he was home, he preferred to sit and look out the window while listening to music—mostly classical or Chicago blues. At one time he had been a symphony subscriber, but had given up his tickets. On weekends he used to cook meals for himself—but no longer.

His work area was the second bedroom. It was equipped with a computer and fax machine. Somewhere under a pile of books he had read or was planning to read was a bed. He hadn't had a guest over since his daughter some seven years earlier. In the corner were his golf clubs. Three summers had passed since his last round of golf.

These were the things that kept him up through the night—the fact that he'd lost interest in hobbies, passions, and social life in general. And it wasn't that he was completely fulfilled by his career; he was losing that passion, too.

Other than the club or the office, he rarely went anywhere. Now, once again, he sat in the middle of the night looking out of the window, inventing lives for strangers driving by. Lives that were better than his own.

When daylight came, the Doe boys were waiting to drive Darcy to the club. After exchanging greetings, Darcy settled into the back seat. It was a quiet ten-minute ride to the club.

Upon arriving, he went through his workout and ate breakfast, skipping his steam, and stepped back out of the lobby to meet the Doe boys. While Darcy had become used to being with them, he still knew nothing about them. He wondered whether they personally had killed Joey "Bag O'Donuts" Battaglia or if that had been the work of one of their colleagues. He never asked them whether or not they had found Mangano. He knew by virtue of their presence that Mangano was still out there.

When he arrived at the office, he accepted a cup of coffee from Irma, then sat at his desk and read a memo from Patrick that was marked Confidential Attorney Work Product. Then he called Patrick in. When Patrick walked in, Darcy had his reading glasses on the tip of his nose and was looking at the memo.

"Good morning, Boss," said Patrick.

Darcy looked at him over his glasses. "Boy, where do you get your information? Tell me about Rona Siegal."

Patrick stretched out on the couch, looking tired. He'd been working almost constantly in Darcy's absence. "Apparently, she's not even a flipper. She just came forward after our ice princess won her state case. Rona thought that justice wasn't served and that she might have known something that would have helped the state's case."

"So how are we going to discredit or impeach her?" Darcy asked.

Patrick yawned. "I don't know. This woman has a great reputation, and she's got no bias or motive. Maybe she just doesn't like our client. Who the hell can blame her?"

Darcy pulled his glasses off and rubbed his eyes. He was already feeling his own lack of sleep.

"You know, Boss," said Patrick, "you won the state case, but maybe we ought to rethink the federal case. Maybe we should consider knocking out related conduct and see if we can get her something so she can still have a life after serving her sentence."

"What? A plea agreement?"

Patrick nodded. "A plea agreement. Or perhaps we ought to look at the possibility that we can't win this case. With all the flippers they're lining up, she may be looking at spending the rest of her life in prison. Maybe I can send a feeler out and see what happens."

"She'll never take a deal," said Darcy. "She's convinced nothing bad can happen to her."

"I guess the death of her husband didn't qualify as bad."

Darcy smiled a little.

The intercom interrupted them. "Ms. Tobias is here," Irma said.

"Send her in."

Patrick stood to leave.

"No, stay," Darcy said, "I'd like your feedback."

Lynne looked younger and happier than ever as she strolled in to Darcy's office. Darcy wondered if she might have had some facial work done since the last time he'd seen her. Or maybe it was just that he was starting to look—and feel— old. Irma closed the door behind her. Lynne looked at Patrick.

"I asked him to stay," Darcy explained. "We need to discuss some things with you."

Lynne sat in the chair directly across from Darcy. She reached into her purse and pulled out a cigarette, then lit it.

"We believe a woman named Rona Siegal is going to testify against you," Darcy said. "What can you tell us about her?"

She took a long drag on her cigarette and let the smoke escape slowly as she rubbed the corners of her mouth with her fingers. "As you know, her husband is a partner at Siegal, Ogden, whatever. We were social acquaintances. I used to work out with her at the East Bank Club, and occasionally we would get massages together."

"Anything else?"

"We had a few lunches, tea at the Ritz."

"So would you say you spent a lot of time with her?" asked Darcy. "Would you consider her a friend?"

"Yes, I would, I guess," she said hesitantly.

Patrick spoke up. "We believe she's going to testify about a conversation between the two of you in which you explained the difference—money wise—between divorcing a husband and having the husband die while you are still married."

Lynne simply took another long drag of her cigarette, so Patrick continued.

"Apparently, she told you that she suspected her husband was thinking of leaving her, and you told her how she would be financially ruined if they were to get divorced. She then said that on a cocktail napkin you laid out the financial advantage she'd have if her husband were simply to die prior to any divorce proceedings."

She looked at Patrick with disdain. "It's simple economics. When you are married to a wealthy man and he divorces you,

you lose access to his wealth. For example, say your husband is worth $10 million. If he was worth $5 million before you were married, then only $5 million of that is marital property. Even if you were to get half of that, he still leaves with $7.5 million and his earning potential. The best you can do is get some maintenance, or maybe some money for training to reenter the job market." She took another drag. "There is nothing sinister about a woman being realistic about the cost of divorce."

"Perhaps, Lynne, but it's not exactly how we want to portray you to the jury," Darcy said.

"And that's another thing, Darcy—explain to me again why trying me a second time is not a violation of double jeopardy clause?"

"It's real simple," he said. "And ask me any questions you want if you don't understand this. Number one, in state court you were charged with murder, conspiracy to commit murder, and solicitation to commit murder. You are now being charged with insurance fraud in federal court. They are using the murder as related conduct, which means that if they can convict you of fraud and conspiracy to commit fraud, they can use the murder in aggravation at sentencing and increase your sentence from the amount of time for the fraud to the amount of time for the fraud plus the time for the murder. If that's the case, you will die in prison. There are different elements of proof for fraud and murder. There are different jurisdictions for state and federal and, although it seems unfair, the courts have consistently held that it does not violate the double jeopardy clause, even when most of the same set of operative facts are being used to prove different offenses."

"So, if we win this case, are they going to turn around and indict me for something else?"

"Let's worry about winning this case first," said Darcy.

She looked over at Patrick. "Would you excuse us? I would like to talk to my lawyer in confidence."

Patrick looked at Darcy, who gave a quick nod of his head.

"I don't appreciate your condescending tone," she said to Darcy after Patrick closed the door. She crushed out the cigarette in an ashtray on Darcy's desk.

"Lynne, I can't be real concerned about your feelings at this point. You're on trial for your life. Although you didn't finish law school, you have a basic understanding of the legal concepts here, so let's not waste time playing games. We need something to use against these flippers. I'm especially concerned about Rona Siegal. I want something on her. I want her to know that I have it, so that she won't testify, or at least will soften her testimony against you. Do you understand me?"

"Yes, I understand you," Lynne said angrily.

Darcy handed her a black vinyl binder. "Here's discovery that I need you to read. I want to know what's bullshit and what we can prove is bullshit. There are dates, times, places, and conversations with various people. I want to be able to disprove as much as possible. I want you to go over this. Compare it to your date books, or however you keep track of your life. I want you to come up with things we can use. Do you understand?"

She nodded. "When do you want this?"

"The sooner the better."

She stuffed the binder into her Gucci bag and stood to leave. "Darcy, you're starting to worry me. You look tired, but I still expect to win this case."

"You just do what I ask, and let me worry about winning," Darcy said, walking her out.

On the way back into his office he poured a cup of coffee. He was standing near Irma's desk, hovering over her, and she looked up and shooed him away. "Go. I can't work with you standing over me."

He had returned to his desk and sat reading files and sipping stale, lukewarm coffee when there was a knock at the door. Irma popped her head in.

"Boss, can I talk to you?" she asked in a whisper.

"Sure, come on in."

She walked in and whispered into his ear. "Owen Dempsey is outside, and he wants to see you."

Darcy was surprised. "He didn't have an appointment, did he?"

"No, he just stopped in. Do you want to see him?"

Darcy leaned back and thought about it. "Sure. I'd like to tell him to go fuck himself. Send him right in."

Dempsey shuffled into the room and took a couple of paces with his outstretched hand reaching for Darcy's. Darcy sat with his hands behind his head and offered him a seat.

Dempsey looked smaller without FBI agents surrounding him. He also looked very tired. Join the crowd, Darcy thought.

"What can I do for you, Owen?"

"Where do you want me to begin?" Dempsey said, leaning forward in his chair. "As you know, I'm in a bit of trouble now. I need representation."

Darcy could barely contain himself. "There are four or five former U.S. attorneys who are partners at large firms. Why me?" he asked, incredulous.

"Actually," Owen replied, "I'm shopping for an attorney. I've already met with three of my predecessors, and, quite frankly, they're all talking about negotiating a deal. They haven't even looked at the evidence yet, and they assume I'm guilty."

Darcy said nothing. He rocked back in his chair.

"They were talking about official misconduct. They were talking about fraud. They were talking felony convictions, Darcy. You know what that'll mean? I'll have no career left. Not only will I not be able to move on to higher office, I won't even be able to make a living. They're going to take my law license."

"You've been in this game for a while," said Darcy. "Do you have a defense?"

He gave a small, nervous laugh, "That's the most intelligent question anyone has asked me. Do I have a defense?" he repeated. "I'm not sure. Do they have proof?"

Darcy shook his head, "I don't know. All I know is what I've seen on the news. What do you know?"

"They're appointing a special investigator," said Dempsey. "Rumor has it that it's going to be the U.S. attorney from Houston."

"Do you know him? What's his slant on this?"

Dempsey shook his head. "I don't know him very well, but hell, federal prosecutors are always looking to convict an alderman, state reps, maybe a state senator. Don't you think he'd have a big hard-on to get a U.S. attorney?"

"What are the guidelines?" asked Darcy.

"The guidelines go out the window in something like this," said Dempsey. "They can do whatever the hell they want. They can say it took more than minimum planning. They can say I conspired with Karen Fowler. They can jack it up left and right for abuse of trust. It can get crazy quickly. I could get prison time for this."

Darcy leaned forward and smiled slightly. "Owen, I don't think I can represent you. After all, we've had quite a few run-ins over the years, and you just recently took some nasty shots at me."

"Shit, Darcy, I was this close to being governor. I'll admit it, I was pummeling you in the press to build myself up. But, god-damn it, we're lawyers. Can't we get beyond that? I need you."

"Again, why me?" Darcy asked.

"In part, it's the message that it sends," Dempsey replied. "Everyone who knows anything knows that we have fought like cats and dogs. If you're representing me, it sends a sub-liminal message that you believe in my innocence."

Darcy laughed, "Yeah, or it could send a not-so-subliminal message that you have a lot of money, which you're now hand-ing over to me."

"How much do want for this case?" Dempsey asked.

"I'm curious. What the hell are the other guys telling you they want?"

"Everything I ever had and anything that I'll ever have," said Dempsey, softly shaking his head.

Darcy glared at him. "Where are they going to try this

case? They can't try it here. Are they going to move it to Houston? Are you going to pay me to abandon my practice while I'm on trial in Houston? Pay for my lodging, my expenses, local counsel?"

Dempsey was sinking deeper into the chair. "I don't know," he said. "I just don't know."

Darcy leaned in toward Dempsey, "What is it that you really want? Do you want a trial? Do you want to make this go away? What do you want?"

"I want to beat this case. Hell, President Clinton gets a blow job from an intern and testifies under oath in a court proceeding that he didn't have sex with her. Two years later, kids are in school talking about oral sex with their teachers. So, I had an affair with a subordinate. It was a consensual relationship between two adults. The whole case rests on the assumption that the only reason she went on those trips was so we could have sex. There's a strong argument that being on those trips was entirely appropriate. I say let's go for it. Together, I know we can win this."

"Listen, Owen, usually a client hires me, and over a period of time I sometimes begin to despise him. In your case, I already do. I don't know that there's not an inherent conflict."

"What conflict could there be?" Dempsey asked. "I was the U.S. attorney. You are a defense attorney. I'm up on charges, it's going to be in another jurisdiction, an independent special prosecutor is going to handle it. Where's the conflict?"

"I'm talking about an emotional conflict, not a legal conflict. You're an arrogant son of a bitch. If I'm representing you, you'll have to put aside your feelings and listen to me."

"I've always respected you as a lawyer," Dempsey said. He shook his head. "Look, we're clearly on the wrong path here. I need your help, and I want you to consider representing me. I'm not sure I can afford you anyway. I'm going to interview a few other lawyers who would be happy to make their name off of representing Owen Dempsey."

Darcy would have to put up with weeks of that attitude. "I'll think about it, Owen, and I'll shoot you a price. It's not going to be the half million dollars that the other guys shot you."

Owen looked at him. "How do you know what they're going to charge me?"

Darcy smiled. "You're talking with former U.S. attorneys at big firms. They'll rape you on the hourly billing, then try to plead you when you run out of money."

"So you'll consider taking the case?" Owen asked while putting on his coat.

"I'll consider it," Darcy said, showing him out.

Kathy ran into Darcy's office as soon as Dempsey left.

"Hey. Interesting meeting?"

Darcy smiled at her. "Can you believe that son of a bitch wants me to represent him?"

Kathy laughed. "Seems he may not be as stupid as we thought." She sat down with an armload of paperwork. "I'm filing our brief in the Rodriguez appeal in the Seventh Circuit. Do you want to read it first?"

Darcy shook his head. "No, I'm sure you've done a good job. Would you like to argue it?" he asked.

"No problem," said Kathy. "It's not complicated. I'll be happy to do it."

"I appreciate that. What are you doing for lunch?"

"I don't know. What are you buying?"

"How about the club?"

"You want to go that far?" said Kathy, mockingly.

They walked across the street with the Does in tow and sat in the main dining room near the fireplace. The room was large and elegant. The forty-foot ceiling accommodated eight large chandeliers. Sunlight splashed through large windows framed in blue velvet drapes neatly pulled back. White linen table-cloths were the perfect backdrop for the china and silver, which had the club's crest on them. The uniformed waitstaff provided seamless service.

Kathy had a chicken Caesar salad while Darcy had fruit salad with cottage cheese and a diet soda.

"Patrick's been telling me about the *Tobias* case," Kathy said.

Darcy ate a piece of cantaloupe and wiped his lips. "You were pretty smart ducking that case, kiddo," he said.

"What are you going to do?" she asked.

"I don't know. She's a cold-hearted bitch. The deeper we get into this, the more people they're flipping on her with corroborating evidence. I've been looking for a common theme or design in the government's patchwork on this case. One could come to the conclusion that their witnesses are telling the truth. How in the hell do you cross-exam witnesses who are truthful?"

Kathy spoke right through her mouthful of food.

"Well, the only thing I can suggest is something you once told me," she said, chewing. "You get them caught up in the minutiae. You treat them like children. You ask them very detailed questions, and by the sheer nature of the detail, they are going to contradict other witnesses even though they're all telling the truth. No one is going to remember each intricate detail. Isn't that what you've told me?"

"You're right. But I'm hoping Collata will dig up something better than minutiae. After all, Lynne Tobias is expecting me to pull a rabbit out of my hat."

"We can only do our best. At least, that's what you've told me over and over again."

Darcy smiled at her. "Gee, Kathy, you sure do listen well," he said sarcastically.

"I have a great teacher."

"Let's change the subject," Darcy said as the waiter cleared their plates. "Tell me about your kids."

The waiter brought the dessert cart, but both Darcy and Kathy declined. They each had a cup of coffee, which became two cups while they talked about children. The dining room was almost empty.

Darcy asked Kathy how she felt about working part time, if she was able to juggle the job with raising her kids. "Oh, I juggle everything," she replied, "But that's not to say I don't drop a ball once in a while. You know, a lunch doesn't get made or a discovery motion doesn't get drafted. . . ."

"What?" Darcy interrupted in mock horror.

"But it's a nice mix," Kathy continued. "You could say I have it all."

"I think I used to have it all," Darcy said, looking into his coffee cup.

"What's up with you, Darcy? You've been pretty melancholy lately. You're not sick, are you?"

He shook his head, "No, I'm just feeling old. I'm seeing all the mistakes I made in my life and where it's left me. You know Judge McGuire who died last December? He was in my law school class."

"Darcy, he drank, he smoked, and he was overweight. You're in good shape."

"But I'm old, sweetheart. I have nothing to show for my life."

"How can you feel sorry for yourself? You're the best lawyer in Chicago. You've made a lot of money. You have a lot to show for what you've done."

"But I don't have anything of substance. You have your children and your husband. You have a life. You have people who care about you. . . ." Darcy's voice trailed off.

"You're not planning to give up law are you?" she asked.

"Then I'd really have nothing," answered Darcy. "I have to figure out what's missing. I'm not going to start making drastic changes."

"You know, Darcy, you are considered a very eligible bachelor," Kathy began.

Darcy interrupted her, "Please, I'm not asking you to scrounge up a date for me."

"That is not my point," she countered. "My point is that the only thing holding you back is you. You can get out and meet people. I thought you and Emily Dwyer made a nice couple, but you dumped her. I liked Judy Wright. You've known a few nice women. You're the one who's chosen this monklike existence."

"Hey, I haven't chosen anything—it's just turned out this way," Darcy said. "And I didn't dump Emily—we agreed to move on."

"Darcy, let me tell you something. If my kids are up all night, I still have to get up and come to work in the morning. On days when the sitter can't come, I have to scramble to find someone else so I can get here. I have to do those things because those are my responsibilities. Your responsibilities are running this law firm. You're responsible to your clients. You constantly tell me how much I've changed since I've been here, going from being single to married with children. You constantly praise me for the job I've done with everything. I praise you for all the things you've done, but that doesn't seem to mean anything to you. You have to take stock in what you have. Stop feeling sorry for yourself."

Darcy smiled and took a sip of his coffee. "How can I with you around?" He set his cup down. "We'd better head back to the office."

"Wait a second," she said. "Let me finish my thought."

Darcy gave her his full attention.

"I chased you down because of your reputation as one of the preeminent trial lawyers in the city. I harassed you into giving me a clerking job, and I've been here ever since. You've treated me like a daughter, and I love you. You took Patrick in after he'd been outed by and booted from the U.S. attorney's office. Now, we may be a dysfunctional family, but we're your family. You've been a godsend to us, so give us a chance to mean something to you."

Darcy smiled. "Well, if you're my daughter and Patrick is my son, does that make Irma your mother?"

"Yeah, and your wife. Why don't you think about developing some sort of social life to augment your career?" she said. "Maybe that's all that's missing."

Darcy looked at his watch. "Maybe you're right," he said, "but now it's time to work. Let's go."

The Doe brothers escorted the two of them back to the office, then took their place in the waiting room.

Darcy picked up his phone messages and called Irma on the intercom. "Irma, hold my calls for a while," he said. He then popped in the Bach Cello Suites CD, leaned back, and closed his eyes.

After a while Kathy knocked on the door and came in. "What are you doing?" she asked.

"I'm trying to achieve balance," he said with one eye open.

She began counting on her fingers. "Irritability, fatigue, difficulty sleeping—those are classic symptoms of clinical depression, Darcy."

"Not a defense," he said, pointing into the air. "Merely mitigation."

"Maybe you should talk to somebody."

She dropped some papers on his desk. "Here's a copy of the appellate brief I filed today. When you get a chance, please read it."

He picked it up and flipped it back to her. "I don't want to read it," closing both eyes again.

Suddenly there was a commotion in the waiting room outside Darcy's office. He opened the door to see the Doe brothers wrestling a man against the wall. He was the kid from the messenger service. Darcy rushed out. "It's okay," he said. "Let him go."

John held on while Jim grabbed a box from the kid's hands. "What's inside?" he asked angrily.

"How do I know?" the kid asked, frightened.

John opened the box, which contained another box filled with cigars. He rifled through them to make sure there were no wires or plastic explosives before he handed them back to Darcy.

Taped to the box was a note that read: "Mr. Cole, please accept this token of my appreciation." It was from Carlos Espinoza.

Darcy held the box open and offered cigars to the Does

and the messenger. John and Jim each took one; the kid took two and rushed out the door. "I'm sorry," John muttered.

Darcy waved them off. "Better to be safe than to have to explain to Mr. Benvenuti why I'm dead."

Back in his office, Darcy placed the cigar box on his desk. He would have liked to smoke one while gazing out over the lake, but there was an oversized Kevlar sheet covering his windows to protect him from snipers.

Patrick came in, grabbed a cigar, and sat down. "Hey, Boss, Dan and I are going to catch a movie tonight and get something to eat. Do you want to join us?"

A faint smile came across Darcy's face. "Been talking to Kathy?"

"Well, she did mention that you were feeling a little down."

"I appreciate it, but I don't want to go to a movie with two guys, whether they're a couple or not."

"Suit yourself. But do you mind if I take one of the cars for the weekend?"

Darcy shook his head, "Be my guest. It doesn't look like I'll be using them."

The firm leased two cars, which were kept in the parking garage across the street from the office building. Darcy reached into his desk drawer and threw a set of keys across the desk. "Take the Cadillac. Have fun."

Just then Dan walked in. "Hi, Darcy."

"Hey, Dan."

Patrick held the keys up and shook them at Dan as he said in a singsong voice, "We got the Caddy for the weekend."

"Thanks, Darcy," Dan said. "But aren't you going?"

"No, you guys go ahead. I don't want to be the third wheel."

Patrick looked at Darcy, "Well, actually, there's another term for it."

Darcy shot him a look. "Get the hell out of here!"

Patrick handed the keys to Dan. "I still have some work to do; why don't you take it home so we have a parking spot."

"Okay. See you at home around six?" Dan said.

Patrick nodded. "Hopefully. Maybe earlier," he said, shooting a glance toward Darcy.

Darcy and Patrick sat at Darcy's desk to look over a list of potential witnesses, dividing up tasks related to each one. At one point, Patrick walked across the room to sharpen a pencil. As he slid the tip into the sharpener an enormous explosion rocked the building. Darcy and Patrick hit the floor and covered their heads. The office was filled with the sounds of breaking glass and car alarms, and there were shouts in the hall as people ran for the stairs.

John burst into the office. "We're getting out of here!" Irma stood in the outer office, her hand over her mouth.

Darcy got off the floor and walked toward the window, staying low. "Holy Christ!" he said, peeking out the window. "What happened?"

"Get down, Mr. Cole!" John yelled. "There's been an explosion across the street. It could be a diversion so they can get to you. I've got to get you out of here."

"You stay here and take care of everyone," John told Jim. "Get some backup. Take them all home and tuck them in. Keep somebody outside their houses until I tell you otherwise."

He turned to Darcy. "Ready?"

Darcy nodded.

They left the office. John opened the door to the hallway and poked his head out, holding his gun next to his ear. He looked down the hall in both directions, then motioned for Darcy to follow. They ran to the staircase, then down three flights, crossed over to the other side of the building, and took the elevator to the third floor. Finally, they descended to a staircase that emptied near the loading dock. A car waited for them there.

"They blew up his car," the driver said to John.

Then Darcy heard the words he'd been dreading.

"The bomb was hard-wired to the ignition."

Darcy felt nauseous.

In addition to the driver there were two guards, one on the front passenger side and another in the back. Both were holding weapons. The sound of sirens filled the air, and dark, rancid smoke billowed from the parking garage.

The guard in the back seat turned to Darcy, "Are you okay?" he asked.

Darcy nodded numbly. He sat in shock as they drove out of the city. As coherent thought came, he realized that the bomb was supposed to have killed him. But that didn't matter. All he could think about was Patrick.

Darcy pulled out his cell phone and called the office. Irma answered the phone.

"Irma, it's Darcy. Is Patrick there?"

Irma's voice broke. "No, he went to the hospital with Dan— with Dan's remains."

"Shit," said Darcy.

"We're waiting for more bodyguards to arrive. They're going to take us home."

"All right, Irma. I don't know where we're headed, but I'll stay in touch. The police and press will be calling, so instruct the answering service to tell them I'm out of the office and that I'll get back to them."

"Okay, Boss," Irma said unsteadily. "Please be careful."

It's the hotel again, Darcy thought, as the car headed west.

He expected to be stuck there awhile, but in fact they were holed up just for the night, and the next morning John told him they were going home. Darcy could only assume that Mangano hadn't been as hard to find as Battaglia.

As they left the hotel and got into the waiting car, Darcy spoke to John.

"Hey, I don't even know your real name, but I really appreciate everything you've done. I hope I can return the favor someday."

John smiled. "No offense, Mr. Cole, but I hope you don't get the chance."

NINE

On Monday morning, Darcy stood in the doorway to Patrick's office. Patrick was on the phone. When he looked at Darcy, it was obvious he had not slept. He looked haggard and tired, and his eyes were bloodshot. He ended his phone conversation abruptly.

"That was Dan's father. Apparently, he doesn't think much of homosexuals."

"But how does he feel about his son?" asked Darcy.

Patrick leaned back in his chair. "Same thing."

"I'm sorry to hear that," said Darcy.

"So," Patrick continued, "here are my choices, neither of which are good. I can ship what's left of him to Iowa for a private burial, where none of Dan's friends from Chicago can attend because his father wouldn't have it, or I can bury him here, in which case his father will have nothing to do with it.

What I would really prefer to do is have him buried next to his mom in Iowa. But to do that would mean none of us could attend the funeral. So what I'm thinking is have a memorial service for him here and then ship the body back to his father."

"Can I help you in any way?" Darcy asked.

Patrick looked at Darcy and shook his head.

"So what does Mr. Benvenuti think of all this?" Patrick asked.

"Well, apparently everything's under control," Darcy answered.

"What does that mean?"

"It means the guys who are after me aren't anymore."

"Does that mean they're dead?"

"Look," said Darcy, "I don't know for sure. I didn't ask. I suppose we'll read about it in the papers soon enough. Obviously, the Doe brothers aren't in the waiting room."

"Yeah, and all the women's magazines are missing," Patrick said without cracking a smile.

Darcy looked at Patrick sadly. "Why are you here today?"

"Because I can't be at home," Patrick said, his chin quivering.

Irma interrupted the conversation through the intercom. "Patrick, the funeral home is on the line." Patrick picked up the phone.

Darcy quietly walked away.

● ● ●

Darcy carried an unopened bottle of Glenlivet down the hall to the office of his friend Seymour Hirsch. He stood in the waiting room for a minute, then knocked on Seymour's door.

Peggy, Seymour's secretary, greeted him. She was happy to see Darcy. "Well, we were hoping we'd see you soon," she said.

"I've been really busy."

"I should say. You've missed two chess games." she paused. "Oh, and I'm sorry about everything that's happened."

104

"Thank you. Is he in?"

She smiled. "He's always in for you."

He walked past her into Seymour's office and navigated the stacks of files strewn about.

"I thought you'd given up on us," Seymour said, smiling when he looked up.

Darcy reached over and shook hands, "Almost, my friend. After all, I can't remember ever winning one of these games."

Darcy worked on opening the bottle as Seymour pulled a couple of glasses from a cabinet. He handed the glasses to Darcy, then started to set up the game.

"You've had quite a couple of weeks I hear," Seymour said.

Darcy handed him a glass of Scotch. "You might say. I've been shot at. My car has been blown up. People have been dying—all because of a spoiled kid with the IQ of a peanut and a hair-trigger temper."

Seymour took a small sip of Scotch, then moved one of his pawns. "You're in a dirty business, my friend."

"Tell me something I don't know."

"I haven't talked to you since you won that crazy case at Twenty-sixth Street," Seymour commented.

"Lynne Tobias," said Darcy, taking a drink. "Now they're going after her in federal court."

Seymour shook his head. "I guess the Constitution is nothing more than a suggestion anymore. Double jeopardy doesn't apply if you change venues and alter the charges slightly."

"Seymour, you should have been a judge."

He gave Darcy a long stare. "You look like shit."

Darcy smiled. "Thanks. You know, Seymour, you start this job and think you're going to be the next Atticus Finch. You're going to save the world. Then you get into it and realize it's just a shitty way to make a good living."

Seymour sipped his Scotch.

"Atticus lost his case," he said. "His client was found guilty, and then he was killed on the way back to jail. I don't think Atticus Finch is a role model."

"Seymour, you know what I'm trying to say."

"I do," he said, "but you have to remember you represent people who have made mistakes. They need your help. Don't ever be ashamed of trying to help someone."

"I know you're right, Seymour, but I just seem to be losing energy. Kathy thinks I'm clinically depressed."

Darcy used his queen to take one of Seymour's rooks and instantly regretted it as Seymour used a bishop to take the queen. He placed Darcy into check.

"And what do you think?" he asked.

Darcy moved his king out of the way of the bishop. "Well, I'm not sleeping well. But how can somebody be kept awake by boredom? I'm up at night thinking about how little I have to think about—how little I have going on."

Seymour ran his rook across the board and again placed Darcy into check. Darcy moved his king.

"Maybe I just need a vacation."

"Ah, vacation," said Seymour. "Where would you go? What would you do?"

Seymour slid his queen into a position to end the game. "Checkmate," he said quietly.

"I don't know. Someplace where I can work on my chess game?"

Seymour pulled his glasses off and rubbed his eyes. "You know, Darcy, it's been said that the two hardest things to deal with are success and failure. I sit in this office and do my work—men's comp cases. I have files that I move from one side of my desk to the other. I work up the paperwork, I make some phone calls, and I settle some cases. I make a nice living, and I'm happy. You, you're a celebrity. You try these high-profile cases. You make a lot of money, and everybody wants to knock the celebrity down. Everybody wants to take your place. All those prosecutors you try the cases against want to be able to say, 'I beat Darcy Cole.'"

Darcy smiled. "I feel sort of like the Wizard of Oz. 'Pay no attention to the man behind the curtain.' It's all a facade, Seymour."

Seymour frowned. "It's not a facade. You're a good lawyer, and there's nothing wrong with that. A lot of people would like to be good at something. You're one of the very best, and that happens to be something our society values. People will pay dearly for a good lawyer. Stop apologizing for it."

Darcy looked at Seymour and envied him. Here was a guy in his sixties who had a successful, low-pressure practice and a happy home life. Darcy got together with him once a week not so much to be beaten at chess but to bask in Seymour's tranquility. At the same time, Seymour got to live vicariously through Darcy—the whirlwind, the danger. But ultimately Seymour wouldn't trade places with Darcy for anything.

"What are you looking at, Darcy?" Seymour said quietly.

Darcy snapped out of it and glanced at his watch. "Well, I've got to run," he said, standing up. "I'm supposed to meet a client."

"Okay, my friend," Seymour said. "See you next week."

"Yep. Next week."

Darcy walked the few steps back down the hallway and entered his own office. Seated at a chair next to a small desk reading a magazine was a slightly built man with round tortoise shell glasses. He had short, curly, gray hair and was clean shaven. He wore a dark suit with a thin gray pinstripe and a perfectly knotted red silk tie. The man rose to his feet and offered his hand to Darcy.

"Mr. Cole, thank you for seeing me."

Darcy shook his hand. "Come in, Mr. Vanek."

Darcy opened the inner door and held it while Peter walked in front of him. Darcy nodded toward the corner office.

"Follow me."

Vanek sat in a chair by the window. Darcy sat behind his desk.

"How can I help you, Mr. Vanek?"

Vanek turned around to make sure the door had shut behind them. "Mr. Cole, as you know, I was a longtime friend of Charles Tobias. His first wife and my wife have been friends for many years. Our children grew up together. We built our law firm together. He was closer to me than my own brother."

Vanek paused, and Darcy waited.

"My interest here is trying to help the family. There are a number of assets that we cannot account for. I believe that your client could be of great assistance in helping us account for those assets. So to get to the heart of the matter, I'm interested in working out some sort of deal whereby your client will help us. In exchange, we will shorten any prison sentence she may receive."

Darcy leaned toward Vanek, stretching his arms on the desk. "Mr. Vanek, I wasn't aware that you had the authority to make deals on behalf of the United States government."

Vanek cleared his throat. "Well, no, Mr. Cole, I can't make a deal on behalf of the government, but I have spent time working for the Justice Department. I do know how things work. I would be happy to ensure that your client gets a reasonable sentence for her crimes."

"Mr. Vanek—" Darcy began.

Vanek interrupted him. "Please, call me Peter."

"Peter, if I were to get a binding written offer for a plea agreement from the U.S. Attorney's Office, I would convey that to my client. Nothing like that has been presented to me."

"Well, that's why I'm here," Vanek said. "I'm making an initial overture to see if there is a possibility of working out something."

Darcy laughed. "Anything's possible, Mr. Vanek. But I don't deal in vague possibilities. I deal in concrete realities. You bring me something in writing from the U.S. attorney, and that will be a starting point for any negotiations."

"Mr. Cole, I want you to know one thing. I don't have any contempt for you in representing this woman, but I do find her contemptible. I want you to know this, though: If I'm able to find what I'm looking for without your help or her help, I'll do everything in my power to see that this woman rots in hell."

"Do whatever you think is appropriate, Peter," said Darcy. "Whatever is in the best interest of the Tobias family. I will represent my client. You represent yours."

"Mr. Cole, I hope we can reach an accommodation that might make the best out of an awful situation. I want you to know, though, that I am a man of influence."

Darcy sized him up. "If she is convicted in this case and the judge accepts the murder as related conduct, she will be sentenced to natural life without the chance of parole. If she wins, she can sail off into the sunset. If there is some middle ground here, please let me know."

Vanek rubbed his chin while he processed his thoughts. "I see your point. What would be acceptable to your client?"

Darcy didn't reply.

Vanek shifted uncomfortably in his chair. "As you can see, I'm a bit out of my element here."

Darcy smiled. "So much for influence. For my client, the key is the related conduct. If the murder is not used and we get reasonable with the amount of money attributed to the fraud, maybe we can find that elusive middle ground."

Vanek was angry. "Without her being held accountable for the murder, she'll do a brief stint in a minimum-security prison. That's entirely unacceptable."

Darcy shrugged.

Vanek stood and offered his hand. "Thank you for your time."

They shook hands.

Vanek eyed Darcy coldly.

"Don't underestimate me, Mr. Cole," he said before walking out.

Darcy leaned back in his chair and reached for the humidor. Pulling out a cigar and rolling it out on his desk, he cut the tip and placed the end in his mouth. He rolled it gently back and forth, moistening it. Finally, he lit it.

He reached down and hit the intercom button. "Irma, get me Collata, please."

"Will do, Boss," she answered.

As he puffed on his cigar, creating clouds of smoke, he turned his chair so he could look out the windows behind him. He stretched back and gazed out toward the lake, over the Harold Washington Library and Grant Park. Buckingham Fountain was glorious, and an occasional plane landed at Miegs Field. The scene was tranquil yet mesmerizing.

Half an hour later Irma cut through on the intercom to let him know Collata was on the phone.

He punched the button. "Collata, I need to see you."

"When and where?"

"Whenever you can get down here, I'd appreciate it."

"I'll be there in about an hour and a half. I got a couple of things I gotta get done first. Is that okay?"

Darcy nodded, then caught himself. "Great. I'll see you here."

He hung up and went back to his cigar and the view. It wasn't to be, though. A few minutes later, Irma poked her head in.

"Boss, can you do me a favor?"

Darcy leaned back and looked at her upside down over the back of his chair. "What do you need?"

"Willie Mae Watkins is here. Could you talk to her for a few minutes?"

"Sure," he answered, sighing. "Send her in."

Darcy was stubbing out his cigar when Ms. Watkins walked in. She saw what he was doing.

"Mr. Cole, don't put that out on my account."

He smiled. "That's okay. Have a seat, please."

She placed a photograph on Darcy's desk. It showed a clean-cut man in a suit. Darcy looked at it, then back at her. Darcy guessed the photo had been taken at a wedding or a church event.

"Mr. Cole, that is John Kennedy Watkins, my baby, my pride and joy. I went to court for him today. They announced that the grand jury has indicted him. He has to go to the chief judge in three weeks to find out who will be his trial judge. Mr. Cole, now is when we need you. I want to know what it would take for you to be his lawyer."

Darcy stared at the picture, trying to get some sort of feel for John Kennedy Watkins.

"Would you do it if I had fifty thousand dollars?" Willie Mae asked suddenly.

"You've got fifty thousand dollars?" he asked gently.

"I've lined up a job on Sundays working at a nursing home. That means I could pay you $750 a month plus a $10,000 retainer, which means that within three months you'd have over $12,000. That's a good start. Isn't it, Mr. Cole?"

"Yes, that's a significant start," Darcy agreed. "But it's well under what we would normally take as a retainer in a murder case."

"Well, I'm doing the best I can. So it's settled? You'll be my son's lawyer?"

"Whoa, hold on, Ms. Watkins," Darcy said. "I'm deep in the middle of an important case, and that's what I have to focus on now. John Kennedy's next court date is in three weeks, and we need to work something out by then. Why don't you come see me in two weeks, and we'll see where we are."

Clearly Willie Mae was disappointed, and it was all he could do to keep from telling her he'd already decided to take her son's case. The events of the past few weeks had helped him remember what had drawn him into law—and it was more than just money.

He stood up, and Willie Mae mirrored him. She reached into her bag, which was on the floor, and pulled out a gift covered in wrapping paper with a bow.

"I got you a present, Mr. Cole, but I must admit I had an ulterior motive. I think that you'll find the answer to all of your questions here."

Darcy smiled. "Thank you. Would you like me to open it now?"

"No, I think you should open it after I leave. You'll do a great job for my son. I know it."

"We'll talk," he said as he showed her to the door.

She gave a little wave to Irma, then disappeared through the door.

Darcy sat down and opened the gift. Ms. Watkins had given him a Bible.

Patrick silently stepped into the office and looked at Darcy. "You'll have to dodge lightning bolts if God sees you with that."

Darcy peered at Patrick. "How are you doing, anyway?" he asked.

"I'm not. I'm just going through the motions."

Patrick had two black vinyl loose-leaf binders in his hand. He gave one to Darcy, then sat down and opened his own.

"I got a list of the witnesses we need to deal with," he began.

Darcy interrupted him. "Are you sure you're ready to do this? You don't need any time off?"

Patrick sighed. "Yeah, but I'm going to need time off when this thing finally hits me. I'll be in the middle of fucking Walgreen's or someplace, and it'll all come crashing down. That's when I'll need a break, but until that happens, I need to work."

"Well, just remember I can do this by myself if I have to."

Patrick laughed. "This may sound trite, but Dan would have wanted me to do it. He always wanted me to be a big-time lawyer, and he believed I had a shot at being one."

"You do," Darcy agreed. "And I'll do whatever I can to help you get there."

Patrick started thumbing through a stack of papers. "I've broken down the witnesses into categories. You've got the flippers—Rona Siegal, Marty Thiel, Mark Thomas. You've got the investigators, cops, and the circumstantial witnesses. I'll write out how each one has hurt us and what we can do to them on cross-examination."

Darcy looked up. "That'll be interesting. I'm especially concerned about Rona Siegal."

"I'm working on her. We'll have something."

"But Lynne is supposed to be doing her homework, too. What's she come up with?"

"I spoke with her yesterday, and she's ready to come in and compare notes."

"But our main concern at this point is to keep her off the stand."

TEN

Darcy was reading the transcript of Mark Thomas's testimony at the state trial when Irma came in.

"Boss, it's Tony Benvenuti Jr."

Darcy pulled his reading glasses off and picked up the phone.

"Yeah, Tony."

"Don't give me that attitude, motherfucker."

"Here we go," said Darcy. "You feel just as macho with dead friends?"

"Hey, fuck you," he said. "You think those two guys are the only ones who can reach out and spank you, motherfucker?"

"What, you're going plant another bomb in my car, ass-hole?" Darcy shouted.

"Oh, fuck you!" Benvenuti screamed. "You bet your ass I'm gonna plant another bomb, except I'm gonna have this one planted up your ass. Sleep well, motherfucker." He slammed down the receiver.

Darcy hung up and immediately hit the intercom button.

"Irma, I need Collata as soon as possible."

He paused a moment, then made one more call before spinning around in his chair and looking out the window, trying to get his thoughts together. He remembered Seymour once telling him that success works for you long after you work for it. Was this what he'd meant? He charged a lot of money to represent people. That was the barometer by which he chose his cases—how much people could pay and how soon. He didn't want some cases. There was no science to it. He just went by his gut instincts. If in the middle of his first meeting he didn't like a prospective client, he would quote a figure four or five times higher than he normally would.

He had learned long ago that the key to being a good defense attorney was having the ability to take the pressure and the heat generated by high-profile cases.

When he'd begun, he was doing murder cases in empty courtrooms, cases no one cared about. Now he couldn't even do a misdemeanor without a full courtroom. He'd once quoted a fee of twenty-five thousand dollars to a man charged with criminal damage for improperly cutting down his neighbor's tree. Darcy had hoped to chase him away, but the man wasn't concerned about the money—it was the principle that mattered to him. Nothing paid more than principle.

He was adrift in his thoughts, thinking of cases long past, when the phone rang.

"Collata, line two," said Irma.

Collata started right in. "Boy, you get your information fast."

"What are you talking about?" asked Darcy.

"They just found a body in the trunk of a car at Midway Airport. I assume that's why you're calling."

Darcy sat back. "So would that be Mangano?"

"Don't know yet. He's kind of puffy."

"There are always the dental records, assuming he ever saw a dentist."

"Who the fuck knows?" Collata laughed. "They might do fingerprints. It's probably Mangano. Not that many people end up trunk music these days."

"Well, I could still be one of them. Junior just called me ranting and raving. He says he's going to kill me."

"Call the old man."

"I did before you called. Uncle Moe called me right back. He's sending a car for me now."

"Well, page me when you know something—or if you need me, okay?"

Twenty minutes later, John and Jim were in Darcy's office. They escorted him down to the street, where a black Lincoln Town Car was waiting.

"Where are we going?" Darcy asked as he climbed into the back seat.

John slid in next to him. "Mr. Benvenuti thought you might like to take a stroll through Lincoln Park Zoo. We're meeting him at the seal tank."

"Seals? Your boss is a soft touch," Darcy said, gazing out the window.

John did not reply. Darcy's mind drifted. He had not been to the zoo since his daughter was a little girl.

They drove east to Lake Shore Drive, then north toward the zoo. The driver let them out at the main entrance, and they walked a short distance to the seal tank. Old Man Benvenuti was sitting on a bench, watching the seals frolic in the water tank. He shook Darcy's hand and motioned for him to sit down. They watched the seals in silence for a minute before Benvenuti spoke up.

"Darcy, the problem with Mangano, the problem with Battaglia—they're over. As far as I know, Tony has no one else who will go against my orders. Face it—he has few friends, and the two he did have experienced such, well, unpleasant deaths, that I seriously doubt that any others will step up. He's powerless now, but that doesn't mean he'll shut his goddamn yap. As much as you can, Darcy, ignore him."

"But, Mr. Benvenuti—"

The old man raised his hand. Darcy shut up.

"I give you my word you'll be safe. And this time I'll deal with Junior myself."

The old man nodded toward John, who was standing some distance away. He walked over and looked at Darcy.

"Time to go, counselor."

Darcy followed him back to the entrance, where the Lincoln Town Car was waiting. John opened the back door and Darcy climbed in.

They drove south along Lake Shore Drive and headed back toward Darcy's office. Why he can't tell me this shit over the phone, I don't know, Darcy thought. Then it occurred to him. The Old Man enjoyed the zoo; he was trying to achieve some balance in his life.

Back at the office, Kathy and Patrick were waiting for him.

"We trust everything's okay," Kathy said. They knew better than to ask for details.

"Everything's fine. Where are we?"

"We're ready for the final pretrial. It's tomorrow at two."

"Okay, what do we have?"

"We need some room to spread out."

"All right, let's go to the conference room."

As they sat around the large round table, Patrick handed Darcy a black binder about three and half inches thick. It was segmented by tabs with names on each tab.

"Okay, Darcy." Patrick began. "First off, let's go behind tab one to Rona Siegal. She seems to be the linchpin in their prosecution."

Darcy flipped to tab one.

"Okay, here's what we got on her. Number one, she had an extramarital affair. We can prove it. We have receipts and witnesses. She had a pretty steady thing every other Friday at the

Drake Hotel. They'd do a two-hour lunch. The guy she was doing used an alias, Steve Dennis."

Darcy shook his head. "Who is Steve Dennis?"

"Guess."

Darcy sighed. "I give up. No, wait, let me guess. Owen Dempsey. No, no, not Owen Dempsey. It can't be that good. I give up. Who is it?"

"Marty Thiel."

Darcy was stunned. "Our Marty Thiel? The flipper, the insurance agent?"

"You got it," said Patrick.

"Okay, what do we have on it?"

"Well, Collata had a couple of guys at the hotel identify photographs of both Marty Thiel and Rona Siegal. Apparently, they were a pretty steady item every other Friday for a long time. So we got it nailed down pretty good. One of the witnesses is an off-duty cop. He gave us a statement and identified him before he realized what the fuck he had done. Now he's stuck. He's on paper. All he can do is deny or lie or try to come off of it, but we got him."

"How long did this go on?"

"Well, they were off and on for a year and a half, two years. We figure that's the way our princess found Marty Thiel."

Darcy was sorting through the possibilities. Proving a link between Marty Thiel and Rona Siegal was important. If he could do it, it would help damage their credibility in front of a jury. If he could show that Thiel was avoiding any meaningful prosecution in exchange for his testimony, Thiel's testimony would be tainted. If he sprang Thiel's affair with Rona during cross-examination of him it would look like Thiel had gotten his lover to perjure herself for him.

"Okay, so tell me this. How do Rona and Marty hook up with Mark Thomas?"

Kathy interrupted, "Well, we think we have a lead there. Get this. Both Marty and Rona drive BMWs. They got them from the same dealership, and they both had them serviced there. Guess who worked as a porter driving cars around the dealership?"

Darcy looked at her. "Mark Thomas?"

"Bingo! For eleven months Thomas was a porter at that BMW dealership," Kathy explained.

"Any evidence they ever met?"

"Not yet, but we're working on it. We've got Collata interviewing people at the dealership—the mechanics, the service manager—and we're trying to find people who got serviced the same day either of them did. So far, the best we can do is confirm that he was working on the days they brought their cars in to be serviced. There were only two porters bringing cars back and forth. So the chances of them never meeting are getting smaller and smaller."

Patrick interrupted. "The government knows we subpoenaed the time records, and they've probably figured out where we're going with this. So they may give a pretty good offer tomorrow at the pretrial. You know Judge Peters is going to push them to get this done. So we might have something."

"She won't plead," said Darcy. "We're going to have to try this thing, so let's push on. Who does Collata have helping him?"

"Don't know," Patrick replied.

"Find out," said Darcy. "We're going to have to get a lot of people out on the streets on this. How are we doing on expenses in the trust account?"

Kathy flipped through the notebook. "We're spending a lot and we still have plenty."

"Good. Here's what I want. Let's see if we can find something to tie any of the witnesses to Mark Thomas. Every job we ask the investigators to do, even if it's to run down records, I want two different guys doing it at the same time. If one screws up, the other should catch it. I want every scumbag who might know something on this. Got it?"

Patrick and Kathy nodded.

"Patrick, are you going to the pretrial with me tomorrow?"

"Absolutely."

"Kathy, you're going to be in charge of the investigators. Make sure they follow up, okay?"

"Absolutely," she said.

"All right. Patrick, you're going to go through the investigators' reports and prepare crosses for the flippers."

"That's right."

"I'm going to reread the transcripts. I'm halfway through Mark Thomas. When I finish that, I'll start on the investigators' notes. You'll get those for the weekend. You think you can get through them?"

"Yeah, no problem. I'll need the diversion."

"Okay, let's get to work," Darcy said.

ELEVEN

Darcy was at his desk talking on the phone to a probation officer for the federal court in Hammond when he heard a knock on the door. He steered the conversation to a conclusion, then rang off.

Collata stepped in with an unlit cigarette dangling from his lips. Without removing it he leaned toward Darcy over his desk.

"You're not fuckin' going to believe it," he said.

"What?"

"I have a witness who wants to talk to you. He's in your waiting room."

Collata turned toward the door and then turned back, almost laughing. "Marty Thiel's out there."

Darcy looked at him. "No shit. Marty Thiel wants to talk to us?"

Collata finally lit the cigarette. "That's right. All I did was leave a message on his answering machine. He called me back and said he'd be happy to talk to us. So I picked him up and brought him down to see you."

Darcy let out a low whistle, then walked over to the window. He looked out across the street toward the federal building.

"It's not often you have a flipper walk into your office willing to tell you what he's going to testify to . . ." Darcy's voice trailed off.

Collata was smoking and grinning when Darcy turned around.

"Well, let's see what he has to say. Remember, you're a prover. Keep your mouth shut. Let me do the talking."

"You got it," Collata agreed. He disappeared into the waiting room.

Marty Thiel walked tentatively into the room. He was tanned and fit and looked like a tennis pro. His black hair was cut short, and he had bright blue eyes that darted around the room.

He walked toward Darcy and held out his hand. Darcy shook it and invited him to sit. Collata sat on the couch near the windows.

"Mr. Thiel, I'm Darcy Cole. I represent Lynne Tobias. I appreciate your returning our call."

"My pleasure," he said. "What can I do for you?"

"Well, can you tell us what you're going to testify to, Mr. Thiel?"

"That depends what they ask me," he answered, laughing nervously.

Collata and Darcy watched him for a few seconds, trying to read his body language.

"What was your relationship with Lynne Tobias?" Darcy asked as he quietly pulled out a note pad and a pen.

"Well, it wasn't what I wanted it to be," he said, cracking a big smile and rubbing his thighs. He seemed unable to sit still.

"Mr. Thiel, I appreciate that humor sometimes helps in

uncomfortable situations, but this is a serious case. I would appreciate it if we could get down to the reason you're here."

"Okay, okay, gotcha," he said quickly. "I'm just a little antsy." This time he tipped his head from side to side, as if he had a sore neck. "I was an insurance agent. She needed insurance. She came in and got it from me."

"She got the insurance or her husband got the insurance?"

"Well, that's the rub, Mr. Cole. You see, she wanted a big policy on her husband, but her husband wasn't interested. It seems he had other plans for his family's insurance needs. So after a few visits we struck a bargain, and I wrote up a big policy. She gave me a cash kickback. I looked the other way when she signed her husband's name."

"Is it unusual for a wife to come in to get a policy for her husband? A policy her husband doesn't want to sign or have anything to do with?"

"Well, it's not exactly common practice."

"When you were doing it, did you think you were doing anything wrong?"

"I thought I was stretching the rules to sell a policy. I never thought things would get so insane."

"Let me ask you this. What's your relationship with Rona Siegal?" asked Darcy.

He suddenly sat still, though his eyes darted around the room. "Rona Siegal? What do you mean, what's my relationship with her?"

Impatiently, Darcy said, "Do you have any type of relationship with Rona Siegal?"

"I'm not aware of ever meeting anyone named Rona Siegal," he answered.

Darcy said nothing as he scribbled notes on a legal pad.

Thiel clasped his hands in front of him and licked his lips. "Look, I don't want to be in the middle of this. Lynne has a lot of money. If she helps me, I can help her. But I'm going to need a lot of help because I'll have to leave the country. I won't have much time, and I won't be able to come back." He was wringing his hands at this point.

Darcy leaned forward. "I think what you're telling me is that you're looking for a bribe. You're asking me to suborn perjury. Is that it?"

"Lynne got me into this. I need a way out."

Darcy stood up and lowered his voice. "I want you to listen very carefully, Mr. Thiel. I am a lawyer. I do not commit crimes; I represent people who have committed crimes. I don't give a pile of shit what you testify to on the stand because I'm going to rip you a new asshole. Do you understand me? That means, don't contact me. Don't come to my office. Don't call me. Don't leave messages. Don't write me. Don't try to contact me in any way because I will turn over everything to the U.S. attorney. Do you understand me?"

"I'm not looking to create a problem. I'm trying to smooth one out. I need some help." Thiel was on his feet and begging.

With that, Collata got up and reached over Thiel's chair. In one motion he yanked up Thiel's shirt to reveal a microphone taped to his chest with a wire that led down to a little recorder inside his back belt loop.

Thiel stood there, stunned.

Collata then grabbed the tape and the microphone, pulling it off and ripping hairs out of Thiel's chest. Thiel jumped back and yelped.

Collata threw an arm around Marty's throat, choking him as he reached down to unhook the apparatus from inside his belt and tear the tape from his lower back. After removing the body recorder, Collata released Thiel and handed the recorder to Darcy, who put it on his desk.

Collata then turned back to Thiel, grabbing him under the arms. He lifted him up and slammed him against the wall.

"You little piece of shit. I oughta break your neck."

Darcy examined the recording device. "It seems the stakes have gone up, Mr. Thiel. I think we have a little bargaining position now, don't we?"

Collata threw Thiel back into the chair and pointed a finger into his face. "Look, you little fuck. I want to know right
now who put you up to this."

Thiel was shaking now, and he began to stammer inaudi-
bly.

Collata took his meaty open hand and slapped Thiel hard
on the cheek.

"Listen, shithead. I'm gonna rip you in two right now
unless you start talkin'."

Tears welled up in Thiel's eyes. "They made me do it. They
made me."

"Who made you do it?" Darcy asked. "Who told you to talk
with me wearing a wire?"

In a quivering, barely audible voice, Marty Thiel looked
Darcy in the eye and answered, "Ira Greenberg."

Darcy stared at him. "Ira Greenberg, the acting U.S. attorney?"

"Yes, that Ira Greenberg," he said nodding. "He put me up
to this."

"What do you mean he put you up to this?"

"Well, he was there when they fitted me for this mike.
You're in big trouble, Mr. Cole," Thiel said, regaining some
composure. "Because this is a transmitter and a recorder. So
they've been listening to everything you've said. They'll be
here any minute."

Darcy reached to the intercom. "Irma, lock the doors
immediately. Don't let anyone in till I tell you."

Irma said, "Here I go, Boss."

Darcy sat on his desk opposite Thiel.

"Okay, let's talk. Why would the acting U.S. attorney send
you in here with a body wire?"

"I don't know. They're worried about something in your
case. I don't think this guy wants to be acting U.S. attorney. He
wants to be the U.S. attorney."

Collata hit him again.

"Hey!" Thiel yelled cowering.

Darcy intervened. "Collata, easy. Why would Ira Greenberg care about this case so much?"

Thiel sighed and slumped in his chair. "After Owen Dempsey got into trouble, Greenberg wanted to be the U.S. attorney. He was named the acting U.S. attorney because he'd been there longer than anyone, but no one takes him seriously. I was told that Mr. Vanek, the law partner of Lynne's husband, used to be some heavyweight with the Department of Justice. He promised that if they get the money back and put Lynne away forever, he'll step up and make sure that Ira becomes the U.S. attorney. So Ira figures that the only way to win the case is to get a judge to issue a consensual overhear order and send me here. They needed someone who you wanted to talk to. I'm the only guy they got by the balls."

"Interesting," said Darcy. "I didn't know you were so well-versed in the law, Mr. Thiel."

"Well, I'm not, really. My appointed lawyer explained everything to me. I think he feels that Greenberg is taking advantage of me. He told me I could have a pretrial diversion if I did this."

"Who told you they would give you a diversion?" Darcy asked.

"Greenberg. That's why I'm in here."

"What do you want?"

"Look, I'm in very serious trouble. All I wanted to do was sell an insurance policy. You tell me how I'm getting out of this."

"There's always the truth," said Darcy.

Thiel let out a little chuckle. "The truth is what Ira Greenberg tells me it is. I need the diversion."

Just then there was banging on the front door.

"That would be our boys from across the street. You want me to tell them to get fucked?" Collata asked.

Thiel looked at them. "What about me?"

"We'll get you out the back door as soon as they're gone,"

Darcy said. "Unless, of course, you want us to just hand you back over to them."

Collata and Darcy stood in front of the door. Irma stepped back. Patrick and Kathy poked their heads out of their offices.

Collata called out, "Who is it?"

"FBI! Open up!"

"Fuck the FBI," said Collata. "You got a warrant? Slide the warrant under the door. Otherwise, get the fuck outta here. This is a private office."

There was quiet conversation outside the door. "Open up, or we'll break down the door."

"Break it down, and I'll shoot you. I told you to go away unless you had a warrant. You don't have a fucking warrant, and you're not getting into this office. It's a private office, you're breaking and entering, and I'm going to shoot you between your fuckin' eyes."

"You're threatening a federal agent," someone said from the other side. "We have reason to believe you have a government informant in there. You can be charged with kidnapping."

Darcy intervened. "This is Darcy Cole. It's my office. Who am I speaking with, and who is talking about charging me with kidnapping?"

"This is Agent Russo."

"Okay, Agent Russo, go get a warrant. Come back when you have one."

Collata and Darcy walked back into the interior office. Collata could not suppress a laugh.

"Those stupid fucks."

"They'll be back."

"Yeah, but the door'll open by then," Collata said.

Marty Thiel was pacing when they reentered the office.

"What am I going to do now?" he said.

"Who's your lawyer?" Darcy asked.

"Some guy they appointed for me. The U.S. Attorney's Office has basically been representing me."

Darcy went around his desk and sat down. He took out his note pad and began writing names and numbers.

"Here, these are names and phone numbers of three good lawyers. I think you need a lawyer."

"Does that mean my deal with the government is off?"

"No, I didn't say that," said Darcy. "It may still be on but clearly you've done some damage. You may have embarrassed them."

"I embarrassed them? They're trying to ruin my life."

"You need a lawyer," Darcy repeated. "Just tell the truth to your lawyer. You'll be okay."

Thiel took the phone numbers and jammed them into his pocket, then stormed out of the office.

Darcy picked up the intercom. "Irma, ask Patrick and Kathy to come in here."

"Yes, Boss," she replied.

"What was that all about?" Patrick asked as they walked in. Then he noticed the listening device on Darcy's desk. "Hey, that's a Nagra body mike," said Patrick. "That's the type I used when I was with the G."

"Precisely," said Darcy. "They sent Thiel in here wearing this."

"Well, how did you get it?" Patrick asked.

"I snatched it," Collata said.

"No shit!" Patrick said. "You know what that means. You grabbed a wire off a guy who had a consensual overhear. They're coming, you know."

Kathy interrupted, "They need a court order for that. They have to have probable cause and an affidavit. How are they going to get probable cause to do a COH with a lawyer?"

"You could get probable cause for anything," Patrick said. "They probably had probable cause to get the wire for someone else. Then they said that this was a tangential rather than a target wire."

"Would you say they were trying to invade the attorney-client privilege?" asked Darcy.

"Absolutely, they were. That's exactly what they were trying to do. I can't believe they would do this. This is way over the edge."

Collata looked at Patrick. "What's so hard to believe? You were one of 'em not too long ago."

Patrick grinned. "Yeah, youthful indiscretion."

Darcy cut in, "Okay, now what are we going to do?"

Kathy raised a hand. "I'm going to call Vernon Peters's clerk and get an emergency motion. I think we're entitled to more discovery on this. We're certainly entitled to whatever tapes have been generated. We need to know if they violated the attorney-client privilege. We need to know what Thiel's deal with the government was and if it included proactive work."

"I'll draft the motion," Patrick said. "After all, I know better than anyone what we're looking for."

"What do we do with this body wire?" Darcy asked.

"As far as I'm concerned, it's evidence for the motion," Patrick answered. "I think we need to keep it in a secure location."

Collata said, "I'll take care of that."

Irma came in over the intercom. "Ira Greenberg on the line for you."

Darcy motioned for everyone to stay quiet, then put the phone on speaker. "Ira, what's going on?"

"Darcy, give us back our wire."

"Well, Ira, I have a problem with that. The problem is that it's now evidence. I have to keep that evidence in a secure location. Chain of custody and all that. You understand, don't you, Ira?"

"Darcy, I'm not going to bullshit you. This is a potentially embarrassing situation for us. So let's put our cards on the table. What do you want?"

"I want everything Ira—the sun, the moon, Uranus. You're going to give them to me?"

There was an awkward pause. "How about a fifteen-year

cap on your girl on a fraud case? We'll drop any issues of related conduct."

"Well, I'll certainly convey that to my client," Darcy replied. "However, it's a bit premature, don't you think? I believe we're entitled to additional discovery. I think Vernon Peters ought to give us a hearing. What do you say we get on a three-way with Peters's minute clerk? We need a time for an emergency motion."

Ira was angry. "Darcy, what do you want? You want to drag us through the mud, or do you want to resolve this in the best interest of your client?"

"Ira, you know me. I want to be an effective advocate for my client. How can I advise her to take a plea when there is so much unknown territory here? Come on, I'll conference us with Peters's office."

"Forget it!" said Ira shouted before he slammed down the phone.

Darcy called Judge Peters's office and talked to his minute clerk. He explained what they needed, and she put him on hold.

Within a few minutes Vernon Peters got on the phone. "What's going on, Darcy?" he asked.

Darcy began to explain what had happened. Peters was incredulous.

"You're telling me they sent one of the witnesses in to talk to you wearing a body wire?"

"Yes, I am."

Peters raised his voice. "Today or tomorrow? When do you want to come in?"

"How about first thing in the morning. That gives us more time to prepare our motions and get them filed."

"Okay. I have a couple of early cases. How about ten o'clock?"

"That's great, Judge. See you then."

"Oh, and Mr. Cole? Be prepared."

Darcy was about to call Ira Greenberg when Irma cut in on the intercom. "Greenberg calling again."

Darcy hit the line. "Ira, ten o'clock tomorrow morning."

"Okay, Darcy, but I'm thinking of placing you under arrest."

"For what?" Darcy said, laughing.

"Theft of government property."

"Well, why don't you? I think that's a great idea."

Ira thought about it. "Look, Darcy, we could both be jerks about this. But why don't we work this out?"

"We can't. I'm holding evidence that belongs to the government. No doubt about it. But I have no intention of keeping it. I intend to bring it to court tomorrow, so if you want to retrieve your evidence, I'll see you there. You'll have our motions by four o'clock," Darcy said.

"I'm looking forward to it," Ira said sarcastically.

Darcy hung up and looked at his crew. "Let's get to work."

Patrick shook his head slowly. "Peters is going to go ballistic tomorrow."

Darcy agreed. "Good thing we're used to it."

TWELVE

Ira Greenberg, Anna Minkoff, and two other assistant U.S. attorneys were seated at a table. Darcy, Collata, and Patrick were at counsel table. Collata had a sealed plastic bag in his hands. A host of federal agents were seated in the first two rows of the gallery.

Sandy Campos and Jim Parker were there, too, directly behind defense counsel table.

The door opened and the minute clerk slammed his hand against the wall. "All rise. This court is now in session. The Honorable Judge Vernon Peters presiding. God save these United States."

Peters strode to the bench, his robes flowing behind him.

"Mr. Cole, I read your emergency motion and the supporting affidavits," he announced as he sat down. "I'm prepared to go forward. Who will represent the government at this hearing?"

Anna Minkoff stood up. "Your Honor, since Mr. Greenberg may be called as a witness, I will represent the government at this hearing."

"Well, well, Ms. Minkoff. You seem to be around all the men who are self-destructing."

"I assure you there is no self-destruction here, Your Honor. Everything was done in a proper manner."

"Okay, let's talk about it, then. How is it proper for you to send a witness to speak to the opposing attorney wearing a body wire?"

"Your Honor, that was inadvertent."

"Inadvertent?" Darcy yelled, jumping to his feet. "This was a deliberate attempt to invade the attorney-client privilege!"

"Ms. Minkoff," Peters interrupted. "How the hell could it be inadvertent when it took two technicians to hook up the body wire in the first place?"

"Your Honor, if you'll allow me to explain—"

Peters put his hands behind his head and leaned back in his chair. "By all means, counsel, explain." Darcy remained standing.

"Mr. Thiel was a witness in the case of *The United States of America v. Lynne Tobias.* He agreed to do proactive work on the belief that Ms. Tobias was going to offer him money to commit perjury. We then got a COH signed by Federal Judge Brentano so that we could do the overhear on her."

Peters leaned forward in his chair. "I'd like to see the complaint for COH to see if it contains anything mentioning Mr. Cole."

"Well, Your Honor, it seems that our confidential informant took it upon himself to go to Mr. Cole."

"Let me get this straight," Peters said with a mock grin. "Your CI, wearing a body wire, being monitored by four or five FBI agents, decided that instead of meeting the target of the COH, he'd stroll over to the target's lawyer and engage him in conversation. Is that right?"

"Your Honor, it appears—"

He slammed the gavel down. "You can do better than that. Come on, Ms. Minkoff, let's get to the reality of the situation. You want to put Mr. Greenberg under oath to give me that line of nonsense? I want a copy of the COH complaint right now."

Minkoff walked over to a wire cart and began thumbing through a box of file folders. She grabbed the one she was looking for and approached the bench.

The minute clerk took the papers from Minkoff, then handed them up to Judge Peters. Peters scanned them, expressionless as he read.

He finished abruptly, then looked down at the government. "So you used Judge Brentano. You lied to him and told him you were doing a COH on a defendant who may have committed a homicide. You didn't tell him she had been acquitted of the homicide, nor did you give him probable cause to know what it was she was supposed to have done this time. You said you had a CI who had initial conversations with the target of the COH and that the target of the COH had offered him money to commit perjury. Isn't that what's in this affidavit for COH, Mr. Greenberg?"

"That's correct, Judge," Minkoff cut in.

"No, Ms. Minkoff, I didn't ask you. I asked Mr. Greenberg. He was the one who prepared the COH complaint. Isn't that right, Mr. Greenberg?"

Minkoff cut in again and Peters glared at her. "Ms. Minkoff, I don't want you to answer. I want Mr. Greenberg to get up on his two feet and address this court. Do you understand?"

"Yes, Your Honor. However, I am the attorney—"

"Ms. Minkoff, do you really want to spend the night in the Metropolitan Correctional Center while I decide whether or not to hold you in contempt?"

"No, Your Honor, but I feel—"

"Ms. Minkoff, sit down and zip your lip."

Anna sat down. Ira Greenberg stood up.

Ira was about five foot six, skinny, with a pencil-thin mustache, dark hair, dark eyes, and an easygoing personality.

Today, he looked tense. He was what they call a lifer. He had come to the U.S. Attorney's Office after law school and had been there ever since.

Peters motioned toward Darcy. "Mr. Cole, you may inquire." Darcy turned to face Ira.

"Mr. Greenberg, how long have you been with the U.S. Attorney's Office?"

"Almost seventeen years."

"Then you should know how a COH works."

"Yes, I believe I do."

"And Mr. Greenberg, your target of the COH was not me, was it?"

"No, it was not."

"And you maintain control over your confidential informants. Do you not?"

"We do our best to. We don't always—"

Peters cut him off. "Mr. Greenberg, would you let the technicians wire up a guy and then send him willy-nilly throughout the city?"

"No, Your Honor, we wouldn't. We adhere to strict guidelines when doing a consensual overhear."

"Mr. Greenberg, it seems we're having a problem communicating here. I asked you a simple question, and you went off in a different direction. Why is that?"

"Your Honor, I'm doing the best I can to answer your questions."

"You know, Mr. Greenberg, it seems to the court that you're doing your best *not* to answer my questions."

Greenberg swallowed hard, "Your Honor, I—"

Again he was cut off. "You know, Mr. Greenberg, we need to figure out what we have here. I'm going to suspend the trial date for *The United States v. Lynne Tobias*. I'm going to enter a few orders. Number one, you have to turn over all COH material—and I do mean all, Mr. Greenberg. You must turn over all the proffers of all of your witnesses in the *Tobias* case. That includes Mr. Thiel and anyone else you're going to be using.

Furthermore, Mr. Greenberg, I want you to get any sealed plea agreements you may have with any of these witnesses and hand them over to defense counsel. Do you understand me?"

Greenberg was upset. "Judge, we can't hand over—"

"Okay, Mr. Greenberg. I'll tell you what I'll do for you. Because I'm a reasonable judge, you can bring those materials to me. I'll do an *in camera* inspection. You'll have the opportunity to tell me how important it is that you keep those items away from the defense team. But understand that I'm probably going to turn everything over to defense counsel anyway.

"That trial date is now a final status date. Does everyone understand that?"

"Yes, Your Honor," Darcy replied.

Anna Minkoff agreed.

"Ms. Minkoff, I don't know what's going on with your office. I won't compensate for your incompetence in this trial by letting improper evidence in. If I find out that your office purposely invaded the attorney-client privilege and attempted to entrap defense counsel without a scintilla of evidence that he was involved in anything untoward, I'll sanction everybody involved. Do you understand me, Ms. Minkoff?"

"Yes, Your Honor, I understand you."

"Mr. Greenberg, Ms. Minkoff, you have twenty-four hours to get this material to me in chambers. After I review it I will summon you for another court date. Do you understand that?"

"Yes, Your Honor," they said.

"Very good. Now get out of my courtroom."

THIRTEEN

It was 3:11 A.M. and Darcy was wide awake, sitting in his chair looking out over the dark lake. There was a considerable wind from the northwest, and every few minutes a streak of lightning lit up the sky. Thunder rumbled intermittently.

Darcy sipped a glass of wine and thought about how his wife had taken his daughter away years earlier. He remembered it very clearly. She had been taken away the Friday before Father's Day. Darcy's former wife had a way of getting her point across. The bitch had found the perfect way to inflict the maximum amount of pain on Darcy. The divorce had been a sham. Darcy gave in on every point with the exception of visitation. Assured he would be able to see his daughter in spite of the distance, Darcy was satisfied to give his ex everything else she wanted.

He remembered bringing his daughter home from the hospital and how, as a baby, she would sleep on his chest for hours. As she got older she would find excuses to come into his room and climb into bed, claiming to be afraid of a boogeyman or a thunderstorm, much like the one he was watching now.

Before she was taken, she had been the focus of his life—his daughter and work. Every day he spent as much time as he could with her, inadvertently driving away his wife. He had no time left for their relationship.

There had been no more children. By the time his wife was ready to have another one, their marriage was already spiraling in ruins.

A lightning bolt cracked across the horizon and splintered into two separate streams, followed by a loud blast of thunder.

Darcy took a sip of wine and sat back. In just over six hours he would need to be in court in front of Vernon Peters.

Wearily, he closed his eyes and waited for dawn.

• • •

The next morning when Darcy walked into court, the first person he saw was the dapper Ira Greenberg. He was in a double-breasted suit and his pocket square matched his tie. Greenberg sat with Anna Minkoff and a couple of case agents. A few other federal people sat in the first row.

Darcy wasn't sure if they were assistant U.S. attorneys, FBI agents, or both. Collata was on his way. Lynne, whose appearance was waived, chose not to attend.

Jim Parker and Sandy Campos were joined by five or six other reporters who had caught wind of the impending showdown between Greenberg and Peters. They could smell blood.

Vernon Peters exploded from the doorway and took the bench. "Well, Ms. Minkoff, Mr. Greenberg. What materials do you have for me today?"

Greenberg handed a collection of documents and one audio cassette to Anna Minkoff. She approached the podium.

"Your Honor, we have one cassette tape of a consensual overhear, the Petition for Consensual Overhear, and all of our reports regarding our confidential informants, as well as their plea agreements."

Peters looked at her sternly. "You tell me you have one conversation that's recorded?"

"Yes, Your Honor."

"And who's that conversation between?"

"Between the confidential informant and Mr. Cole."

Peters raised his eyebrows.

"You're telling me that you have a COH for your confidential informant to record conversations between him and Lynne Tobias, and the only tape that you have—the only conversation you have—is between your confidential informant and Ms. Tobias's lawyer?"

"Well, Your Honor—"

"Ms. Minkoff, I don't have to listen to that tape. Everything on that tape is excluded as being outside the parameters of the COH unless you want to tell me that Mr. Cole was the target of that COH."

"No, Your Honor, he was not."

"This is egregious conduct on the part of the prosecution."

"Your Honor, we would disagree—"

Again, he interrupted her. "Well, whether you agree or disagree, you can take it up to the Seventh Circuit, but nothing on that tape is coming in. I'm taking the rest of the documents into chambers. You will wait here for me. When I've read all of the reports and the plea agreements, I will decide what I'm giving to Mr. Cole in preparation of trial. Is that understood?"

"Yes, Your Honor."

Minkoff walked up to the bench and handed the judge the paperwork. He accepted them. "Is this everything you have?" he said, not bothering to look at her.

"Yes, Your Honor. It's everything I have."

"All right, then. We'll take a brief recess."

Darcy stepped out into the hallway and saw Collata coming from the elevators. He carried the recording device in a heat-sealed plastic bag.

Anna came out of the courtroom and headed toward them. "Darcy, you okay?"

"Fine, Anna. Are you?" Darcy asked.

"I've been better."

"What was it Peters said—something about men who self-destruct around you?" Darcy asked jokingly.

"Actually, he said all the men around me self-destruct. There's a big difference." A tired smile spread across her face. "It hasn't happened with you yet, has it, Darcy?"

"I'll tell you after the trial," he replied.

Ira Greenberg came out of the courtroom and walked over to meet them. "Darcy, I'm sorry about all this. It's my fault."

"Ira, you know me better than that—you know I'm not going to commit a crime. And you're right, it is your fault."

"Darcy. I didn't expect this to happen. I let these FBI agents run wild with the wire. They were supposed to follow the parameters of the COH and just go after your client. I should have sat all over them and made sure that's all they did. They got smart. You know what happens when an agent gets smart. Now here I am with my ass exposed."

Collata pulled out a cigarette and popped into his mouth. He held the pack up as an offer. There were no takers.

"You want to return that body mike to us now?" Ira asked.

Collata lit his smoke. "I don't think so. I think I'm going to wait until the judge orders me to give it back."

"Well, he already suppressed the tape, so there really is no reason for you to hold on to it. If that's what you want to do—"

Collata smiled. "Oh, yeah, that's what I want to do."

"Collata, what's your beef with us? I understand Darcy's problem, but what's yours?"

Collata chuckled and Darcy interrupted. "You know what, Ira? You have no idea what my problem is, but I'm going to tell you. You guys are all the same. You're always lookin' to hammer somebody—a cop, a lawyer, or a politician. You want to take them down to make your own career. Every time one of you fuckers runs for office, all you talk about is who you convicted. You don't look to do justice. You look to get feathers in your cap. You're all despicable."

Anna cut in. "Darcy, don't hold back. Tell us how you really feel."

"You guys will spend a million dollars and flip thirty-five bad guys to get one clean guy. You ruin his life. Do you ever think what it's like when your FBI agents crack down someone's door and pull him out in front of his kids or send a letter to him saying he's the target of an investigation? Did you ever stop to think what it does to him? Hell, no. You've got an insurance agent who took a shortcut to sell a policy. He wasn't part of a conspiracy to commit murder, and yet you tell him he's going to go away for the rest of his life unless he does exactly what you tell him to do. He becomes your lap dog, and he'll live the rest of his life knowing that he's a gutless pussy. You fry the cop who's dirty, but you take down every one else who's around him whether they're dirty or not. You just want those numbers. You want scalps. I'm a lawyer who's representing a client, and you send in some asshole with a wire trying to get me to say something that will give you the opportunity to fuck with me."

Greenberg straightened his tie. "I'm proud of the work I've done," he said. He looked at Collata. "You used to be a cop. Don't you think bad guys should be punished?"

Collata's arms were folded, and he simply grinned as he smoked hands free. Darcy continued. "Absolutely! Bad guys should be punished. I think somebody who robs somebody, sticks a gun in their face, should go to prison. Someone kills someone, he should go to prison. But you assholes, you get some little Mexican kid who gets five hundred bucks to take a flight from LA to Chicago with two kilos. You tie him up on a conspiracy with related conduct and give him forty years. Do you think that's justice? The kid was making five hundred bucks. I like the deals you make with really bad guys like Sammy the Bull. How many murders did he cop to? What did you give him? Fucking vacation. You let him keep all his mob money. Come on, who's shinin' who here? To get the guy who ordered the hits, you let the guy who did all the hits go. What kind of sense does that make? I like it better in state court. There's a crime, and the police try to make an arrest. They prosecute someone for committing a crime. Here you target someone you want, then you go about trying to find a crime to tag on him."

"What is all this, Darcy? You were once a prosecutor just like me."

"No," Darcy replied, holding up his finger. "I was a state prosecutor. We waited for the crimes to be committed before we prosecuted."

"Hmm," Ira said. "I guess when you switched sides you really embraced the role of savior. Money can do that, huh, Darcy?"

"Yeah, I'm just like you guys," Darcy replied. "You're here 'til you get a job offer with some silk-stocking firm. Then you do "white-collar criminal defense," as if somehow that makes it better than representing some punk with a bag of dope. I'm working to make sure that anybody you guys send to prison actually deserves it. I want to keep you guys in line. Remember, you're just suits filling an office. Don't ever think you are the source of all the power, because that's when you get your shorts in a knot.

"I don't want to hear it, Ira." With that, he strode away. After a moment's silence, so did Greenberg.

Anna looked at Collata, who shrugged and grinned.

"Would you call that an antigovernment diatribe?" she asked in disbelief.

"Well, you know," Collata said, "I think Darcy was a hippie back in the sixties."

They both laughed out loud.

FOURTEEN

Darcy had finished his morning swim, taken a steam, and was now seated poolside in a bathrobe having a breakfast of grapefruit juice, Irish oatmeal, wheat toast, coffee, and the morning *Tribune*.

He thought about Patrick and the pain he must be feeling. He thought about Kathy and the time spent away from her children, writing briefs or preparing cases for trial. He thought of Irma and all the nights she had stayed late because she was needed and all the mornings she came in early for the same reason. He felt uncomfortable with the idea that the only people he really felt close to were people he paid, who worked for him.

Many of his contemporaries had found their passion in hobbies or possessions. Yet Darcy had little interest in golf or a Mercedes. And then something occurred to Darcy. The thing that was really missing from his life had nothing to do with hobbies or possessions; what he really craved was a solid, unconditional relationship—like the one he'd had with his daughter when she was little. So it wasn't a romantic liaison he wanted—first things first, after all—but instead a closer relationship with those who were already in his life.

Patrick, Kathy, Seymour, Irma—these folks were his family, and it was about time he started treating them as such. He had grown closer to Patrick since Dan's death, and he'd come to appreciate Kathy and all that she sacrificed for him. And Irma—Irma had been a rock throughout the events of the past weeks. She was a caring soul and a devoted office manager who had helped Darcy build his practice.

It's settled, then, Darcy thought. Family comes first. Relationships had to be nurtured, and he was ready to put some energy into it.

He finished his coffee, got dressed, and headed into the office feeling unusually invigorated. He even stopped at the bagel shop and picked up breakfast for everyone. Taking the elevator, he burst through the door of the office and saw Irma on the phone. She smiled at him, and he gave her a huge smile in return.

"Good morning," she said cheerfully.

"Good morning, Irma. Round up Patrick and Kathy and meet me in my office in twenty minutes."

Darcy then headed to his office, slapped on his headphones, and turned on his stereo. The Bach Cello Suites CD was still in it from the last time he'd tried to listen to it. He turned up the volume, leaned back in his chair, and put his feet on his desk. He liked the way he was feeling.

When Kathy and Patrick walked into his office, they stopped in his doorway and watched him curiously. Darcy's head bobbed to the music; his eyes were closed and he had a genuinely peaceful look on his face.

"Darcy?" Patrick said loudly. "You okay?"

Darcy's eyes popped open and he pulled off the headphones.

"Ah! You're here!" he said. "Sit down."

Irma walked in with a platter of bagels and cream cheese and a pot of coffee.

"What's up, Boss?" Kathy asked.

Darcy slapped his hands down on the desk. "I've made a decision," he said happily. "I think that we need to make some changes around here."

He had their attention.

"I think it's time for the two of you to become partners. Let's put your names on the door and letterhead. I haven't figured out what we're going to do with the money, but obviously you guys will make more as partners."

Kathy and Patrick sat in stunned silence. Irma smiled and passed out bagels.

Darcy looked at them. "So? What do you say?"

"I'm speechless," Kathy said. "I never imagined it."

Darcy thought he even noticed a hint of excitement in Patrick's tired eyes. "Wow. It's great, Boss. But how are we going to structure this?"

Darcy waved him off. "I haven't the faintest idea. I haven't really thought it through. Why don't you think about it, and tell me what you feel is fair. In the meantime, put your names up! How about Cole, Haddon & O'Hagin, or Cole, O'Hagin & Haddon? You guys figure it out. Get your names up on the door, and get the letterhead changed. And do it before I change my mind. Irma, it's your turn. I'm giving you a raise."

"Thank you," she said. "I appreciate it Darcy, but you don't have to do it."

"Oh, but I do. You've taken care of me all these years, and now I want to do something for you."

"Honey, thank you," she said softly. "That's so sweet of you."

"So, . . . he said hesitantly, "how much would be a really good raise?" He felt silly asking, but Irma knew more about these things then he did.

"Darcy," she said, puzzled. "I don't know what's gotten into you, but I'm sure whatever you give me is fine. In fact, just seeing you in such a happy mood is worth more than any amount of money."

Darcy smiled. That's exactly what he'd been thinking lately.

FIFTEEN

Terre Haute, Indiana, hadn't always been a small town on the banks of the Wabash River. When railroads were king, the town had thrived, but as the railroads' significance waned, things began to tumble. Factories closed, and people moved out. Over time, new industries moved in: chemical factories, manufacturing. Indiana State University grew, and a federal prison was built.

While not quite prosperous, Terre Haute was holding its own and even growing at a reasonable pace. One of its newest residents was Anthony Benvenuti Jr. Tony had been released from the segregation unit and had gone back to his cell in the general population as a seething, vicious man. He threw his weight around with the other prisoners, particularly those who were uncertain enough about his background to be afraid of him. He brutalized and stole from them. After being there for less than a year, he was the most hated man in the prison.

Ray Wells didn't want to be in Terre Haute, either. He had hoped that when he left Jasper, Indiana, as a high school baseball phenom that Indiana State would just be a stop along his way to the major leagues. It never happened. Injuries and a fundamental lack of talent ended his dream. Instead, he was working at the prison. Today, his job was to put shackles on some jackass from Chicago named Anthony Benvenuti. Wells tightened the leg irons around Tony's ankles and checked to make sure they were closed. Next, he put on the leather belt and tightened it around Benvenuti's waist, then pulled the chain to the end of the handcuff, which he clamped on his wrist. He did it on the other side and double-checked everything.

"Snug as a bug in the slammer," he said to Benvenuti.

Benvenuti's expression didn't change.

Wells's partner was Al Davis, from Evansville. He had an associate's degree from Vincennes University and was quite happy to be working for the federal government. He watched as Wells tightened everything on Tony. It was a warm spring day, and he was glad to have transport duty, even if it was a trip to the dentist.

Wells led Benvenuti to the van, opened the door, and helped him climb up and onto the bench seat. He then took another pair of handcuffs and attached it to the metal ring at Tony's waist, then cuffed him to a hook on the side of the bench chair. After checking to make sure it was secure, he nodded to his partner.

Davis got in on the passenger side of the van. Wells slammed the door, then got into the driver's side and hit the automatic locks. He rolled the van out of the loading dock into the courtyard of the prison, then down an alleyway through a series of doors. One by one the doors opened, and the van inched its way to the outskirts of the prison, toward the road.

Davis turned back and looked at Benvenuti. "Hey, little fish, we have a tradition. When we take you on a dental run, you get a choice of Burger King or McDonald's. We'll buy."

Benvenuti scowled. "That's big of you, fellas. Aren't you worried about using up half your paycheck?"

Ray looked at him in the rearview mirror. "Hey, if you want to be an asshole, we don't have to do it."

Benvenuti relented. "Yeah, I'm sorry. You guys are just doing your job. I appreciate that. Burger King or McDonald's, either one would be great."

He dropped his trademark swagger; he had other things on his mind. He leaned forward and reached under the front of his seat until he felt a piece of tape, which he quietly pulled off. Three handcuff keys were stuck to the inside of the tape. One of them had to fit. He deftly pulled each key off the tape and manipulated one of the keys to his fingertips while the other two remained in the palm of his hand. He slid the key into the keyhole on the cuff on his right leg iron, then he turned it and watched the iron pop open. He quietly pulled it closed without locking it, and put the keys into the pocket of his workshirt.

Heading north on U.S. 41, they passed flatlands and fields after they left the prison. At the intersection of U.S. 40, they headed east.

Wells steered the van into the drive-through at a McDonald's, where they ordered burgers, fries, and Cokes to go. They pulled into the parking lot with their food and parked in the far corner. No other cars were nearby, only a dumpster enclosed by a brown wooden fence.

Wells rolled down the windows and Davis leaned back, putting his feet up on the dash of the van. Wells grabbed a Big Mac, an order of fries, and one of the Cokes and stepped out of the van. He set everything on top of the van and opened the sliding door.

"Okay, chief, you're not going to fuck around if we let you use your hands to eat, are you?"

"Nah, actually, I'm pretty hungry," Tony said.

Wells reached in and undid the handcuffs. Then he reached up for the Big Mac and fries, which he handed to Benvenuti. He pulled down the Coke and handed that to him last.

"All right, buddy. Enjoy."

He slammed the door and locked it.

Wells got back into the front and began to eat while telling Davis about his plans to take his wife to Chicago for a Cubs game. Occasionally, Davis tried to engage Benvenuti in the conversation, but Tony was busy with his own plans.

Benvenuti had been studying the parking lot as he ate. When he finished, Wells went back to retrieve his garbage, which was thrown into the McDonald's bag. Wells set the bag outside the van and began to put Benvenuti back into the handcuffs. Tony pleasantly thanked him for the food.

"No problem," Ray said. "Every now and then you need something that reminds you you're human."

As Ray reshackled Benvenuti, he couldn't help but think that he'd like to do the same thing to his wife in a hotel room after the Cubs game. He grinned at the thought.

"This dentist must really be a hack," Benvenuti said. "Otherwise, why's he doing all the prisoners?"

"He's not so bad," said Al. "I go to him myself."

"Like I said," Tony replied.

They all had a good laugh.

As the van got underway and they talked and joked, Benvenuti used the three keys to quietly remove the shackles. First, he undid the one on his waist, then the leg shackles, and finally the handcuffs. He then reached under the seat and felt around until he felt a long, hard object taped to the inside of the bench. It was a shiv. He had paid a lot of money to one of the men who worked on prison vehicles. He then reached along the window behind the bench seat and felt a long, small, round tube—a zip gun. He pulled that down, too.

The zip gun was nothing more than a small piece of metal conduit that had been bored out to the size of a .38-caliber bullet. The other end had a firing pin, which consisted of a nail tip hooked to a spring. Tony had a shiv and one shot that would ensure his freedom.

The van drove past a rundown storefront with the dentist's name in neon letters out front. Wells pulled around back into the parking lot.

Benvenuti looked around. "Okay," he muttered to himself.

Wells came around and slid open the door, then reached in to release the handcuffs. As he did, Tony put him into a fast, tight headlock, then thrust the sharpened metal stick deep into Wells's eyes. Blood sprayed everywhere as Tony pulled out the shiv and gouged it into Wells's throat. What began as a deafening roar turned into a gurgling moan as Wells fell near Benvenuti's feet.

Up front, Davis had seen everything but was unable to move. Benvenuti's blood-soaked hands fumbled with the zip gun as he jumped out of the van and around to Davis's door. Al had managed to roll up the window and lock the door and was desperately reaching for his gun. Benvenuti smashed the glass with the end of the zip gun and jammed it into the back of Al's head. Just as Al released his gun from his holster, Benvenuti pulled the pin back and let it go. The bullet exploded into Al's head, and he slumped forward. Benvenuti reached in over his body and pulled Al's gun free.

After a look around the parking lot, Benvenuti pulled Al's body out onto the gravel. Wells's body was dumped next to it.

"Nothing personal, guys," he said, breathing hard. "I just need to borrow a few bucks." He emptied their wallets.

Tony ran around the front of the van and jumped in. He drove steadily away with forty-three bucks in his pocket and blood everywhere.

About half an hour later he crossed the border into Illinois and looked for a place to stop. He chose the large parking lot of a grocery store, which also had a drive-through cash station. He parked the van and watched for a while, looking for his best opportunity to switch cars and get more money.

Twenty minutes later he found his mark. A woman in her early twenties drove her Saturn through the cash station and took out what appeared to be a considerable stack of bills. As she pulled out of the parking lot, he followed her down a two-lane road toward the town of Marshall. She then parked directly across from a drugstore on the town square, ran in, and came back out carrying a small white bag. He waited to make his move until she was well out of town.

A few minutes later, the young woman checked her rearview mirror and saw that the van was tailgating, so she drifted over to the right to allow him to pass. He smiled and started to pass and when he was alongside her, turned his wheel toward her car, forcing her to the side of the road. She slammed on the brakes, swearing, then screaming as he jumped out of the van pointing a gun at her.

Jerking open the door, he placed the gun's barrel against her head. "Don't make a sound," he ordered.

"Don't hurt me! Please don't hurt me."

"That's up to you," he yelled. "Now shut up and move over."

When she saw the dried blood on his clothes and hands, she screamed again. She immediately covered her mouth with her trembling hand.

"What's your name?" he demanded.

"Sarah," she said, whimpering.

"Give me all your money."

She reached in her jeans pocket and pulled out the wad of twenties she had gotten from the cash machine.

"Now listen very carefully, Sarah. If you do everything I tell you to do, I'll let you live."

He ordered her out of the car and took her by the arm to the van. He then turned the steering wheel all the way to the right and slammed the van into drive. It jumped into gear, rolled down into the ditch, and fell on its side.

"Who do you live with?" he asked as they walked back to her Saturn.

She just stared at him.

"I said who do you live with?"

She mumbled, "I live by myself," and began to cry.

"Where?" he demanded.

"Back in town."

"What town is this?"

"Marshall."

"Marshall what?"

"Marshall, Illinois."

"Is that where you're from?"

"No. I'm from Effingham."

"Effingham, Marshall—Jesus Christ. Are there any big towns near here?"

She was sobbing. "Charleston."

"Honey, you and I have a different idea of what a big town is. Now, let's get in the car. We're going for a ride. If you fuck up, I'll shoot you."

He put her on the passenger side, and he got behind the wheel.

"Who do you know around here?" he asked as he pulled onto the road.

"No one, really. Most of the people I know live in town or further out."

"What do you do for a living?"

"I work at a chemical factory in West Terre Haute."

"Why do you live here?" He was agitated.

"Because I want to stay in Illinois. It makes things easier," she said. He didn't bother to ask what she was talking about.

"Look, honey, I need to wash up and change my clothes. Then we're going for a ride. I have no reason to hurt you, so don't give me one. You understand?"

She had calmed down a little. "Okay," she said quietly.

Tony took U.S. 40 west until they hit a small town called Casey. He drove around a neighborhood until he saw a guy working on a car in his garage. The house was off by itself at the end of a cul-de-sac. Everything else looked quiet.

He pulled the car in front of the house, got out, and went around to the passenger side. He warned her again, "You fuck up and I'll kill you. Understand?"

Sarah nodded.

They walked over to where the man was working. "Hey, how you doing?" Tony said. "I'm a little lost here, and I'm trying to get back to I-70."

"No problem," the man said, looking Sarah up and down. "All you gotta do is take 49 North, and you'll run right into it."

"Hey, I appreciate it," Junior said. "They got any gas stations that have rest rooms? My wife here needs to go."

The man began wiping the grease off his hands with a rag. "Come on. You can use the one in the house."

Tony made sure to stay behind Sarah as much as possible. The man wasn't paying much attention to him anyway. He walked them to the side door. "Come on in."

"Your wife home?" Tony asked.

"Shoot, my wife ain't been home in years," the man said, laughing. "I'm all alone."

Sarah walked in, followed by Tony. It wasn't until then that the man noticed the blood.

"Hey, what happened to you?" he asked Tony.

"Hmm, got bad news for you, old-timer. It's going to happen to you, too."

The man looked at him. "What's that supposed to mean?" he asked.

Junior pulled his gun out. "Sit down at the table."

"Whoa! What the hell you doin'?"

"Well, for starters I'm going to shoot you in the head if you don't shut the fuck up. Tell him, Sarah."

"He will," she agreed.

Tony went over to the kitchen sink and began washing his hands, keeping an eye on both of them.

"Listen, old man. You want to live, here's the deal. I need a fresh shirt. I need some money, and then I'll tie your ass up. Otherwise, you can take what's behind door number two, which is a bullet to the head. Now which one do you want?"

"Shit, I got all kinds of shirts," he said, shrugging.

They walked together through the two-bedroom house, as

Tony checked every room. There was no basement and no attic, so it didn't take long. When Junior was convinced they were alone, they went into the bedroom.

The old man started to open the closet, but Junior stopped him, "No, no, no. You sit on the bed, and I'll take care of that."

Junior opened the closet and grabbed a blue long-sleeved shirt. He took off his blood-soaked workshirt. The T-shirt underneath was clean, so he threw the blue shirt on top of it and buttoned a few buttons.

"Thanks a lot, old-timer. Now, how much money you got?"

The man reached into his pocket and pulled out a wad of twenties, tens, and fives. He reached into his other pocket and pulled out three singles.

"Sarah, grab the money," Junior ordered.

She reached over and took it. "I'm sorry," she said. "He kidnapped me. I'm not—"

"Shut the fuck up!" Junior screamed.

She was quiet instantly.

"So, old man, what do you got to get tied up with?"

Junior looked around the bedroom and saw a bathrobe hanging on the back of the closet door. He took the belt off it.

"Okay, lie down on the bed." He roughly tied the man's hands behind his back.

"I sure am glad I don't have to kill you, old man. Do yourself a favor and keep your mouth shut for a while. I'm going to rip the phone out of the wall."

He used the phone cord to bind the man's ankles.

"Now, how did you say I get back to I-70, old man?"

"Take 49 North for a few minutes, then you'll hit 70."

"You got any more money anywhere?"

"Nah, nothin'!"

Junior walked over and pointed the gun at him. "You sure, old man?"

"Yes. I don't even have a job." He smiled at Sarah.

Junior then walked about six feet, turned around, and fired two shots into the old man's head.

The smell of gun powder wafted into the air.

Sarah became hysterical. Junior slapped her hard. "Shut up, or I'll kill you, too."

"What'd you do that for? What'd you do that for?" she sobbed.

"Shut up and get your shit together. We're going to Chicago."

He went to the dresser and tore through each drawer until he found a stack of money, close to eight hundred dollars, stuffed into a sock. "Let's go. I gotta see a lawyer in Chicago."

He grabbed Sarah by the arm, led her outside, and threw her into the car. She was crying softly. He put the gun in his belt.

"If you do not shut up, I will kill you. Do you understand?"

"No, I don't understand," she screamed. "You told him you wouldn't kill him, and now look. What do you want?"

"Like I said, I want you to shut up," he yelled as he started the car.

He drove out of the cul-de-sac and backtracked to U.S. 40 until it intersected I-49, then went north to I-70. He followed the signs for South St. Louis.

"What's the best way to get to Chicago?"

"I-57," Sarah replied.

"Where do you get that?"

"We'll run into it before we get to Effingham."

"Oh, going home, huh?"

"Yes, I'd like to, please," she said quietly.

"Do you know who I am?" he laughed.

"I have no idea."

"Does the name Tony Benvenuti mean anything to you?"

She shook her head.

"Do you ever get out of these cow towns, or do you spend all your time with plow fucks?"

The road was clear, and Benvenuti was doing about 70. After ten minutes, he saw signs announcing the junction with I-57. They passed several exits and finally got on I-57 North.

"Here's the deal," Tony said, looking at Sarah. "I'm going up to Chicago. I got a score to settle. After I settle that score, I'm leaving the country. I'm going to drop you off someplace safe with instructions that you're not to be hurt. When it's all over if you don't try to escape, I'm going to leave you with $20,000 in cash for your effort. How's that sound?"

"I just want to live," she said, wringing her hands.

"That's the spirit, honey," he said, smiling.

They were approaching a town called Rantoul, north of Champaign-Urbana, when they heard on the radio the news about Tony's escape from Terre Haute. After the brief report, he looked at Sarah.

"Now you know who I am?"

Her tears began to flow again. "You're going to kill me, aren't you?"

"I don't know. I haven't decided. And when I do, I might change my mind." He chuckled in a way that made her skin crawl.

They pulled into a truck stop and gassed up north of Rantoul in a town called Paxton. He told her to switch places with him.

"Drive," he ordered.

They headed north toward Chicago.

He knew the cops would be looking for him, but they'd be looking for the van, and it would take awhile before they found it. No one would be looking for a blue Saturn and a female driver. He sat low in the passenger seat and watched the cornfields roll by.

"I'm not a bad guy once you get to know me."

Sarah said nothing.

"Think of it this way. You're going to have one hell of a story to tell your grandkids."

She squeezed the steering wheel tightly. "I just want to go home. I don't care who you are or what you did. I want to go home." She said it calmly.

As they were going north on I-57, they passed two state

troopers headed south. They drove through Kankakee and eased toward the southern suburbs of Chicago.

"Why me?" she asked, breaking the silence.

"Because you were alone. You had a new car, and you had cash. Ever been to Chicago?" he asked.

"Once," she said, "but I was ten."

"Oh, you'll like it," he said, grinning. "I promise."

Sarah followed his directions, but she was completely lost. They had gotten off I-57 at a sign that said Bradley-Bourbanais. He directed her to a two-lane highway, which she guessed she was taking north for about an hour. The area became more populated, and he had her turn off at a stoplight. They traveled a few blocks, then pulled into a subdivision.

She followed the road until he told her to pull into a driveway.

"Get out," he ordered.

He walked her up to the front door and knocked.

A short, thick man answered. He had an olive complexion and plug marks on his scalp from a hair transplant that hadn't taken.

"Tony, what the fuck are you doin' here?"

"What, you don't listen to the news?" Tony replied.

The man at the door was wearing an open silk shirt, and gold chains tangled in thick, matted chest hair.

With two fingers he pointed to his heart. "Just fuckin' shoot me right now."

Tony stepped back. "Angie, what the fuck? This is me, Tony."

Angelo Cavelli had been a fighter at one time, with the scar tissue around his eyes and nose to prove it. Forty years later, he was closer to 250 than to his fighting weight of 150. He put his hands up and cocked his head. "You know I love you, but your Dad said anyone who helps you is an enemy of his."

"Angie, come on, I need your help. I need money to get out of the country."

Angie slowly got down on one knee and then the other. He

bowed his head. "Shoot me. Fuckin' shoot me. You know how I feel about you. I can't do it for you. Your old man said no. This thing of ours, we have to follow the rules. You broke the rules, Tony. If I help you, I'm fucked. My family is fucked. I can't do it for you, kid."

Tony was angry. "Angie, how can you turn your back on me?"

"God knows I don't want to. I have to."

"Come on, you old fuck, you owe me. Look, gimme some cash and I'll get the fuck out of here. Once I'm out of the country, I can get to my money."

"I can't give nothin' to you," Angelo objected. "But I'll tell you this. I got a couple grand in my pocket. I ain't got no gun, so I can't fuckin' stop you from takin' it. You know what I'm sayin'?"

Sarah watched the exchange in disbelief. She looked for a way to escape, but Tony had a tight grip on her elbow. She prayed someone else would come out of the house—a woman, hopefully.

With his other hand, Tony reached into his pocket and took out his gun. Sarah tried to pull away, but he yanked her back. He looked at Angelo, who seemed to be at peace. With his gun hand he swung back and cracked Angelo across the bridge of the nose. Angelo went down in a pile, blood spraying from his nose. Now there was a deep gash over the mangled cartilage and scar tissue.

Tony reached down and started rummaging through Angelo's left front pocket.

Angelo muttered quietly, "The other pocket . . . the other pocket."

Tony grabbed a wad of money—hundreds, fifties, and twenties. He looked down at Angelo, who was lying on the front porch, bleeding. "I love you, Angie. I'm sorry I had to do this."

Angie looked up at him and just shook his head.

Tony pulled Sarah back to the car. She was still frightened, but at least Tony hadn't killed this guy, too.

"Please, just let me go here. I promise I won't do anything. I won't say anything. Just let me live. I won't tell anyone what happened."

Tony looked at her as if he was giving it some thought. "What are you worried about? See? I didn't kill him. I'm not such a bad guy after all."

SIXTEEN

Darcy made his move, dropping his rook to the center of the board. He absentmindedly looked around Seymour's cluttered office, at the credenza, which was loaded with family pictures. File folders were strewn about his desk, dozens of phone messages.

There was a rap on the door and John Doe walked in. Darcy was startled to see him again. This can't be good, he thought.

"Mr. Cole, can I talk to you for a minute?" John asked.

Darcy stood up. "Seymour, I'll be just a moment." Then he walked over to the doorway where John was standing.

John bent his head toward Darcy's ear and in a voice just above a whisper said, "I'm afraid I have some bad news for you. Junior has escaped."

Darcy looked confused. "From prison?" he said.

"I'm afraid so, Mr. Cole. So it looks like you have company again."

Darcy stood there for a moment, then turned back toward Seymour, "Sorry, friend, but I have to cut the game short today."

John began to step out of the office and back into the waiting room. "I'll wait for you out here, Mr. Cole."

Darcy looked at Seymour. "You got lucky today, Seymour. Take care of yourself. I was winning."

"I don't want anything to happen to you," Seymour replied. "It's very hard to break in new chess partners"

Darcy smiled and shook his hand. "I'll be here next week," he said unconvincingly.

"You going to be all right, Darcy? I thought this whole mess was cleared up."

"So did I, actually. But this knucklehead kid is determined to get at me. They'll find him fast, though. He's too stupid to not get caught. And as soon as he is, I'll be back, okay?"

"I'll keep the board just as it is." Seymour said, putting his arm around Darcy.

Darcy laughed. "You were two moves from beating me anyway, so we'll start a new game."

They walked together out to the waiting room, where John Doe was standing. "Let's go, John," Darcy said.

• • •

At the Doe boys' insistence, Darcy worked the rest of the day in the windowless conference room, with John just outside his door. Jim sat in the waiting room, studying the new magazines that had come in.

Darcy couldn't concentrate. He told Kathy, Irma, and Patrick of the escape, and they stayed with him to talk about it. Patrick turned on the radio to a news station. They got details about the escape and the ensuing manhunt, but learned that no progress had been made in locating Tony.

Darcy's office was transformed into a fortress as John gave

orders to several men inside and outside the office. The constant crackle of radio transmissions came from the walkie-talkies used by John's men. Finally, after hours of this, Darcy had had enough. He caught John's attention and signaled him over. "What's the point in being here? Can we leave?"

John shrugged. "Suit yourself, sir. I'll arrange things."

Twenty minutes later, Darcy said good-bye to Irma, Patrick, and Kathy, and John instructed his men to escort them home. Then they headed down the stairwell to the loading dock and shot out to a waiting car.

Once on the street, the driver did a couple of maneuvers to determine if they had a tail. Satisfied they didn't, he went north on Lake Shore Drive. They skipped Darcy's exit and kept traveling, then got off at Montrose, spun around, and went back on the drive headed south.

"Mr. Cole," John said. "We can't take you home. It's just not worth the risk. We're going to take you to a hotel for the night."

They drove to the Guest Quarter Suites near O'Hare Airport and dropped John off. The driver circled around the block, went down Mannheim Road, went off on another road, turned around, and came back. By that time John was standing just outside the front door of the hotel.

The driver pulled the car over and Darcy and Jim got out. Jim put one hand on Darcy's arm and the other into his jacket pocket. His eyes scanned everybody and everything in the lobby. Darcy looked around as well. They all walked to the elevator without incident and rode up alone to the thirteenth floor.

As the door opened, Darcy looked at John. "All they had was a room on the thirteenth floor?"

John said nothing and showed Darcy to the suite. They ordered room service, and Darcy sat on the couch, reading the transcripts he had taken from his office.

"You like being a lawyer?" John asked as he ate his club sandwich.

Darcy was surprised at the question. It was the first thing he could remember John asking him. "It has its ups and downs," he answered. "Why, you thinking of becoming one?"

John bristled at the suggestion. "Nah, lawyers fuck everything up."

Darcy and the Doe boys spent the rest of the evening reading the newspapers and watching TV. There wasn't much more conversation.

Darcy wondered how John had come to work for Mr. Benvenuti. He wondered where he had grown up and what sort of family life he had. He wondered what the brothers did in their spare time. He wondered, but didn't ask any questions.

He looked John over carefully—dark hair, dark eyes, a strong nose and jaw. The kid was probably Italian, maybe Greek. He had the thick shoulders and the neck of a lineman. His hands were big. He was moderately overweight, though he moved gracefully.

Jim Doe was a little thinner with lighter and shorter curly hair and light brown eyes. Jim was the less talkative of the two—he said nothing at all.

Darcy couldn't fall asleep. He finally nodded off after two o'clock and awoke at four. He got another good hour between five and six.

He had slept in his boxers and a T-shirt. He got dressed in the same suit, socks, and shoes he had worn the day before, then stepped out into the living room where the Doe boys were dressed and waiting for him.

On the elevator, John explained the plan to Darcy. "Frankly, we can't hide forever," he said. "Junior's going to make a move. We just need to be there to stop him. If we put you on ice for a week, he'll stay on ice for a week. He'll wait until you're back to your schedule. So unfortunately, we're playing cat and mouse, and we have to be really careful.

"We're going to take you to the Union League Club, and you can go ahead with your morning routine. Afterward, we'll walk you back to your office like usual and you can go about your day. If he hasn't learned your schedule yet, he will. That's how we'll draw him out. Then we'll nail him. But you have to do precisely what I tell you. Do you understand, Mr. Cole?"

"Absolutely," Darcy said.

Darcy had a great workout and afterward sat in the steam room reading the *Sun-Times'* account of Junior's escape. As he read about the two dead guards, Wells and Davis, he thought about their grieving families. People were dying because Junior had a score to settle with Darcy. A rational escapee would try to get out of the country, but Junior wanted Darcy first.

The police couldn't help. Hundreds were looking for Junior, but they wouldn't find him. One FBI agent said he believed that Junior's dad had a plane waiting for him at some remote airstrip. Sure, Darcy thought, but only if the plane had a faulty engine. There was no way the old man would help Junior get to another country. In fact, there was no way Benvenuti would let Junior get away alive.

When Darcy finished his workout and breakfast, he met John down in the lobby. John was seated in a leather wing chair with his hand inside his suit coat. He sprang to his feet when he saw Darcy.

They sat together for a few minutes to discuss the day ahead.

"You should be okay down here," John said softly, looking around as he spoke. "There are too many cops hanging around the Federal Building, and they're all looking for him. Our guess is that he's going to hone in on your condo. We've got guys there now, and we've alerted your building security. The weekend is here, so as much as you're able you should go about your business. All we ask is that you don't do any Cubs games or concerts—nothin' in a big crowd like that."

Great, Darcy thought. There goes my renewed subscription to the Symphony. "Sounds like a plan, John," he said. "We're basically just waiting for him to take a shot, then, right?"

"That's right, sir."

"And if he hits his mark?"

"Well, Mr. Cole, that's why I'm here. He's no crack shot, we know that. So you just let me worry about who takes a hit."

John smiled slightly as he stood up, and Darcy resisted the urge to shake his hand and thank him. It seemed inappropriate at this point.

As they walked through the revolving doors, John turned and looked at him one last time. "You stay right on my ass, you understand? I'm your protection."

"Yes. Just be careful."

John poked his head out of the doors and looked up and down the street. He saw nothing to the north, which was just twenty feet to Jackson Street. As he'd waited for Darcy to finish his swim, he'd surveyed the situation and determined that the route from the door of the club to the loading dock of the office building was the best bet. Jim was across the street waiting for them, and it was still early enough that there weren't a lot of people on the street.

Darcy came through the door behind him. "All right, you ready?"

Darcy nodded. "Ready."

"Not to be weird, sir," John said, "but put your hands on my back and hold on."

"Okay, John," Darcy said playfully. "But I don't think this is the right time for the Bunny Hop—"

John stopped dead in his tracks, and as Darcy peeked around him to see why, he too froze in disbelief. Walking toward them quickly was a wiry, dark-haired guy who John and Darcy recognized immediately as Tony Benvenuti Jr. In an instant, Tony reached inside his jacket and pulled out a gun, leveling it at John and Darcy. As John turned around to tell Darcy to get back inside the club, the first shot tore through his rib cage. The force knocked him back into Darcy, who tried to break his fall.

As Darcy knelt on the sidewalk holding John, another bullet ripped through John's right foot, causing Darcy to look up. He stared into the end of Junior's gun, then into his eyes. Junior grinned widely.

Of course, Junior hadn't finished his homework. He never saw Jim across the street, and he likely didn't feel the bullet that shattered his skull.

As Junior's head came apart, a fine red mist sprayed John and Darcy, and Junior hit the cement, sprawled out over the club crest in the sidewalk.

Jim ran across the street, kicked the gun out of Junior's hand, and grabbed John out of Darcy's arms.

"Mike, you okay?" he asked frantically.

John's jacket and shirt were ripped apart and soaked with blood. His right foot quivered in a strange, bloody tap dance.

Darcy leaned him forward a little, trying to get a look at the damage, and found an exit wound in the back.

"Well, you got a through-and-through," Darcy said. "You're going to be okay."

"I don't feel okay," John groaned.

He looked up at Darcy. "You asked me once if you could do me a favor. If I don't make it, I want you to talk to my mom. My name's Michael Landini. I'm from Elmwood Park. My mother's name is Marie. You tell her I was okay. Deal?"

"Deal," Darcy agreed. "But you're going to make it, Mike."

Mike smiled faintly. Darcy helped him lean back against the wall of the building.

They heard the sirens of the ambulance in the distance and sat back and waited.

SEVENTEEN

Darcy sat in his office, having a hard time pinning down just one emotion. He was relieved Junior was dead; he was oddly exhilarated about surviving a shootout; he felt guilty and worried about John Doe.

There was a loud knock on the door, and Collata walked in, carrying a new bottle of Glenlivet and two tumblers. He sat on the couch, wrestled the bottle open, and poured two healthy glasses. After he handed one of the glasses to Darcy, he leaned back on the couch and sipped from his.

"You know," he said, sniffing comically. "I've been in my share of shootouts."

"Really," Darcy said suspiciously.

"Oh, yeah," Collata continued. "And I know just how you're feeling."

Darcy sipped his drink and glared at him.

"Seriously, Darcy," Collata said. "You just survived this

trauma, one you weren't supposed to live through. It's like being a kid and having to run from the school bully, who really wants to kick your ass. The bully was after you, but you happened to have a couple of big goon friends who stepped up for you. Now the bully's gone, and he's not coming back. It's every kid's fantasy."

"Yeah?" Darcy said, feeling the soothing effects of the Scotch. "What do you know about being bullied?"

"Nothing, actually," Collata replied. "I was usually the big goon friend."

"Look, I know you've been through this," Darcy said, "but this is my first time. I've got to tell you, it's something I'll never forget. I'm going to remember every second of that shootout."

Collata stared into Darcy's eyes, making sure he had his full attention. "You'll never feel so alive as you do after an episode like that."

Irma broke in on the intercom. "Boss, there's a woman on the line who has something to tell you. She refuses to tell me what it is, but she sounds as if she knows something."

"What's it about?" he asked.

"She won't say. She says you should talk to her, and that it'll be worth your time."

Darcy looked at Collata.

Collata shrugged.

"All right, I'll take it."

He pushed the blinking button as he cradled the receiver against his shoulder. "Yes, this is Darcy Cole. May I help you?"

"Darcy, do you recognize my voice?"

"Yes," he said.

"Good. I have something to tell you. Does Collata still work for you?"

"Of course he does. He's here with me now, as a matter of fact."

"Great. Get out a pen and paper and take down this information."

Darcy leaned forward and grabbed a note pad off his desk,

then pulled a pen out of his pocket. "Okay, shoot."

There was a slight chuckle on the other end. "Nice expression, considering."

Darcy smiled.

Collata drank his Scotch and watched Darcy as he made notes, occasionally glancing up. The phone call lasted less than a minute. When Darcy hung up, he pulled the paper off the pad and handed it to Collata.

"I have a job for you that's going to require some finesse," he said.

Collata looked at the piece of paper and saw three addresses. The first one was in Westchester, a suburb west of Chicago. The other two were in Oak Park and in the far southwest suburb of Burr Ridge.

"Yeah, so what's the deal?" Collata asked. "Am I going on the parade of homes?"

Darcy leaned in to him. "When Junior broke out of prison, he killed those two guards. Then he grabbed a hostage, killed another guy in central Illinois, and drove the hostage from central Illinois to Chicago. My source was informed by a flipper inside the organization that the hostage is stashed in one of those three houses. They're betting on the Westchester house because it's small. It's at the end of the street, and it abuts a forest preserve."

"So dial 911," Collata said. "Let the cops find the hostage."

"It's not that easy," Darcy said. "I've got to protect both the flipper and my source."

"Why not call in a tip to the cops?"

"Because," Darcy said slowly, "if the cops go breaking down the door to find the hostage, then someone's going to know who the flipper is."

"So you want me to grab the hostage and quietly make everything go away?"

"If possible."

"I don't get it," said Collata. "Why would we give a shit if someone knows there's a flipper? I mean, if the guy's a flipper and they find out who he is—bam, two in the back of the head. Who gives a fuck?"

"I can't go into it," Darcy answered. "All I can tell you is that it's in my best interest if this hostage is released unharmed without police intervention. This is important to me."

"So, what? Am I going to get keys to these places, or am I supposed to break into 'em?"

Darcy said nothing.

"What the fuck? Let me guess. These are safe houses that Junior had access to."

Darcy nodded.

"You gotta be shittin' me. You want me to break in to some mob safe houses, looking for a fuckin' hostage, to protect some snitch? If they find me, I'm gonna get capped."

"No one knows about these houses."

"Bullshit!" Collata exclaimed. "How would you have gotten the call, then?"

"These houses are houses the flipper controls," Darcy explained. "Look, if you're apprehensive, I'll go with you."

Collata slammed the rest of his Scotch. "Gee, that makes me feel better. How do I know you're not all jacked up, looking for another shootout?"

"C'mon, Collata. I need your help."

Collata stuffed the piece of paper into his pocket.

"What do you want me to do when I get the hostage?"

"First of all," Darcy replied, "her name is Sarah West. She's going to be pretty shaken. Make sure she understands she's safe. Let her know Junior's dead. Take her wherever she wants. Take her home."

"What if she wants to go to the cops?"

"Then take her to the cops. I'll give you five grand," Darcy said. "That ought to get her started. If she needs more or whatever, let me know."

"What if she's not interested in money?" Collata asked.

"Then you just made five grand."

Collata smiled. "I'll see if I can find her."

176

EIGHTEEN

Collata rolled down a quiet, tree-lined street. At the end, he saw a small ranch house with a large backyard surrounded by a chain-link fence. The forest preserve lay beyond the fence. Collata pulled up all the way at the side of the house so no one could see his van. From the van he could see two windows to the basement. He noticed they were darkened out. He got out of his car and walked to the side door. Just inside the door he saw a security alarm keypad. As he looked closely through the window, he could see the blinking lights on the keypad. They spelled out the word "disabled."

"Why does this smell like a setup?" Collata muttered to himself.

He looked at the door and the lock, then went back to his van and opened it. Bypassing his lock pick kit, he reached for a crowbar, then walked back to the door and placed the edge of the crowbar against the bolt. He ripped as hard as he could.

The wood door splintered and popped open. He shut the door behind him, glancing outside, then pulled out his gun and started to make his way through the house. There was no one and nothing unusual in any of the three bedrooms, the living room or bathrooms. Then he walked down the rickety stairs to the basement, holding the crowbar out in front of him. He flicked on the light with his elbow, and a dim haze fell across the room. The basement was unfinished, its steel I-beams supported by cement poles. Boxes were stacked on and around an old pool table. A curtain hung across the doorway leading to the laundry room.

Collata saw the young woman slumped against a pole. She was handcuffed to it and her mouth was taped shut. She watched with wide eyes as Collata approached her, and then she began to whimper. He realized she was staring at the crowbar in his hands.

"Ma'am, my name is Collata," he said as he set the crowbar down. "I'm a private investigator. I'm a retired Chicago cop."

He pulled out his badge and showed it to her, holding it close enough that she could see.

"Ma'am," he said gently. "I'm here to get you out of here, but you have to cooperate with me. You can't go crazy when I take off the tape and undo the handcuffs. Do you understand?"

She nodded.

He examined the duct tape, wrapped completely around her head. "There's no good way to do this. It's going to hurt when I pull the tape off, but do your best not to scream."

She nodded.

"By the way, there's no one else in the house, is there?"

She shook her head, then shrugged.

"Well, we'll deal with that when it comes," he said.

He could tell she had been working on the tape but hadn't gotten very far. He worked his thumb and forefinger along it until he was able to get a grip on the corner of the tape.

"Are you ready?"

She nodded.

"Okay. One, two, three."

He ripped it fast. Clumps of hair came out, and little dots of blood formed on her upper lip. She squinted in pain, grinding her teeth and trying to hold in a scream.

Collata talked to her softly. "Tell me your name. Is it Sarah?"

Her eyes watered as she tried to answer. Finally she answered, "Yes, my name is Sarah West."

Collata studied the handcuffs. "These are Smith & Wesson cuffs," he said. "I have to go to my van and get a key for them. I'll be right back."

"No, please don't leave me," she pleaded.

"I'll be right back. I need the key to get you out of here."

"Just hurry," she begged. "Please, oh, God, hurry."

Collata pulled out his gun and walked back upstairs. He moved quietly through the living room and kitchen, and then outside to the van, where he retrieved a ring of keys, then went back into the house.

When he knelt down next to Sarah, she was shaking. "Okay, Sarah, you have to work with me here. I gotta get you the hell out of here to someplace safe as quickly as possible. I don't have time to chase a hysterical woman around."

She gave him a dirty look. "Hysterical woman? Do you have any idea what I've been through?"

"We'll talk about that," he said. "You got to promise me."

"Just get these things off, please."

He popped the handcuffs off her wrists, then opened the second set, which was around her ankles. He helped her to her feet.

"You okay?" he asked. She was a little unsteady.

"Yeah, I'm fine. Can we just leave?"

As they walked up the stairs and through the house, Sarah looked around. Junior had brought her here when it was dark, and he'd never bothered to turn on any lights. He'd shackled her in the basement and, without saying a word, left her there.

In the hours that she had been cuffed to the pole, her terror-fueled imagination had created gruesome scenarios. They'd kept her company through the long, cold night—it was only the next morning that she'd been able to sleep at all. Now, as she looked around the house in the daylight, she saw that everything was perfectly normal.

Once outside, Sarah jumped into the passenger side of the van, and Collata got behind the wheel. They backed out onto the street.

She looked around the van and back to Collata. "Do you live in this thing?"

"Sometimes."

"Where are you taking me?"

"Wherever you want, young lady. You want to go to the police, I'll take you there. You want to go home, I'll take you there."

"Where are we, anyway?"

"Westchester, a suburb of Chicago."

"I live three and half hours from here," she said.

"I know."

"Why didn't the police come get me?"

"I don't think they knew where you were."

"How did you know where I was?"

"Like I said, I'm a retired cop. I'm a private investigator. I work for a lawyer. He got a phone call from an anonymous source telling us where you might be. So I came to find you."

"I don't know any lawyers in Chicago."

"The guy who took you, Benvenuti—"

She nodded.

"He wanted to kill this lawyer."

"Why?"

"It's a long story. Benvenuti was killed earlier today in a shootout."

"Oh, my God," she moaned. "Thank God."

"Yes, and that means you're safe. Now for the hard part. You have to figure out what you want to do. If you want to go to the police, I'll take you to the police. If you want to go home,

I'll drive you home. If you want to go to the airport, I'll buy you a ticket. Anywhere you want to go, whatever it is, you tell me."

"Can we start with something to eat?" she asked.

"Absolutely. What do you feel like?"

"Just something hot and decent. I don't care."

Collata smiled. "Well there's a Baker's Square down the block and a Burger King across the street."

"Baker's Square."

They were seated at a booth near the window and had ordered before Sarah felt like talking.

"Where's my car?" she asked.

"I haven't the faintest idea," Collata answered. "We'll report it stolen. It will turn up. It's gotta be someplace near where Benvenuti showed up."

"It was brand new, you know."

"Don't worry. You'll get a new one."

The waitress brought their drinks and salads, and they ate eagerly and silently. As they waited for their entrées, Collata asked Sarah if she felt like talking about what she'd been through. She jumped at the chance.

"Well, for starters, he forced me off the road," she said, motioning the waitress for another soda. "Then he drove me all over hell trying to find some money. He beat and robbed one old guy—I think it was even a friend of his. And the other old man . . ." She gazed quietly out the window. "Tony said he wasn't going to hurt him."

The waitress brought her soda, and Sarah took a lone sip. "So then he made me drive," she continued. "Don't ask me why. He kept saying he wasn't going to hurt me if I cooperated. But how could I believe him? So I just drove, and he seemed to sort of lose interest at that point. He stopped talking and just stared straight ahead, like he was in a trance."

The waitress brought their food—club sandwiches and fries for both—and they dug in as soon as the plates hit the table.

"Anyway," Sarah said with her mouth full, "he directed me

to the house and marched me inside. Then he shackled me in the basement. I wanted to make one last plea for my life—I was sure he'd kill me—but I didn't say anything. I didn't want to set him off. So he just cuffed me and went upstairs without saying anything. I had no idea he had even left the house."

Collata was clearly uncomfortable. "Sarah, do you need to go to the hospital or see a doctor or anything?"

She shook her head. "No, he didn't do anything like that," she replied. "I'm okay."

They continued to eat, with Collata already looking at his pie options.

"Oh, my God," Sarah said suddenly. "I've got to call my family."

Collata pulled out a cell phone and pushed it across the table.

"Be my guest."

She took another quick bite of her sandwich, then dialed a phone number. It appeared to Collata that she was trying to talk with several people at once.

"Yes, Mom, I'm okay. No, Dad, don't call the police yet. The police are there? All right, tell them I'm going to the police here. I'm in Westchester, Illinois—I'll call you from the police station. Okay, bye."

She slid the cell phone back to Collata.

"Way to keep it together," he said appraisingly.

"Had to," she said. "They were falling apart. This is certainly the biggest thing that's ever happened in that town."

"Ooh," Collata said. "You'll be a celebrity then."

She smiled.

"What do you do, anyway?" he asked curiously.

Sarah sighed. "Well, I work at a factory in West Terre Haute, and I have an apartment in Marshall, Illinois. A few nights a week I wait tables—I'm saving up some money."

"Yeah?" Collata said, signaling for the waitress. "What for?"

She let out a sad laugh. "You know, it's funny. I've been saving up to move to Chicago. I wanted to get out of Hicksville and start a new life someplace exciting. I just didn't figure I'd be brought here at gunpoint."

"Well," Collata said. "It doesn't get much more exciting than that."

The waitress stepped up, and they both ordered pie and coffee. Sarah ordered hers à la mode.

"I eat when I'm nervous," she said, slightly embarrassed.

When the pie and coffee arrived, Sarah looked at Collata.

"Okay," she said, "I've told you my story, so how about you tell me how this whole mess came about?"

"From the beginning?"

"That's a very good place to start," she said with a mouthful of pie.

"Well, let's see. I work for a guy named Darcy Cole. He's the best lawyer in Chicago, a damn fine man. Anyway, Darcy's represented a lot of important people. When Tony Benvenuti Jr. got arrested for drugs, racketeering, and conspiracy, his old man asked Darcy to represent him. The kid was a screw-up. The father was an old mustache pete. He kept his mouth shut and did everything the right way. The government had been after him for years, but they could never lay a glove on him. They knew the old man had done everything you have to do to get to be the head of the Chicago mob, and yet they couldn't touch him. So along comes Junior, shooting his mouth off, acting like a big shot, and wearing his stupidity on his sleeve. He threw money around like he was important.

Eventually, the government gets him on tape saying a bunch of stupid things, and they pinch him. Darcy represents him. He gets a copy of the tapes, listens to them, and tells the kid there's no way we're going to win this. Let's cut our losses and work out a deal, Darcy tells him. The old man tells the kid to keep his mouth shut, take the hit, do his time, and get out. But the kid says, fuck you, I'm not takin' no hit. I'm going to trial. Well, the jury hears the tapes. It embarrasses the hell out of the father and puts a lot of heat on the organization. Junior goes down like a brick. He goes off to Terre Haute Federal Penitentiary to do a forty-year bit. He's pissed, so he sends out a kite—"

"A kite?" Sarah interrupted.

"Yeah, you know—he sends out notice from inside that he wants someone to do a hit for him."

"You mean he wanted your boss killed?"

"That's it. So his old man puts the word out that no one better pick up the contract, but there are two freelancers he can't stop. They make a run at Darcy and end up dead. Now Junior's cut off, so he breaks out of the pen, comes up here, and ends up with a tag on his toe."

"So how did you find me?"

"Somebody in the organization is a flipper. They dropped a dime to somebody in the government, and that somebody tipped my boss."

"Why didn't they call the police?"

"Like I said, whoever gave the information is a flipper. That means they're inside the mob, but they're giving information to the government. So whoever it is—the FBI, the DEA, whoever—calls my boss and says, "Hey, this woman is out there. Take care of her." There can't be that many people who knew where you were. If the cops got you, the mob might figure out who the flipper is. My boss didn't want that to happen."

"Why would your boss do that?"

"Probably in exchange for something down the road."

"I don't understand."

Collata lit up a cigarette.

"Well, I don't know exactly what happened, but there's probably some snitch who called an FBI agent who in the past has given Darcy some inside dope. So then they call in the marker. They say, get this woman out so we don't burn the identity of our flipper. If the mob finds out he snitched, they'll probably kill him."

"I still don't really get it," Sarah said, shaking her head.

Collata smiled and finished his coffee.

"Doesn't matter, anyway. You're safe, and you're gonna tell your side to the police, right?"

"Right," she said.

NINETEEN

Darcy finished his workout and walked across the street to his office. No Doe boys. No threats. Just early-morning solitude.

Irma was there already and had coffee brewing.

"Boss?" she said, holding up a cup.

"No, thanks," Darcy replied as usual.

He stood over her desk and looked down at the appointment book. "What do I have today?"

She put on her reading glasses and glanced at the book. "You're free until 9:30, when you have a status hearing across the street on Wysocki. Patrick said he'd cover it. Then you have appointments starting at 11:00 with Owen Dempsey, 11:30 with a prospective new drug case, and noon with a prospective insurance fraud."

"What's after that?"

"Lunch with Seymour."

"Bless your heart," he said. "You scheduled that?"

"I sure did. I figured the least you could do is buy the man lunch. After all, you drink all his Scotch."

"Okay, then," Darcy instructed. "From now until my eleven o'clock appointment, I need some peace and quiet. I have to get some work done on the *Tobias* case, so would you hold my calls?"

"You bet."

Darcy's desk was littered with transcripts, black binders, and file folders. He pulled a legal pad from a folder and began reading the notes that Lynne had written in the margins. She had photocopied pieces of police reports and passages from trial transcripts, which she'd then taped on to the pages of the legal pad. Darcy read the sections she had highlighted with orange and yellow markers, as well as the notes she had made in red ink in the margins. Most of the notes were merely comments, such as "liar" or "not true." He scanned page after page of this, looking for something intriguing. Toward the end of the documents, his eyes landed on a one-word comment next to a list of additional witnesses for the government. Next to Rona Siegel's name Lynne had written "slut!" As Darcy stared at the word, Irma announced over the intercom that Owen Dempsey had arrived.

Dempsey wore a pair of khaki Dockers, a golf shirt, and a blue blazer. His hair was longer, and the curl was breaking out on all sides.

"Darcy, let me get to the point," he said as they shook hands. "I'm closing on my house in five weeks. I'll have a cashier's check for $250,000. Tell me to put your name on it. You're my lawyer."

"What about your predecessors? Isn't there one of them who wants to represent you?"

"Oh, yeah, they want to represent me. Those big-firm bastards. They want half a million dollars to work out a plea for me. It's $200,000 for the trial and $50,000 for the appeal. And that's up front. I sat down and figured it out. This trial can't take more than two weeks. So don't give me the bullshit that you can't do a two-week trial for $200,000. You're not making a $100,000 a week, are you, Darcy?"

"No, I'm not."

"If we win, then I get the $50,000 back," said Owen.

Darcy looked at Owen and saw a deflated man. He had put on weight, he looked disheveled.

"How are you holding up?" Darcy asked.

"It's the worst experience of my life," Owen said. "I was going to be governor, now I'm looking at going to prison. This is so goddamn stupid," he said. "A guy can't get a little action on the side? Someone has to ruin his life?"

Darcy shrugged. "Hell, you should talk. You've gone after scalps, famous people. That's how you were getting so close to the governor's mansion."

"No, Darcy, I went after guys who were dirty."

"You went after me," Darcy said.

"Goddamn right I went after you. I went back ten years on your ass. It's a hell of thing to go after a guy and then come to the conclusion that he's honest."

"Or good," said Darcy.

"Or good. But I don't know anyone who's that good. I was on you with a microscope and couldn't find a thing. So what do you say? Are you my lawyer?"

"Let me know when you get the money; we'll talk then," Darcy answered. "You know, things have a way of changing quickly around here."

"I'll take that as a yes."

"You can take it any way you want," Darcy replied. "I'm not filing an appearance until I'm paid."

"That's what I wanted to hear."

● ● ●

Seymour and Darcy were seated at a table against a large pillar in the main dining room of the club. The pillar offered them some seclusion, and the two tables next to them were vacant.

"Thanks for lunch," Seymour said.

"You haven't eaten yet," Darcy replied.

"Oh, but I will. And believe me, I'll save room for dessert."

"Did you suggest this to Irma?"

"No, it was her idea. She thought you needed a break."

"Well, she has always known what's good for me."

Seymour looked at Darcy intently. "How are you, my friend?"

"Since the last time we spoke? Well, I was almost killed, but other than that, things are actually better. Seymour, you have a good practice and a great family life, and I really admire that about you. It's something I'd like in my life. I've been through the ringer, Seymour. As I was telling you last time, I'm sort of lost."

"What are you doing about it?"

"Nothing, really. I'm just trying to keep one foot moving in front of the other."

"How's your health?"

"Good. I need some joy in my life."

"And you deserve it, Darcy," Seymour said. "But it usually doesn't just drop in your lap. It takes some work."

"Yeah, I've started to realize that."

"And another thing, Darcy. Don't rely too heavily on other people to fill some sort of void you might feel. Only you can do that."

"You're not preaching spirituality, are you Seymour?"

"You have no money problems. Business is good. Your health is good. What's missing?"

Darcy ran his hand through his hair. "If I knew that everything would be fine."

"Are you sleeping any better?"

"Not really."

"Well, you know, most guys our age have to get up a lot to piss in the middle of the night. Is that your problem?"

"I wish it were," he said. "I get up to piss, but I can't go back to sleep."

"You know what you need? You need to do something spiritually."

"Spiritually?" Darcy asked.

"Yes, you have to get in touch with yourself. Darcy, subconsciously you've probably come to the conclusion that you have less time left on this earth than you thought. You're facing your mortality. You have to find peace with that."

"But I'm not a real God person—"

"Who said anything about God? I'm talking about your need to reconnect with yourself. You need to get a center, a core to your life. You need to get in touch with your values. Do you have values?"

"Yes, I do," Darcy said, smiling. "In fact, I'm going to be taking a case that I'd normally turn down. It's an older woman who came to see me about representing her son, except she can't afford me. But there's something about it—well, taking the case just seems like the right thing to do. For once I'm saying screw the money. How's that for values?"

"I'm impressed," Seymour responded.

"As a matter of fact," Darcy said, "the woman who wants me to represent her kid gave me a Bible."

"Really?" asked Seymour. "King James, Old Testament, what?"

"I don't know. I haven't really looked at it."

"I'll tell you what," said Seymour. "Next time you can't sleep, why don't you crack that Bible open and read a few pages? You can read it in a secular way with a secular frame of mind, but read it. There's a reason it's been the bestseller for the last two thousand years."

"I was kind of leaning toward Prozac," Darcy said.

"Well, take the Prozac and read the book," Seymour replied.

They finished lunch and walked back to Darcy's office. Seymour stopped in to thank Irma for lunch before heading down the hall to his own office.

"Irma," Darcy said as he walked into his office. "Call over

to Northwestern Hospital and see what room Michael Landini
is in. Also find out the visiting hours."

"Will do."

• • •

John Doe was wearing a hospital gown, sitting up in his bed
watching *Jeopardy*. A tray of untouched food was next to his
bed. Darcy knocked on the open door and stepped through.

"How are you, John?"

"Mr. Cole, it's great to see you."

"I'm sorry to show up empty-handed but I couldn't figure
out what to get you. Somehow you don't seem like a flowers-
and-candy type of guy. So what do you need? I'll be happy to
get you anything."

John laughed. "I need to get out of here. I got a buddy coming with some sandwiches from Fontano's." He pointed a
thumb toward the tray of uneaten food. "Who can eat this
shit?"

"John, I wanted to come by and thank you."

"Mr. Cole, you can call me Mike now. The old man would
understand."

"How is the old man?"

"He had to bury his son. That can't be easy."

"Can I ask you a question John—Mike?"

"Go ahead."

"How do you feel?"

"I feel pretty good. They tell me I'll be out of here in a couple of days."

"No, I mean how do you feel after surviving a shootout?"

"I feel lucky to be alive. I feel stupid for being in a position
to get shot in the first place. It wasn't like it was a big surprise.
I just reacted slowly."

"Mike, the only thing you did wrong was underestimate
Junior's stupidity. Who imagined he'd come out in the cops'
backyard? Not me."

"No, that's our job, sir."

"C'mon, Mike. The fact that I'm standing here talking to you proves that you did your job. Right?"

"Yeah, I guess so, counselor."

"Listen, when you get out of here, maybe I can take you out for a steak. What do you say?"

Mike smiled in appreciation of the gesture, though they both doubted the dinner would ever take place.

TWENTY

Clouds blocked the moon, creating a darkness that made the sky look almost purple. Darcy sat in a chair in his apartment looking out over the tranquil lake.

He didn't even bother to look at his watch. He knew it was around 3:00 A.M. After his visit with Mike in the hospital, he had done some more work on the *Tobias* case. The trial was to start in two days, and he was at that point where he was ready but nervous, reviewing his notes for anything he may have forgotten to do. He knew that once the jury was selected and opening arguments began he would be relaxed and confident. Before that he was always filled with lingering doubts.

He was stepping into battle once again. He fretted over every detail. He knew every word on every transcript for every witness who had testified in the state case. Each witness's testimony was cross-referenced with items he wanted to confront them with during his cross-exam. Kathy and Darcy had demanded prior approval of Lynne's wardrobe for the trial. Lynne didn't like it, but she cooperated.

Darcy took a Tagamet and washed it down with warm club soda, then paced for a few minutes before retrieving his reading glasses. He turned on the lamp next to his chair and waited for his eyes to adjust to the light, then sat back in the chair and put on his reading glasses. He turned the book over, looking at both sides. The only thing it said on the cover was Holy Bible. He opened it, marveling at the thinness of each page, and started to read. "In the beginning God created the heavens and the earth. . . ."

• • •

The day before the trial, Darcy shared the pool with his friend the bankruptcy judge and someone he guessed was an out-of-towner staying at the club. He finished his swim and threw on a bathrobe, then ordered grapefruit juice, Irish oatmeal, and coffee, which he ate at one of the tables near the pool. He thumbed through the *Tribune,* but nothing caught his eye.

The judge finished his swim, put on a robe, and walked toward Darcy. He stood on the other side of the table, beaming. "Morning, Darcy."

"Good morning, Your Honor."

"Well, are you ready for trial?"

"I suppose I am."

"Hell, I know you are!" the judge exclaimed. "You ever think of taking the bench, Darcy?"

"No one has ever offered," Darcy laughed. "Besides, I'm too old a dog to learn any new tricks."

"Oh, bad state of mind, Darcy. Look at me—I'm a spring chicken!"

The judge began to shuffle away. "When I get a little time, I'll pop down to see you try this case."

Darcy drank his coffee and watched the solitary swimmer struggling through the water. He was trying very hard to stay afloat.

The waiter approached with a coffeepot, but Darcy waved him off. He finished his grapefruit juice and got up to get ready for the day.

Fifteen minutes later, he bounded through the doors of his office.

"Good morning, Boss," Irma said.

"Good morning, my dear," Darcy replied.

He strode into his office and took off his coat. Irma had followed him, and she handed him a stack of messages. He dropped them on his desk and walked around it to sit down.

"Patrick had an 8:30 in DuPage County, and he is doubling back to do the 10:30 in federal court. He asked that you be available in case he gets hung up in DuPage."

"Who's covering the cases in Skokie?"

"Kathy got them bumped over the phone."

"Did she speak with the clients?"

"Yes, it's all covered."

"Good. What else?"

"You have appointments at 11:00, 11:30, 2:00, and 4:30. With prospective clients."

"Anything good?"

"Hmm—bank fraud, money laundering, a drug case, and a reckless homicide. We also got a phone call about an insurance fraud case in federal court in San Antonio. You interested?"

"Not likely, but bring them in anyway. Anything else?"

"No. Do you need anything?"

"No, I'm good."

"All right, then. If you need something, buzz me. Otherwise I'll see you when the mail gets here. And Darcy?"

"What?"

"Stop worrying about the *Tobias* case. You'll do a good job."

• • •

It was close to 5:00 when Darcy walked into the conference room. Patrick, Kathy, and Collata were already there. Two pizza boxes were on the countertop near the sink.

"Okay, everybody set for tomorrow?" Darcy asked.

Various forms of "yes" rang about the room.

Kathy had a set of eight manila folders, which she handed to Darcy, and an identical set that she gave to Patrick.

"Okay, issues," she said. "Each file contains case law regarding a certain fact or issue that we expect to arise during the trial."

Patrick handed Darcy three black plastic binders, each tabbed with different names. "Here's each witness, broken down into the report we have for them and the impeachment."

Darcy looked it over. "Very good. You guys do nice work."

Collata had a tattered brown cardboard accordion file with manila folders inside. "These are my original reports on all the interviews I did. Do you want copies?"

"No, I don't need them. As long as they're available, that's all I care about. You keep the originals so there's no issue as to custody. Anything else?"

No one spoke up.

Darcy said, "Well, in that case, what do you think about this?" He handed Patrick, Kathy, and Collata each a packet of stapled papers.

It took about thirty seconds of reading before Patrick exclaimed, "Jesus Christ!"

Collata began to chuckle loudly.

"I don't fucking believe this, Darcy," Patrick said.

"Where did you get this?" Kathy asked.

"Every now and then you get lucky," Darcy said. "My source with the government doesn't like Greenberg."

Darcy waited until everyone had finished reading the five-page memo.

"Okay, here's how I look at it," Darcy said. "Since we have our hands on this memo, let's use it to our advantage."

"This is internal work product," said Patrick. "Vernon Peters isn't going to let you use it."

"Oh, but he will," Darcy replied.

Patrick shook his head. "This is a To/From memo from an FBI agent to the acting U.S. attorney saying that the star witness in the *Tobias* case is an inveterate liar. According to this, everything Marty Thiel says is subject to intense scrutiny, so they need corroboration for everything. It lists specifics where they have questions as to whether or not he's being truthful."

"Exactly," said Darcy. "It's clearly relevant. It's great for impeachment. I can perfect it by calling the FBI agent and that little shit, Ira Greenberg."

Darcy shot a couple of pieces of paper across the table to Collata. "I want you to serve the agent and Greenberg. I don't want you serving their office. Hand it to them in person."

"Ira's easy," said Collata, "but I have no idea what Special Agent Rob Ewing looks like."

Darcy raised his eyebrows. "You know the guy's name. You know where he works. You know he parks in the federal garage on the other side of the MCC. Those are what we call clues. You're an investigator. Get out and investigate. I want that subpoena thumbtacked to his forehead by tomorrow morning. Got me?"

Collata saluted him.

Darcy turned to Patrick. "I know you have the list of every U.S. attorney's home address from your glory days. So give Collata Greenberg's home address. I want him served late tonight so he can't do anything about it. I'm going to shake them up tomorrow morning."

"I'll pull cases on the admissibility of the memo," Kathy said. There may be an issue of privilege regarding the testimony of the agent and Ira. I may have to go on-line at home, and if I do, someone is going to have to swing by and get it early tomorrow morning because I don't have a sitter until 10:30."

"Not a problem," Patrick said. "I won't be sleeping much tonight anyway."

"We're going to give Ms. Tobias a vigorous defense," Darcy

said. "Just think," he said Patrick, "you can return in a blaze of glory. Now Ira's tit is in a ringer, and Owen is going to be indicted. If we can pull this case off, you're going to be just like Lazarus."

Collata lit up a cigarette. "Oh, shit, he's going biblical on us."

TWENTY-ONE

Darcy dropped his briefcase on the floor next to counsel table. He walked over to the first row of the visitors gallery to talk with Sandy Campos.

"Hey, Darcy, I understand Collata laid paper on Ira Greenberg," Sandy said.

"That's correct," Darcy said. "Mr. Greenberg was served with a subpoena late last night."

"Cut the crap, Darcy. I'm not going to hold you on the record."

"Oh, in that case, yeah, we served the fucker on his front lawn."

"And an FBI agent?"

"Yes. He's the other side of it."

"So what do you expect the G's going to do this morning?"

"If I were prosecuting this case, I would file a motion to

quash the subpoena. I would want to know why there was a subpoena for the U.S. attorney and an FBI agent."

"And the answer to that is?" Sandy asked.

Darcy walked back to his briefcase. He rummaged through it and pulled out a sheaf of papers.

"I thought you'd ask me that. Don't say I never gave you anything." He handed her the five-page interoffice memo. She spent a moment glancing through it.

"Okay, I won't ask your source," she said. "But I'd sure like to have a source like that. This is a confidential interoffice memo. Isn't this work product?"

Anna Minkoff entered the courtroom, followed by three or four federal types. She walked over to Darcy and handed him a few court papers.

"You do make things interesting," she said angrily.

Sandy flipped open her reporter's note pad and popped the button on her pen.

"You are a piece of work. I don't know how you get the shit you do, but you are unbelievable." Anna was seething.

"Well, Ms. Minkoff, I was going to ask you to join me for coffee during a break in the trial, but apparently you won't be up to it."

"Is this some kind of joke, Darcy? You're privy to more information in my office than I am. I don't know who your source is, but if I find him I'm going to make it my life's work to ruin him."

"Anna, I'm surprised that a veteran trial lawyer like you would let something get personal."

Don't be," she said. "I'm going to ask that you be held in contempt of court."

"Do what you must."

Sandy was writing furiously when Anna turned her attention to her.

"Let me ask you something, Ms. Campos. Do you get your information from Darcy, or does the source feeding Darcy feed you as well?"

Sandy smiled. "If I had his sources my life would be a lot easier."

Anna started to reply to her, but turned to Darcy instead. "Did you bring a toothbrush, or will you have your secretary run one over to you at the lockup?"

Darcy smiled. "That's what I like about the government. You are our friends. You're here to help us."

"Go to hell, Darcy," she said as she walked over to counsel. She threw her files onto the table as hard as she could.

Vernon Peters entered and stood behind his chair for a minute surveying the crowded courtroom. He nodded to his minute clerk, who called the court to order.

"Well, we can't just try a case anymore. We got to have all the hoopla, don't we, Ms. Minkoff," he said, dragging out her name.

"Step up to the podium, children. Let's resolve this. Mr. Cole, have you read Ms. Minkoff's motion to quash your subpoena on her boss and her minion in the FBI?"

"Yes, Your Honor, I have."

"What say you, Mr. Cole?"

"Your Honor, I have a report generated by the FBI agent to Ira Greenberg, as the acting U.S. attorney, indicating defects in the proposed testimony of their star witness, Martin Thiel. I believe that it's relevant and admissible for cross-examination purposes—not only on Martin Thiel, but on the witness who authored the report, since he did the investigation, and Mr. Greenberg, who was aware of these problems. He is ultimately responsible for the proposed plea agreement for Mr. Thiel. Bias or motive for him to testify as the government would like him to is clearly relevant."

"Okay, Ms. Minkoff. Your response?"

"Your Honor, I don't know how Mr. Cole gained possession of this internal memo, but it is work product. It is privileged, and his possession of it constitutes theft of United States property."

"Ms. Minkoff, let's get serious here. Someone in your office obviously gave this to Mr. Cole. He didn't commit burglary. So if someone in your office is giving it to him, I assume the person in your office waived the privilege and the confidentiality. Now move on."

"Your Honor, you can't dismiss the confidentiality and the privilege associated with this because someone unlawfully handed it to Mr. Cole."

"It's your assumption that it was handed to him unlawfully. Perhaps someone in your office believes in the rules of discovery and believed this to be Brady material. So unless you're going to present witnesses to testify that Mr. Cole stole this document, move on to the effects of the content rather than how he appropriated it."

"Your Honor, this document is nothing more than concerns raised by an FBI agent. It was prepared for trial purposes, trial strategy, and it has nothing to do with the credibility of Martin Thiel."

"Give me the document, Ms. Minkoff."

Anna handed the document up.

Vernon read it without any expression.

"Well, Ms. Minkoff, I would say this is quite an explosive document. I can't in good conscience quash those subpoenas because I think Mr. Cole has every right to call those witnesses."

"Your Honor," Darcy cut in, "under *Brady v. Maryland* they had to tender this document. Work product or not, it's information that tends to negate the guilt of my client. So I don't know how they could complain that my receiving this document is improper. It would have been improper if I had *not* received the document."

Judge Peters spoke up. "On the other hand, Mr. Cole, let me warn you of this. You put both the agent and Mr. Greenberg on, and I promise you I will give wide latitude during cross-examination by the government. In effect, you're going to allow Ms. Minkoff to testify if you get too far afield. Do you understand me, Mr. Cole?"

"Loud and clear, Judge."

"Now, children, are there any other little tussles to deal with before I call up the prospective jurors?"

Lynne, who had been glaring at Anna the entire time, leaned in to Patrick and whispered, "You'd think a woman who has nothing else in her life would be better at what she does."

Jim Parker snuck into the courtroom and sat in the third row directly behind Sandy Campos.

"Okay, then, enough of this nonsense," Peters ordered. He looked at his minute clerk. "Let's bring in a panel." He returned his attention to the courtroom.

"Ladies and gentlemen in the gallery, you are all going to have to move to the right side of the courtroom."

The reporters and the usual throng of court watchers all stood silently and moved across the aisle. Half the courtroom gallery was suddenly empty. A few U.S. marshals, wearing their gray slacks and blue blazers, stepped through the courtroom door and within moments returned, leading jurors silently into the pews.

Darcy was impressed with the panel of prospective jurors. It was a good cross section of the community. There were people from Chicago, the suburbs, and the counties that made up the judicial district of northern Illinois. It included men and women and a reasonable number of minorities. He liked his chances of getting a fair jury from the group.

They packed the empty side of the visitor's gallery, then put fourteen in the jury box. After all the jurors had filed in and the door to the courtroom was shut, Judge Peters smiled.

"Now, let's get to work, ladies and gentlemen."

TWENTY-TWO

It took about a day and a half to complete the jury selection process. When the twelve jurors and two alternates were finally seated, Anna Minkoff came out blazing in her opening statement, racking up points as Darcy waited his turn. She began by telling the jury about Charles Tobias, a man who had put himself through college and law school with the help of his wife. The young couple struggled to make ends meet while the husband finished school. Gradually, after he became a lawyer, the couple's fortunes began to rise. They started a family and pursued the American dream. Through hard work and skill, the business took off. A small firm, started by a few friends, exploded into one of Chicago's most influential law firms. It was that unbridled ambition and success that caused Lynne to target Charles Tobias as her ticket to the good life. She was young and beautiful and knew how to use that to her advantage.

The jury watched Anna as she strolled through the courtroom, accentuating her point by directing their attention to Lynne Tobias. Lynne sat at the counsel table staring ahead, when she wasn't looking Anna up and down in disgust.

Judge Peters watched from his perch eight to ten feet above them all.

It was a large courtroom, eighty feet long with a ceiling twenty-five feet high, elaborate wood trim and the United States seal. Three counsel tables filled the well of the court-room. A new assistant prosecutor sat at the first table in front of the jury, but this was Anna's case. Because he had become a potential witness, Ira Greenberg couldn't be in the court-room.

Darcy, Patrick, and Lynne sat at the middle table directly behind the government. The third table was empty. The spec-tators' gallery had filled in. In addition to the press, trial watchers, and the victim's family, a large group of lawyers had come to see the heavyweights slug it out.

Anna proceeded to tell the jurors about the murder. She explained how the police and FBI had unraveled the plot and how the witnesses were located. She told them about the mur-der trial and how the proof needed to convict in the fraud case was different.

"She's the ultimate con artist," Anna declared, as she pointed to Lynne. "She's going to play the role of an innocent victim and try to con this jury. But you will see her for what she really is. Remember, if you don't like Mark Thomas or Martin Thiel, don't blame us. She chose these people, we didn't."

Darcy rose to give his opening statement. He stood behind the lectern briefly, then began to stroll in front of the jury box.

"This is not a fraud case—that is a ruse. Mr. Tobias was a powerful man with powerful friends. This is about an older man who left his wife for a young woman. He wanted a trophy wife. When he was tragically murdered, somebody had to pay. Mark Thomas was caught. The police had him in an open-and-shut case. It was a stupid and senseless murder. Unfortunately, it happens every day. Mark Thomas wanted to rob the guy in the expensive car. Things went bad, and Mr. Tobias ended up dead. After being in custody several days and not once mentioning Lynne Tobias, Mark Thomas went to court and was assigned a defense lawyer. The lawyer helped him cut a deal to testify against Ms. Tobias in exchange for a deal—an incredible deal. Although they had never met, Mark Thomas began to talk about Ms. Tobias, and the government began to purchase the testimony it wanted from a murderer and scumbag to create a case against the trophy wife. The jury in state court didn't buy it, and you won't either."

Anna shot to her feet. "Objection!"

Peters spoke over her in a deep, annoyed voice. "Sustained."

Darcy explained the consideration the government had given each of their witnesses. He pointed out the lack of corroboration for the witnesses' testimonies. He tore into the government for feeding the witnesses the testimony they wanted to hear, but he didn't tell the jurors everything. He didn't want to let on what he had up his sleeve.

Peter Vanek testified first for the government. He laid out his credentials and explained his longtime friendship and partnership with Charles Tobias. His job was to humanize Charles Tobias, to make him something other than a rich guy who dumped his family for a young babe. The Charles Tobias he described was a family man, a loving husband, a hard-working, honest lawyer who amassed a fortune—a fortune, alas, that was now missing. The devil who had taken Charles Tobias's soul and ultimately his life was sitting at counsel table next to Darcy. Vanek was the setup for Marty Thiel and the others who would explain the fraud and the extent of the fraud committed by Lynne Tobias. He was very effective.

In cross, Darcy concentrated on two issues. The first was that early on in the marriage Charles had been happy with his new bride. The second point was that after Mark Thomas' arrest, Vanek—on behalf of Charles's family—sought charges against Lynne, despite a lack of evidence of her involvement.

After Vanek, the government put on an insurance company official who testified to paying off the insurance policy that Marty Thiel had written. The checks had been made out to Lynne Tobias, the widow.

Next was a bank executive who testified that the proceeds of the insurance policies were deposited into his bank. The money, per the instructions of Lynne Tobias, was wire-transferred to an asset funds management holding company in the Cayman Islands.

Darcy trod carefully on cross-examination. He wanted to make it look like Charles was responsible for setting up the offshore accounts.

They finished the first day of testimony with an IRS agent who carefully went through the Tobias financial web and was able to demonstrate the looting of at least $6.9 million in assets. He explained how the trail of money had been lost.

Through it all, Lynne sat stoically, staring at her manicure or twirling her hair. She was barely interested, and clearly bored.

Sandy Campos, Jim Parker, and a few other reporters stepped toward Darcy after the trial broke for the day to ask him a few informal questions.

"Mr. Cole," Sandy began. "Your cross-examination of the IRS seemed to suggest that Charles Tobias was responsible for putting his assets offshore."

Darcy responded. "By all accounts, Charles Tobias was a brilliant attorney. If anyone were to consolidate his assets and move them so that they were undetectable in an offshore account, perhaps for retirement with his beautiful young wife, it would be Charles Tobias. Isn't that a logical conclusion?"

Collata stepped into the courtroom, his massive body filling the large oak doorway. The lights above glinted off his freshly shaved skull.

Darcy begged off from answering any other questions and walked toward Collata.

"I thought I'd have you and Tinkerbell buy me some dinner," Collata said, chewing on a toothpick.

Patrick was packing up materials. He glared at Collata and gave him a mock frown.

"But I'd be happy to carry your shit back to the office," Collata continued. "After all, I don't want an unearned meal."

The three of them headed for the door and Darcy noticed Lynne Tobias leaving on the arm of an unknown and attractive man.

Collata looked across to the opposing counsel table and saw Anna talking with a case agent. She noticed him and nodded slightly.

"Ma'am," he said.

"Collata," she replied.

"You should be careful who you associate with," he said, removing the toothpick. "You don't want your reputation turning to shit."

The agent gave Collata a hard look but had no idea how to respond.

Anna smiled broadly. "Why, Mr. Collata, imagine you being worried about someone's reputation."

Outside the courtroom, Sandy Campos and Jim Parker stood with Darcy, Collata, and Patrick, waiting for the elevator. A reporter from a radio station who tried to get on the elevator with them was abruptly pushed back by Collata.

"Take the next one, pal. We're talking."

The elevator doors shut and the five of them rode down together.

Kathy and Irma were waiting at the office.

"Well?" Kathy asked, as they walked through the door.

"They put on Vanek, the insurance company guy, and an IRS agent as to asset liquidation," Darcy said, loosening his tie.

Patrick immediately chimed in. "Darcy did a good job with the asset liquidation. It could have been Tobias himself getting ready to blow town without having to pay taxes on his retirement nest egg."

Darcy cut in. "It was not a stellar day for us. Anna was very effective. The jury loves her."

"And our client?" asked Kathy.

Collata lit a cigarette. "Well, it seems our client has a new friend. Right after court he walked her out."

"Yeah, it looks like shit," Darcy said. "He sat in the back of the courtroom. The jury thinks he's the new jocker."

"I'm sure he is," Patrick replied.

"Tell her not to bring him again," Darcy instructed.

"Will do."

"Anyway, that's where we stand. Tomorrow they'll probably put on Marty Thiel and his girlfriend, Rona Siegel."

TWENTY-THREE

Marty Thiel strolled into the courtroom, took the oath, and sat in the witness chair. He wore a gray sport coat over a black knit shirt that was buttoned at the top. He had gray slacks, black loafers, and fancy Italian socks.

Anna Minkoff led him through direct examination and didn't pull any punches. She had him tell the jury of the fraudulent policy. He told in detail about the cash he was paid and that he didn't report the cash as income. He didn't tell his company or the IRS. He knew exactly what he was doing. She didn't try to clean him up. She had Thiel explain how he originally lied to the police and the FBI. She went through the deal he was receiving for his testimony.

A small smile crept across Darcy's face and he leaned over to Patrick. Lynne, who was on the other side of Patrick, leaned in to hear what Darcy had to say.

"He's coming off as a complete scumbag," said Darcy. "The jury is going to hate this guy.

"Lawyers, used-car salesmen, and insurance agents," Lynne muttered.

Patrick and Darcy looked at her.

"You know, the three biggest scumbags." She leaned back.

Patrick whispered to Darcy. "Are husband killers fourth?"

Anna tried to minimize the damage to be done on cross by having Marty explain the variations in his testimony. He explained how he agreed to cooperate, then tried to back out by telling different versions. There was even an explanation for the ill-fated bribery attempt by Marty when he had gone to Darcy with the wire.

Darcy rose for the cross-examination.

"Mr. Thiel you were looking at sixty months in prison for your part in this insurance fraud, correct?"

"Yes, sir," Thiel said confidently. He knew what was next.

"Now, based on your testimony, you'll get a pretrial diversion. That means you won't even get prosecuted for your criminal acts, correct?"

"My truthful testimony. I'll get a pretrial diversion based on my truthful testimony. Yes, sir."

It was just as he had practiced it with the government lawyers countless times before the trial. He was still confident.

Darcy smiled at him. "The only people who will decide if your testimony was truthful is this woman here and her fellow prosecutors, correct?" Darcy pointed to Anna.

"Yes," Thiel said hesitantly.

"They have gone over your testimony with you many times, haven't they?"

"Yes," Thiel agreed.

"They told you what questions they would ask and what questions to expect from me, correct?"

"Yes."

Darcy shifted gears. "Do you know Rona Siegel?"

"I've met her," Thiel said.

"When?"

"I don't know. Maybe a few months ago. I met her in the U.S. Attorney's Office."

"So you had no prior relationship with her? By that I mean you met her for the first time while you were being prepared to testify in this trial?"

"I may have met her someplace before, but I don't remember," Thiel said dismissively.

"I assume that means you didn't socialize with her?"

"Oh, no, nothing like that," Thiel said, shaking his head.

"I'm sorry to have to ask you this indelicate question, but you weren't her lover, were you?" Darcy asked, feigning embarrassment.

"Of course not," Thiel said with a slight chuckle.

Darcy walked back to counsel table and picked up a folder. "Mr. Thiel, have you ever gone by any other name?"

Thiel looked amused. "You mean like an alias or something?"

"To be more specific Mr. Thiel, have you ever used the name Steve Dennis?"

Thiel's eyes darted around the courtroom. He thought briefly, then looked at the judge. "I refuse to answer that."

"You have to answer that," Peters replied.

Darcy held up the file. "C'mon, Mr. Thiel, or Mr. Dennis. You know I wouldn't ask the question if I didn't already know the answer. So why don't we tell the jury the whole story?"

Thiel was shrinking into himself. "I have used the name Steve Dennis," he admitted.

"Steve Dennis was the name you used when registered at hotels with Rona Siegel, correct?"

Thiel looked toward Anna for help. The muscles in her jaw flexed as she tried to keep her composure.

"Yes," he said meekly.

"You had a long-term sexual relationship with Mrs. Siegel, didn't you?"

"Yes," Thiel's voice was getting softer.

"When you got arrested, you discussed this with your lover, Mrs. Siegel, correct?"

"Yes."

"She wanted to help you, correct?"

"Yes," his voice was now barely audible.

"Did you bring her to the U.S. attorney in an effort to help yourself?" Darcy was firm but not aggressive. He knew he was getting what he needed. He didn't want the jury to think he was bullying the witness.

"Yes," Thiel replied.

"The U.S. attorney gave you a way to buy yourself out of trouble. All you had to do was testify and get your lover Mrs. Siegel to testify the way they wanted, and you'd get a diversion, correct?"

Darcy liked to use speech questions—he'd give his version of the facts in question form, a tactic difficult to get away with.

"Objection, Judge! Objection!" Minkoff shouted.

"I'll allow it. Go ahead and answer," Peters said, leaning in for the response.

The question lingered. Finally Thiel came up with an answer. "They told me I had to tell the truth. . . ," he said without completing his thought.

"I have no further questions for this witness."

Darcy tossed the folders onto the table in disgust, then sat down and looked at Peters, who returned his glance. Peters appeared to be relishing this latest development.

After the jury's obvious repulsion toward Marty Thiel, they were eager to see Rona Siegel. She was well manicured and expensively dressed. She was also doomed. Rona was called immediately after her secret lover had slithered off the witness stand; Judge Peters refused Anna's request for a brief recess. He wasn't going to let the government tip Siegel that Thiel had given it up. She sailed through her direct examination, answering Anna's questions as they had rehearsed. Anna could think of no way to prepare the witness for what was coming. Finally, Anna had to tender her for cross-examination;

she had no choice. She had told the jury about Rona in her opening statement. If she didn't call her, Darcy would. The jury would then think Anna had orchestrated the whole perjurious mess. She was being forced to sacrifice Rona Siegel to try to win the case. Now she envied Darcy. He had a witness who could only continue to lie or admit the lies. Darcy's going to treat her like a pinata, Anna thought, and each question will knock out more candy.

"Mrs. Siegel, you are a married woman, correct?"

"Yes," she said proudly.

"You took a vow when you got married, much like the oath you took when you took the witness stand, correct?"

"Yes," she said. Now she fiddled with the gold chain around her neck.

"Did you ever tell your husband about your affair with Marty Thiel, also known as Steve Dennis?"

The jury seemed to enjoy the moment. They had watched patiently, waiting for Darcy to confront her.

She was stunned. "That's not true. I never had an affair with Marty Thiel or anyone else. I take my vows seriously," she protested.

"Marty Thiel told us about your long-term affair. It's been going on quite a while."

"He's a damn liar."

"That's probably the first truthful thing you've said since you told us your name."

"Objection!" Anna said, jumping to her feet.

"Ask a question, Mr. Cole," Peters said.

"Okay, here's a question, Mrs. Siegel. Ever been to the Drake Hotel?"

She put her hands over her face. Her world had just collapsed.

Darcy continued, softening up a bit. She had been broken as a witness.

"You wanted to help your lover, so you agreed to testify, correct?"

"I wanted to help Marty, but what I said about your client is true. I just didn't want to admit to adultery. I didn't want to hurt my husband."

"Funny thing about lying, Mrs. Siegel—once you start, it's hard to stop, wouldn't you say?"

She didn't answer.

Darcy let it go. Finally, Peters told her she could step down. She walked through the center of the courtroom, out the doors, and into the unknown. Her extramarital affair would be front-page news in the morning. It would be on the ten o'clock news tonight. Her marriage had probably ended in less than ten minutes.

Mark Thomas, the actual killer, testified next, and he brought his own baggage to the stand.

During Anna's direct examination, Thomas had admitted the murder. He went into detail, explaining how he had prepared for the crime. Anna stuck to her plan of presenting the flippers for what they were. She made no effort to clean him up for the jury.

By the time Anna had finished, Vernon Peters had had enough. He ended testimony close to 5:00, and Darcy asked Lynne to go back to the office with him and Patrick.

They found Collata in the hallway outside the courtroom smoking a cigarette. He looked out at the plaza below.

Patrick carried two catalog briefcases, Darcy a third. Collata walked over and took one from Patrick.

Sandy Campos was in the plaza below getting ready to give a feed for the five o'clock news, and Jim Parker was just a few feet from Darcy, trying to get his attention. When they arrived at the elevator, Darcy nodded for Parker to join them.

Parker dropped his reporter front for a moment. He looked at Darcy and said, "You destroyed them. You had a great day today."

"We'll see," Darcy said. "They have a lot of corroborative evidence."

Jim pulled a pen from behind his ear, flipped over a few pages in his note pad, and found someplace to write. "Well, how about some questions?"

"Can you call me later?" said Darcy.

Parker shook his head. "I have a deadline."

"Give me just an hour, will you?"

"All right, I'll call you."

They walked the press gauntlet back to their office. At one point, a reporter who got too close received a shove from Collata. Normally that would have elicited howls of protest from the other reporters, but no one said a word. They just stared at Collata, who glared back at them.

Irma handed Darcy a stack of messages when he arrived at the office. Collata escorted Lynne to a conference room, and Darcy looked through his messages as he hung his coat up in his office.

Irma stepped in. "Do you need anything?"

"I'd love some ice water," he said.

"No problem. I'll get something for Ms. Tobias, too."

Patrick and Darcy walked together to the conference room. Lynne was sitting at the table, smoking a cigarette.

"Things went pretty well today," Darcy said.

"That's an understatement," Lynne said confidently.

Darcy raised his eyebrows. "My suggestion to you is that you do not testify," he said. "I think we have good momentum, and a very good chance of winning this case. If you testify and do not do well, we could lose everything."

"I have to testify," she said. "This jury isn't going to cut me unless they hear from my own mouth that I didn't do it. I'm going to testify, Darcy."

"Well, understand that it's against my wishes," Darcy warned.

"I understand," she replied. "It's my ass, and I'm going to testify."

"All right, then. I'm guessing we have three days before

your testimony," said Darcy. "They'll probably have two or three days before they rest. I want you with Patrick every night. He's going to put you on the stand."

The announcement caught Patrick by surprise. He was pleased. Up to now he had pretty much been a bystander while Darcy and Anna Minkoff went head to head.

"Why him?" Lynne asked. "Why not you?"

"Because he's great at this. He was a U.S. attorney, so he's used to doing directs. He's very thorough. He'll be able to prepare you for cross. And he's doing it because I say so. I'm running this trial."

She stomped out her cigarette indignantly. "Wrong, Darcy. I'm running this trial. I'm paying for it."

"You're paying for it," he said, "but I'm trying it. Remember, you didn't even finish law school."

At that she tossed her head back and laughed. "You're right, Mr. Cole. I may not have finished law school, but I essentially ran a law firm. And let me tell you, it was a hell of a lot more of a firm than Darcy and his flunkies." With that, she stormed out the door.

At that point Darcy looked at Patrick. "That reminds me. Did you guys ever add your names to the letterhead?"

● ● ●

After a restless night, Darcy was back in the courtroom by 8:30 A.M., ready for the cross-examination of Mark Thomas. He wanted the jury to see Thomas as a lying, murderous thug, someone who would kill for money, certainly someone who would lie to escape punishment. Darcy called attention to numerous inconsistencies in Thomas' testimony.

"Mr. Thomas, when you first got arrested for the murder of Charles Tobias, you confessed to the police, is that correct?"

"Yes."

"You told them you killed the guy in the Mercedes, correct?"

"Yes."

"In fact, on four different occasions you referred to the victim as 'the guy in the Mercedes,' correct?"

"I'll take your word for it," Thomas said, grinning at the jury.

"Oh, don't do that," Darcy countered. "Let me show you a copy of the court-reported statement you gave to Chicago police detectives the night you were arrested."

Darcy asked for and received permission from Judge Peters to approach the witness. He walked across the courtroom holding the typed confession by the corner, as if he'd just plucked it from the trash. The jury watched intently as Thomas shifted nervously in his seat, reading the confession.

"You can see there," Darcy continued, "that you made the reference four times. Was that because you didn't know the victim's name at the time?"

"No, sir. I mean, I knew his name. I just couldn't remember it at the time."

Darcy frowned in disbelief.

"How could you forget the name of your murder victim?"

"Objection!" Anna shouted, rising to her feet.

Judge Peters leaned back in his chair, enjoying the show.

"I'll sustain the objection. Move on, Mr. Cole."

"Mr. Thomas, some nine months after the murder of Charles Tobias, your lawyer cut a deal for you. You would tell the government what they wanted to hear, and they'd reduce your sentence. Is that correct?"

"Objection!"

"No, Ms. Minkoff. Your objection is overruled," Peters said.

"No, I wouldn't put it that way," Thomas answered. "I was in jail and she did nothing to help me. So I figured it was time to help myself."

Darcy tore into him. "C'mon, Mr. Thomas. There isn't a phone record in existence that can prove the two of you ever spoke on the phone, is there?"

"None that I'm aware of," Thomas said sheepishly.

"And there isn't a single witness on this earth who can testify that they saw you speak to Lynne Tobias, is there?"

"None that I know of," Thomas said, looking at Anna.

"Furthermore, Mr. Thomas, you never received any money from Lynne Tobias, did you?"

Thomas looked at Lynne. "She promised, but, no, I never got the money."

The jurors kept shifting their gaze from Darcy to Thomas. With each new question, Thomas nearly bristled. The top two buttons on his shirt were now open. Darcy held the confession above his head.

"Based on what you've testified today, this prior statement is a bunch of lies—except, of course, when you admit to killing *the guy in the Mercedes*!"

Thomas was trapped. He had been prepared to take his hits and get off the stand. He'd just hoped the jury would find him credible for his admissions. Now he was being held accountable for what he'd done.

"From the time you were arrested—up to and including today—you've told a lot of lies, haven't you?" Darcy asked.

"Um, a few, I guess. But not a lot," Thomas conceded.

"And you consider yourself a good liar?"

Anna wanted to object, but she feared the jury would think she was trying to hide something from them. Darcy was excited. He knew Thomas was way off the practiced answers he had gone over with the government lawyers. But Thomas managed to answer the last question.

"Yes, I do," he said.

"So it'd be hard for someone to tell if you're lying or telling the truth, right?"

"I'm telling the truth now," Thomas insisted.

"Well, we'll have to take your word for it, won't we?" Darcy looked at the jurors. Thomas was silent.

"Won't we?" Darcy repeated loudly.

"I guess so," Thomas said sheepishly.

● ● ●

In the days that followed, the government finished its case with a series of filler witnesses who testified about financial transactions, cancelled checks, and how money moves from the United States to an offshore account before it disappears.

Patrick did the cross-examinations, and the government rested its case.

Darcy called a former client of Charles Tobias, who proceeded to testify to a series of intricate financial dealings, which included moving money legally from the United States to the client's offshore accounts in the Cayman Islands. Darcy used his testimony to show that Charles Tobias not only had the means and ability but also experience in moving money offshore. One juror, an accountant, took copious notes.

Darcy then called a hostile Chicago detective who moonlighted at the Drake Hotel. He was forced to testify consistent with his prior statement of the affair between Rona Siegal and Marty Thiel.

Next on the stand was Ira Greenberg. He was a dangerous witness, and Darcy was careful in the questions he posed to him.

"Mr. Greenberg, you knew Marty Thiel was a liar, didn't you?"

"We are always concerned that witnesses testify in a truthful manner."

"So, you wanted some corroboration to Thiel's testimony?"

"Of course. We always look for corroborating witnesses or physical evidence."

"You had no corroborating physical evidence in this case, correct?"

"Correct," Greenberg admitted.

"You couldn't document a single phone call between Mark Thomas and Lynne Tobias so you—"

"Objection!" Anna shouted.

"Sustained," Peters said, raising his eyebrows at Darcy as if to say "Nice try."

"Even though you knew Thiel was a liar you offered him a pretrial diversion in exchange for his testimony?"

"Yes."

"Did Peter Vanek contact you after the acquittal of Lynne Tobias?"

"Yes, he did."

"He wanted Lynne Tobias prosecuted, is that correct?"

"He wanted our office to investigate certain aspects of this case."

"Is it true that Charles Tobias did some legal work for clients who had corporations and bank accounts in the Cayman Islands?"

"Yes, he did."

"Mr. Tobias knew how to move assets offshore, correct?"

"I don't know what he knew."

"But he represented clients who moved assets offshore, correct?"

"He represented clients who transferred money to Cayman banks. That's true."

"He was a smart lawyer?"

"I believe so."

"Mr. Greenberg, you're aware that Marty Thiel lied to federal agents or members of your office after entering into his plea agreement with you, correct?"

"Yes." Ira was making a concerted effort to maintain his cool. He knew that if he let his guard down, Darcy would pounce.

"You're also aware that Mr. Thiel neglected to tell you certain things—important things—since entering into his plea agreement with you?"

"Yes, sir."

"His agreement required him to be truthful and to tell you everything, not to hold back any information, correct?"

"Yes," Greenberg said.

"Is he still getting his pretrial diversion?" Darcy asked.

"Yes, he is," Greenberg answered with a sigh.

Darcy let the answer linger before turning toward Peters. "I have nothing else for this witness."

Ira Greenberg stepped off the stand knowing he would never get beyond acting U.S. attorney.

After Ira's testimony, Vernon Peters called the lawyers up to the bench.

"Well, what do you have left, Darcy?"

"I have my client."

"She is going to be long, I suspect," Peters said. "I don't want to start her and have to kick it over to tomorrow. Why don't we do her first thing in the morning?"

Everybody agreed.

"After that, what do you have, Darcy?"

"I'm done."

"Government, are you going to have any rebuttal?"

"Depends on her testimony, Judge. If she testifies truthfully, then no," Anna said.

"Please," Vernon said, impatiently. "How many rebuttal witnesses do you have?"

"At least one," she said.

"Fine. We'll assume Ms. Tobias is going to testify truthfully, and you'll still put your witness on. Let's get moving so we can close tomorrow afternoon, okay?"

"Well it depends on how long her testimony goes," Anna began, "and then I'd like the opportunity to prepare my closing argument."

"Ms. Minkoff," Peters said, "you've been preparing this closing argument since the day you picked up the file. You don't need any time for that. We're going to go right into closing. We're going to do the jury instructions tomorrow morning before court. Understood?"

"Fine," she agreed, rolling her eyes. "Tomorrow morning."

"I have the instructions on disks, so let's not dink around," Peters said. "Darcy, I want your instructions first thing in the morning. Government, I want you to be ready to make any alterations, including defense instructions. Understood?"

"Yes, Your Honor," they both agreed.

TWENTY-FOUR

Lynne Tobias was in Patrick's office, preparing for her testimony. Darcy was in his own office, staring out the window, when Collata strolled in. He walked to the credenza, opened the drawer, and pulled out his bottle. He poured three fingers and held the bottle up to Darcy. Darcy declined.

"They're going to walk this bitch?" Collata asked.

Darcy turned back toward the window. "Well, we have a shot at it. Her testimony scares me."

"Why?"

"Because she's a lying bitch."

Darcy nodded toward the door. "Close it, would you?"

Collata walked over to the door and pushed it shut with his boot.

"I don't know what they have by way of rebuttal," Darcy said. "They don't have to disclose rebuttal witnesses, so I'm afraid our princess is going to say something that's going to blow up in her face."

"Tell her not to testify."

"I did," Darcy said. "But she knows she has a constitutional right to testify, and she thinks she's smarter than everybody."

"She has a constitutional right to be stupid," Collata said.

Darcy rubbed his eyes. "I'm tired of this shit, Collata. I'm taking a break. I'm going on vacation after this."

"Vacation?" Collata echoed. "You don't know how!"

"I can learn," Darcy said, smiling.

Collata lit a cigarette. "Well that's the first step—deciding to do it. Of course, I'd like to take a trip, too. You going alone?"

Before Darcy could answer, there was a knock at the door.

"You got some good momentum going," Kathy said enthusiastically as she entered.

"Yep. We got a problem tomorrow, though."

"She's insists on testifying, huh?" Kathy said.

"You got it."

"So tell her she can't," Kathy said.

"You tell her she can't," Darcy told her. They both eyed Collata.

"Don't look at me," he said, shaking his head. "I'm not that brave."

TWENTY-FIVE

A buzz arose throughout the courtroom when Patrick called Lynne Tobias to the stand. Everyone watched as she walked to the witness stand, faced the judge, and raised her right hand to be sworn in. She took her seat.

Her hair was pulled back severely, and she wore a string of pearls. Clasping her hands together in front of her, she answered Patrick's questions coolly, in a clear firm voice.

"Did you love your husband?" Patrick began.

"Yes, I did."

She did a convincing job of explaining how she had fallen in love with her late husband. He was a successful man. He usually got what he wanted. The fact that he wanted a younger, prettier wife shouldn't surprise anyone. She felt lucky that she had been the object of his attention. She made the jury understand that when he applied his charm, there was no way she could turn him down.

She described an idyllic honeymoon period, followed by an exciting life full of social opportunities and friends. They seldom argued, and she went so far as to describe the two of them as soulmates, asking forgiveness for using such a cliché. She was convincing as she told the jury how her life would have been better had Charles lived longer. There was no motive to have him dead.

One by one she answered Patrick's questions, each of which prompted an answer that built her credibility. He skillfully led her through the testimony while at the same time trying to humanize her to the jury.

Patrick was nearing the end.

"Ms. Tobias, did you have anything to do with the death of your husband?"

"Absolutely not," she said, looking directly at the jurors.

"Did you pay anyone to have your husband killed?"

"Absolutely not."

"Did you commit fraud with Marty Thiel?"

"Absolutely not."

"Did you sign the document?"

Lynne then explained how, in fact, she'd signed the document with the full knowledge of Marty Thiel and the consent of her husband. He had just been too busy to sign himself.

"Did Mr. Thiel contact you after your husband's death?"

"Yes, he did. He called me and told me he wanted money from me or he would go the police with information of fraud."

"How did you respond to that?" Patrick asked.

"I told him that I'd done nothing wrong. I told him to go ahead and go to the police because he wasn't going to get a dime from me."

"Was that the last you heard from Mr. Thiel?"

"Yes," Lynne said softly.

"Did you have anything to do with your husband's death?"

Lynne began to cry. "No. I loved my husband. I miss him. I did not have anything to do with his death."

Lynne looked Darcy directly in the eye, then shifted her

gaze to the members of the jury. In the process, she managed to coax out two large tears, which sat in her unblinking eyes, waiting for the entrance.

"My husband was my life," she said, emphasizing each word. "Nothing will be the same ever again." The tears rolled, one by one. "And no, I had nothing to do with his death."

Anna showed no mercy in cross-examination. She bored in over and over again trying to trip Lynne up on details. "How many vacations did you take alone last year?"

Lynne remained cool. "I don't know, three or four? I liked to travel, but my husband was a very busy man."

Anna was sarcastic. "It must have been hard for you to travel to the Cayman Islands all by yourself."

A few jurors perked up.

Lynne didn't flinch. She was determined to make the jury believe she had nothing to do with the death of her husband or the disappearance of his money.

Anna herself put on quite an act. She stood behind the podium checking her notes, then walked over to the counsel table and set her notebook down. She then walked back to the podium, as if she had thought of one more thing to ask.

"By the way, Ms. Tobias, do you know someone named Dave Anderson?"

Darcy felt a cold shiver go down his spine. "Objection, Your Honor."

"Overruled. Please answer, Ms. Tobias."

"The name is familiar. I just can't quite place it at the moment."

"Well, do you recall going to a conference in the Cayman Islands in November of 1997?"

"Yes, I was there at a conference that year."

"Can you tell the ladies and gentlemen of the jury what kind of conference it was?"

"It had to do with money and banking, I believe," she answered.

"Offshore money and banking?"

"Yes, it was about the banking laws in the Cayman Islands."

"Do you recall meeting someone named Dave Anderson there?"

"Ah, that's why the name is familiar. I did meet a man named Dave Anderson there."

"At the time you were married to your husband. Is that correct?"

"Well, we were married until the time of his death, so the answer is yes," Lynne said sarcastically.

"Oh, yes," Anna replied. "Till death do you part."

Lynne nervously smoothed back her hair.

"Well, is it true, Ms. Tobias that when you met Dave Anderson at this conference you began having a sexual relationship with him?"

"Objection!" shouted Darcy. He and Patrick stood up together.

"Sidebar," Judge Peters ordered.

The lawyers approached and stood at the side of the bench out of earshot of the jurors. The court reporter was in the middle.

"Where are you going with this, Ms. Minkoff?" Peters asked.

"Judge, she conspired with Dave Anderson to have him kill her husband. When he backed out, she found someone else."

"This is preposterous," Darcy exclaimed. "There's no Dave Anderson on the witness list."

"This is a rebuttal witness, Mr. Cole," Anna said. "Surely you understand that I don't have to tender all my potential rebuttal witnesses. That's absurd."

"Mr. Cole, you'll have to accept the fact that Ms. Minkoff sandbagged you. Now move on."

"That's a bush league move, something I'd expect from Owen Dempsey, but not you," Darcy said.

"Please spare me the show, Darcy. I'm shocked that you let your client take the stand. Perhaps the game is slipping by you, Pops."

"We're going to try this case without any further non-sense," Peters said. "Understood?"

"Understood, Judge." They agreed. Anna continued her line of questioning.

"From November of 1997 until February of 1998, you had a sexual relationship with Dave Anderson, correct?"

Lynne searched for an answer, shifting in her chair before replying. "Yes."

"You told him your marriage had been a mistake, correct?"

"No, that's a lie. I never said that. I loved my husband."

"How does having an affair fit in with your love for your husband?"

"Objection!" Darcy and Patrick said in unison.

"Sustained. Ask your next question, Ms. Minkoff."

"You offered him money to kill your husband, correct?"

"Never," Lynne said defiantly.

"When he refused to kill your husband, you ended the affair, correct?"

"I ended the affair because it was a horrible, regrettable mistake. But I never asked anyone to kill my husband."

"It must have been a big surprise to you when you heard that your husband had been murdered," Anna said sarcastically.

"Objection!"

"Sustained."

"That's okay, Judge, I'm through with the grieving widow."

When it was over the jury knew two things. One was that Dave Anderson was going to testify and two, that Lynne had tried to use sex and money to lure Dave Anderson into killing her husband. When that had failed, she'd moved on until she found Mark Thomas.

Darcy looked up at the court. "No redirect, Your Honor. Thank you."

Lynne walked back to counsel table shaking. Patrick helped her to the chair next to him. With no other option, Darcy rose to his feet.

"Your Honor, at this time the defense would rest."

Peters looked at Anna. "Are you ready to proceed or do you need a break?"

"No, Your Honor, we're ready."

"Proceed."

"We would call Dave Anderson."

Dave Anderson had a deep tan and close-cropped light brown hair. He was clean shaven and wore a conservative navy blue suit, crisp white shirt, and colorful silk tie.

He strode to the witness chair confidently and sat before taking the oath. Judge Peters asked him to stand. He rose, took the oath, unbuttoned his coat, and sat back down.

Patrick reached over and tugged Darcy hard at the elbow.

"Oh, Jesus, Darcy," he whispered. "I know this guy."

"What do you mean?" Darcy asked.

"I know this guy. We need a recess. Now."

Darcy rose to his feet. "Your Honor, may we approach for a sidebar?"

Anna, Darcy, and Patrick stood before the judge.

"What is it, Darcy?"

"We need a brief recess."

"Why didn't you say that before?"

"We didn't know who they were going to call. Now that we know who he is, we want to have a few moments to prepare for his testimony."

"Your Honor," Patrick added. "I would like to have this person's photograph from the government file."

"What file?" Anna asked.

"The file your office creates when you use a cooperating individual. You take his picture and run his fingerprints so you know whether he has any wants or warrants."

"Do you have the file here, Ms. Minkoff?" Peters asked.

"Yes, I think I do."

"Good. Tender the picture. I'll give you fifteen minutes."

"Ladies and gentlemen of the jury," Peters said as he walked back up onto the bench. "We're going to take a fifteen minute break to let you stretch your legs or use the bathroom, and then we'll get right back to it."

"Counsels," he said as the lawyers were walking back, "approach, please."

The U.S. marshals escorted the jury out as the judge leaned in to Anna, Darcy, and Patrick, "You have fifteen minutes. You give him the picture. We're going to wrap this up, then go to argument. You understand?"

"We'll try, Judge," Darcy answered.

"No, trying leaves open the possibility of failure. We are going to do it," he demanded.

Patrick and Darcy stepped out of the courtroom. Patrick already had the photograph in his hand. He saw Collata and motioned him over.

"I gotta take a piss," Collata said. "Why don't you guys join me?"

They followed Collata into the men's room.

"What's up?" Collata asked as he relieved himself.

"How do you know Dave Anderson?" Darcy asked.

"He's notorious in the gay community," Patrick replied. "He likes to seduce old men, then he steals their money. But he goes by the name Carlson."

Collata looked at Patrick and quickly zipped up. "No shit," he said.

"Right, so the guy we need to find, and fast, is named Don Simon," he said. "He owns two bars, one called the Boy's Room and another called Fur Traders."

"Ah, subtle," Darcy said. "Why do we need him?"

"Well, he also owns a shitload of property in Boy's Town—he's a rich old fag. Anyway, this guy Carlson, or Anderson, burned him out of a ton of money and ended up burning a bunch of Simon's friends, too. If I tell Simon that he has a chance to confront Carlson, I guarantee you we're going to bust Carlson in half."

Patrick pulled out his cell phone and walked out of the men's room, already dialing. When Collata and Darcy caught up with him a few moments later in the hallway, he announced, a note of triumph in his voice, "He's getting a cab right now and heading over here. Collata, you meet him at the front entrance and get him up here as soon as you can. I described you to him, so he'll be looking for you."

Darcy and Patrick walked toward the courtroom. Darcy put his hand on Patrick's shoulder. "If this pans out, you're going to be a hero."

"Well, unfortunately our client still looks like a lying murderer," Patrick replied.

"Yeah, but if you blow this guy out of the water, at least I have an argument."

They walked into court and went to counsel table. Anna stepped up to Darcy.

"Do I see another trick up your sleeve, old man?"

Vernon Peters came back into the courtroom. "Okay, lawyers, let's go. We're going to finish this."

Once the jurors were seated, Anna led Dave Anderson through direct. He told of how he had met Lynne Tobias at a seminar in a bank on Grand Cayman. After the first day of the seminar, they had drinks and dinner and ended up in bed. They spent the next three days going to seminars and having sex. Toward the end of their stay Lynne began to bring up the subject of a job she needed done, for which she would pay a lot of money. He was immediately interested, and before long she laid out a scenario for him in which Dave would kill her husband in exchange for a large sum from the insurance proceeds. Anderson testified that at first he didn't think she was serious, but after a while she convinced him she was.

He had never come forward because he didn't know what to do. He had no evidence to prove what she had done. It wasn't until after she had been acquitted in state court that he thought it was important to tell authorities what he knew. He also testified that he received reward money from Peter Vanek and some expense money from the U.S. attorney. Anderson seemed sincere. Darcy worried that the jury was buying his act.

Patrick leaned into Darcy. "He's my witness. I'm crossing him. You wouldn't know what to ask."

Darcy nodded. "That's fine with me."

Patrick rose for his cross-examination. He looked at Dave Anderson, who did not recognize him.

"Sir, have you ever used the name Dave Carlson?"

Anna jumped to her feet. "Objection, Your Honor. Not relevant."

"I don't know. He hasn't answered the question," Peters said. "Let's hear it. Overruled."

"Have I ever used the name Dave Carlson?"

"Yes, sir, that was the question. Have you ever used the name Dave Carlson?"

Anderson stared at Patrick, obviously trying to place his face.

Just then the door at the back of the courtroom opened, and Collata walked in with a well-dressed man in his late sixties. He was silver-haired, distinguished, and casually dressed.

Anderson saw the man in the back of the courtroom and sunk into his chair, as if trying to hide.

"Again, sir, have you ever used the name Dave Carlson?" Patrick asked.

"Yes, I have," the witness responded quietly.

Patrick turned and nodded to Collata, who then took the man with him out of the courtroom to wait.

Patrick smiled. "Do you know a man named Don Simon?"

Anderson sat staring at Patrick.

"Sir, did you hear my question?"

Still nothing. Peters leaned toward the witness.

"Sir, please answer the question."

"Yes," Anderson admitted.

"You've testified about a sexual relationship with Lynne Tobias, but you also had a sexual relationship with Don Simon, correct?"

"Objection. Side bar," Anna was furious.

The lawyers met Judge Peters in the corner of the court-room away from the jury.

"Where's this going, counsel?" Peters asked.

"This man is a criminal," Patrick said. "He has defrauded a number of people. Don Simon is one of his victims. This evidence will destroy his credibility and is clearly relevant."

"I have no notice of this witness, Don Simon," Anna protested. "What kind of game are you guys playing?"

"Maybe it's just that you haven't played the game long enough, sweetie," Darcy said gleefully.

"Okay, children, let's get back to work. Don't stray, counsel, or I'll shut you down," Peters said pointing a finger at Patrick.

Patrick dropped a note pad on the podium that faced the witness.

"You had a sexual relationship with Don Simon and stole over $50,000 from him by writing yourself checks from his account. Isn't that right, Mr. Carlson?"

"I refuse to answer that question."

"Is that Carlson or Anderson?"

"I refuse to answer that question."

"How many men have you had sexual affairs with and stolen money from?"

"I refuse to answer that question. I assert my Fifth Amendment right to remain silent and I demand a lawyer."

Patrick pushed forward. "You mean you will not answer my questions because a truthful answer would incriminate you?"

Carlson kept repeating his refusal to answer questions.

"I refuse to answer that question. I want to consult an attorney."

Dave Anderson refused to admit to the jury that he was a liar, a con man, and a thief. Then again, he didn't have to, thanks to Patrick.

Anna Minkoff sat fuming as her witness unraveled before the jury.

After Patrick's cross-examination of Anderson, Anna declined to ask any more questions. She was disgusted. She had given Darcy an unintended break. Don Simon's testimony was almost anticlimactic, as the jury already knew all they needed to know from Carlson's witness-stand meltdown. They proceeded to closing arguments.

Anna rose to her feet and went on the attack.

Anna stood behind the podium. She had no notes. The jury watched as she gathered her thoughts.

"You know, ladies and gentlemen, this was like two separate trials. The government gave you evidence of insurance fraud. We're asking you to convict Lynne Tobias for insurance fraud. Mr. Cole and Mr. O'Hagin have concentrated on the murder of Charles Tobias. I think they wanted to remind you that a different jury did not believe that state prosecutors proved Ms. Tobias guilty of murder beyond a reasonable doubt. Of course, you should remember that being found not guilty is not the same as being declared innocent."

"Objection!" Darcy said.

"Overruled," Peters replied.

"She gets a pass on the murder. We also know that more than six million dollars is missing from the estate of Charles Tobias. The adulterer, the opportunist, the woman signing her husband's name on insurance forms."

Anna began to pace. She walked toward Lynne and pointed her finger.

"Look at her. That's the true face of evil. She has never shown any true sorrow over her husband's death. She never felt the slightest remorse when she broke up Charles's marriage and family. You saw the real Lynne Tobias. She lied to you. She was caught lying and responded by blaming everybody else. According to her Marty Thiel is a liar, Rona Siegel is a liar, Dave Anderson is a liar, everybody's a liar. But she has some problems. Even if you throw out the testimony of these witnesses, you're still left with the fact that even Ms. Tobias admits she signed Charles's name on the insurance policy. A policy which pays her upon Charles's death. Shortly after the policy goes into effect, her husband is murdered. Remember, this is not a murder case. We don't need to prove the murder. We have to prove insurance fraud. We did that. She signed her husband's name to the policy. Now it's time for you to sign your name to a guilty verdict."

Anna took one last look at Lynne. The jurors followed her lead and studied Lynne. She sat still with her hands folded on the table in front of him. Anna wanted the jury to notice Lynne's lack of emotion. They did. Anna took her seat.

Finally Darcy had his moment. He strolled to the podium and looked over the jury.

"This case is about money and power. Lynne Tobias married an older, wealthy man. That was what he wanted. He always got what he wanted. He reached a stage in his life where he wanted a trophy wife. That left bitterness among a host of people close to him. His ex-wife, his children, his law partners, and their spouses all were furious with Lynne. They would never accept her and placed the blame for this marriage at her feet. When Mark Thomas tried to rob a rich old guy in a Mercedes and ended up killing him, none of these people could accept the fact that this stupid, tragic crime took Charles from them. They needed to blame Lynne. Mark Thomas didn't know it when he first talked to the police, but he was going to get an enormous break. Instead of the death penalty, he would have a chance of getting parole one day. All he had to do was tell them what they wanted to hear. The liars were bought and paid for. The government didn't take witnesses that Lynne Tobias had selected. They took witnesses who would say anything.

"Ladies and gentlemen of the jury, what you've seen in this courtroom is the most despicable display of purchased perjury I have ever witnessed. Mark Thomas killed Charles Tobias. He was caught by the police and promptly confessed. At the time he confessed, he had never heard of Lynne Tobias. He didn't know the name of the guy in the Mercedes, the man he murdered. But as with everything else in this case, there's a strange twist. He got handed a get-out-of-jail card—all he had to do was parrot out a speech, written by the government, to you jurors. But, hey, what's a little perjury? It's not like shooting a man. So nine months after the murder, Mark Thomas cut a deal with the people who had the key to his prison cell.

"The government realized that no jury in the world would believe Mark Thomas. What to do? Get some corroboration. Uh-oh, another problem. Try as they might and using the Chicago Police Department, the FBI, Secret Service, the U.S. marshals, the Postal Inspector, the CIA, the Navy, the psychic network, and public television, they couldn't come up with any corroboration for Mark Thomas's fantasy testimony. Enter Marty Thiel. The FBI threatened Thiel, then offered him a way out—tell us what we want to hear and we'll let you go, no charges filed.

"But Marty Thiel had his own problems. Enter Rona Siegel. What a wonderful stroke of luck for the government that Rona Siegel, the good Samaritan, stepped forward to give testimony to corroborate Thiel and Thomas. But then, *kaboom,* the case exploded because we exposed Rona. She wants you to excuse her perjury because she was trying to spare her husband's feelings. Sorry, Mrs. Siegel. Try the Oprah show."

"Ladies and gentlemen, look at this beautiful courtroom. At first glance you would think that this room and this courthouse are monuments to justice in America. Well, you'd be wrong. These are monuments to the business of justice. The government had a theory. To try to convict Lynne Tobias on that theory, they were willing to spend any amount of money necessary. They spent it on agents, investigators, and lawyers they've used in this case. They bought witnesses with promises of sentence reductions or dropped charges. While the burden was, is, and will remain with the government to prove this case beyond a reasonable doubt, we have gone beyond simply defending Lynne Tobias. We have exposed government witnesses as liars, perjurors, and, in the case of Mark

Thomas, murderers. This case demonstrates how the government has perverted the justice system. It's no longer about justice. It's about winning.

"You will soon get this case. It will be yours. Neither I nor the government will be there with you while you deliberate. Judge Peters will not be there. Your verdict will be solely yours. Is it possible to find Lynne Tobias guilty beyond a reasonable doubt in a case where the three star witnesses are Mark Thomas, Marty Thiel, and Rona Siegel? Can the government buy a verdict in this case? If you believe in the business of justice, then you'll let the government buy your verdict. If you believe in justice then you must let them know. Find Lynne Tobias not guilty."

There was so much adrenaline coursing through Darcy's body, he didn't think he'd be able to sit down. It was a wonderful, familiar feeling, an odd mix of excitement and tranquility.

He walked back to his table, stopping a moment to wrap his arm around Lynne before sitting down. It was a gesture for the jury. He wanted them to see some emotion even if it had to come from him. Lynne's cool facade had him worried.

Peters nodded toward Anna. "Ms. Minkoff, your rebuttal argument." She popped to her feet.

Anna place her note pad on the podium, then began to pace before the jury.

"Boy, that was some performance by Mr. Cole. I really enjoyed it. One thing struck me during his show, though. Let me remind all the members of the jury that this isn't a murder trial. We all know that Lynne Tobias will never have to answer for the murder of her husband. No, she was acquitted of that and in this country our justice system does not allow a person to be tried for the same crime twice. If they're convicted they can get the case reversed on appeal, but we can't get an acquittal reversed. So, no, this isn't a murder trial. The question you have to answer is whether Lynne Tobias committed insurance fraud.

"But don't you find it odd that Mr. Cole avoided any reference to insurance fraud? The three witnesses Mr. Cole calls perjurors are primarily motive witnesses. And believe me, if we hadn't given you evidence of motive, Mr. Cole would have screamed about the lack of motive. We don't need to prove motive; we only need to prove fraud. In fact, we have proven all the elements of fraud, all beyond a reasonable doubt. So what about these three witnesses? If you don't like them, blame Ms. Tobias. She selected the witnesses when she asked Mark Thomas and Marty Thiel to help her carry out this criminal enterprise. She chose them; we merely caught them. I assure you if I could buy witnesses as Mr. Cole has suggested, I'd have bought better witnesses at less cost.

"Ladies and gentlemen, don't let Mr. Cole confuse you. This case comes down to one simple question: Did Lynne Tobias commit insurance fraud? The evidence of fraud is overwhelming and beyond any reasonable doubt. Please feel free to accept for sake of argument the testimonies of Mr. Thiel, Mr. Thomas, and Mrs. Siegel can be discarded. You still have the handwriting expert's testimony that Ms. Tobias signed her husband's name to that policy application. She was the only beneficiary. And shortly after her husband was murdered, she made a claim for the proceeds of the policy.

"Ladies and gentlemen, the time has come to hold Lynne Tobias responsible for her actions. Based on the evidence and the law, you must find Lynne Tobias guilty. I ask for your verdict."

TWENTY-SIX

Lynne Tobias sat in the client chair across from Darcy's desk.

"How long have they been out?" she asked, putting out one cigarette and fishing through her bag for another.

Darcy looked at his watch. "About five and a half hours."

"Will Peters send them to a hotel, or will he make them deliberate all night?"

"He'll probably keep them there until about ten, then send them to a hotel. He'll bring them back in the morning to start over."

"Well, I just hope you convinced them," she said, suddenly changing her demeanor. "Now, let's talk about what we're going to do after this is behind us."

Darcy looked at her curiously.

"What did you have in mind?"

"I was thinking maybe I could take you somewhere—a

trip," she said, ignoring his pessimism. "It's the least I can do after everything you've done."

"Whoa," Darcy said, shaking his head. "Let's get through this verdict first."

He walked her out to the waiting room.

"It could be minutes, or it could be hours," he said. "You don't have to stay here. Just make sure we know where you are."

She put her arm on Darcy's shoulder, leaned up, and kissed him on the cheek. "It's going to be okay. I'm confident."

Darcy walked down the hall to Seymour's office. Seymour immediately cleared off his desk to set up the chess board.

"Scotch?" he asked.

"No, I'm waiting for a jury," Darcy said.

He moved a pawn and the game began.

"Guess what? I'm going on vacation."

Seymour countered Darcy's move and looked up at him, "Really? When are you leaving?"

"After the verdict," he said. "I'm spent. I need a break."

"I think it's a great idea," Seymour said, watching Darcy ponder his next move.

"Other than that, how are you doing?" Seymour asked.

"Well, I've been reading the Good Book. I've come to one conclusion."

"What's that?"

"There's no answer there for me."

Seymour chuckled. "Well, I don't know that there are answers there, but sometimes there are guidelines. So, do you have a particular vacation spot in mind?"

"Actually, I think I do."

"Care to share?"

"Not really," said Darcy. "There's someone else involved. I have to find out how she feels first."

It wasn't Seymour's style to pry.

Darcy moved a queen. "Checkmate."

Seymour looked at the board, stunned. "You son of a bitch! You beat me."

"Yes, I did," Darcy said. "And I just hope it's an indication of what's to come."

Darcy walked back to his office. Lynne was gone, but Owen Dempsey was seated the waiting room. Since there was no way of avoiding it, Darcy invited him in.

As they were walking into Darcy's office, Patrick appeared.

"Nothing yet, Boss," he said.

Owen looked at Patrick. "I heard you did a fantastic job—great cross-examination, couple of good directs. Congratulations."

"Well, we don't have a verdict yet."

"That doesn't change your performance," said Owen. "You still did a great job. By the way, I'm sorry I didn't do more for you when things got out of hand."

Patrick shook his hand. "Please. You did me a favor. I'll leave you two gentlemen to your business." He went out, closing the door behind him.

Owen handed Darcy an envelope. It contained a cashier's check for $250,000, made out to Darcy.

"That'll get you started, won't it, Darcy?" The old Dempsey swagger flashed just for a moment.

"Yeah, I suppose," Darcy said. "You got yourself a lawyer. But I'm going on vacation, so Patrick's going to work it up until I get back."

"Okay with me. Besides, they still haven't charged me or given me a grand jury letter, so we still have time. If I get contacted, I'll let them know your office is representing me."

"Fine."

Owen looked at him. "All bullshit aside, you're the best, Darcy. I know you'll go to the mat for me. Not because you like me, but because I'm a client. That's what you do, Darcy. You're a lawyer."

Darcy shook Dempsey's hand and watched him leave, then turned and looked out the window. He stared at the Federal Building. Somewhere in the upper floors behind a courtroom, twelve people were deciding the fate of Lynne Tobias.

At 8:40 P.M., Patrick knocked on Darcy's door. "We got a verdict," he said.

"Where's our client?"

"She's downstairs in the bar."

"Get her," Darcy said. "Let's go."

It was close to 9:15 by the time everyone had assembled. The gallery was full of news media. Vernon Peters sent the U.S. marshals out to let everyone in the courtroom know there were to be no outbursts when the verdict was returned.

Darcy looked over to the far corner and saw the Tobias family, along with Peter Vanek and James Ryan, seated in the first row. No one was there for Lynne.

Darcy could almost hear his heart pounding and his blood pumping. Anna was writing furiously on a note pad. Darcy assumed she was doodling—he'd done the same thing in this exact situation.

Peters entered the courtroom. He looked at Darcy, catching his eye and giving him a very slight nod. He then did the same to Anna. He was letting them know he thought they had done a good job. In a moment the jury would rule, and there would be a winner and a loser. Peters didn't care about the verdict. He wanted them to know that they had both tried the hell out of the case.

He looked at his clerk.

"Bring the jury in."

The jurors found their seat, and the foreperson, a dentist from Wheaton, held the verdict form.

"Madam Foreperson, have you reached a verdict?" Peters asked.

"We have, Your Honor."

"Is it unanimous?"

"Yes, it is, Your Honor."

"Would you hand it to the marshal, please."

The marshal took it and strode across the courtroom to Peters. The judge looked it over, then handed it to his clerk.

"Will the clerk read the verdict, please?"

The clerk stood with the verdict in hand and in a loud voice read, "In the matter of the *United States of America versus Lynne Tobias,* on the count of insurance fraud, we the jury find the defendant, Lynne Tobias, guilty."

Anna's expression didn't change, but below counsel table, she gently pumped her fist.

Lynne put her hands over her face, shaking her head. Darcy put his hand on her shoulder. He was shocked and disappointed, and he asked that the jurors be polled. One by one, they were asked if that was their verdict. One by one, they affirmed it.

Lynne Tobias was going to prison.

The jurors were whisked back into the jury room with the promise that the judge would speak to them.

Post-trial motions were now at hand. The first was the government's request to revoke bond. Judge Peters granted their request, and Lynne Tobias was taken into custody. Peters allowed Darcy a moment with her in the lockup.

"You've got to get me out of here," she pleaded.

"I'll do what I can. The only thing we have now are the post-trial motions and appeal."

"You know the money is there, Darcy. Get me out of here. I'm not staying in prison."

"I'll come to see you soon."

"Tomorrow," she said emphatically.

"Well, actually, I'm going out of town. I won't be able to see you until I get back."

"No, you're not!" she screamed. "You're staying here to finish your job! I'm not paying you all this money so you can take a goddamn vacation!"

"You're right, Lynne," Darcy said. "You are paying me a lot of money. But unlike you, my life won't be ruled—and ultimately ruined—by money."

TWENTY-SEVEN

Darcy cleared customs and walked to the taxis. It would be easier to take the underground, but he wasn't going to let his first moments in London take place inside a subway.

He got into one of the old-fashioned black cabs and gave an address in Kensington Gardens, then he sat back and watched the scenery, grateful for the silence from the driver. As he took in the sights, he felt relaxed, with a sense of direction he hadn't had in years.

He paid for the ride and tipped well, then entered the luxury condo building. He was met by a doorman.

"My name is Darcy Cole," he said. "I believe Mr. Espinoza made arrangements for me."

"Yes, sir," the doorman said, directing him to an elevator. "You have the penthouse."

The elevator opened to a short hallway with double doors.

Darcy knocked on the doors and was greeted almost instantly by a manservant.

"Mr. Cole," he said. "Welcome to London."

"I left my bags with the doorman," he said. "Will they be okay?"

"Yes, sir, I will tend to them. We have tea waiting for you on the balcony."

Darcy walked through the massive, exquisite penthouse and onto the balcony. The evening was dry and cool, but the sun was still shining. He heard someone approaching and turned around, then he smiled broadly.

"You made it," he said.

Anna Minkoff strode onto the balcony. Darcy threw his arms around her. She held him tightly.

"I'm so happy we're here," she said.

Darcy looked at Anna fondly. "You tried a great case."

"It's in my blood," she said. "And, Dad? You made me very proud, as usual."

"Good, then. You'll join me at my firm? You would be a partner."

"Dad," she said. "You know we've talked about that—"

"Hey," Darcy interrupted, "it's every father's dream to build a business to share with his children. Besides, you're not a bad trial lawyer."

"Seriously, Dad, I have to tell you. Most of the people in the office think you took all of Lynne's money."

"What do you think?" Darcy asked.

"I don't think so. First of all, she is a client and, corny as it sounds, I don't think you would betray the attorney-client trust. Second, money isn't that important to you. Last, it would make you no different from the rest of the thieves in our profession."

"You do have a high opinion of me. Of course, the attorney-client privilege precludes me from ever telling you the true answer to that question."

"Sure," she said, rolling her eyes. "But I do have one other question. Who took care of the tapes for you in the *Espinoza* case?"

"Anna, I'm surprised. You know I can't give up the identity of a flipper. Let's just say that when Patrick was forced out of the prosecutor's office, he wasn't the only one who didn't want his sex life revealed."

"You blackmailed someone?" Anna exclaimed.

"No. One of the bigshots over there didn't like what happened to Patrick. He felt bad that he didn't have the courage to step forward. He didn't want to lose his wife and kids. He didn't want anyone to know his secret. So instead of stepping forward, he sabotaged the *Espinoza* case. He wanted to bring down Owen Dempsey and Ira Greenberg."

"He sure did that," Anna said.

They drank their tea, looking out over the city.

"Now what?" Anna asked. "We both deserve a break. After this, why don't we travel a little bit?"

"Hmm. I don't think so. I'm going back to Chicago."

"Why? You've done everything there is to do in Chicago. You have enough money. And it's not like you have any friends." She smiled and sipped her tea.

"Exactly, Anna. I've come to a conclusion about my life. It's not a flattering conclusion, but it rings true. Law is my identity, and I like being a lawyer. It's not about money. I've finally figured out what's been missing. It's simply justice. If there's a case I want to try, I'm going to try it whether I get paid well or not. Once in a while, justice has to be served. Don't get me wrong, it's still a business, but it's not going to be just business anymore.

"The first thing I'm going to do is to represent John Kennedy Watkins."

"Who is that? It's not another rich guy from a screwed-up family, is it?" she asked.

"No, definitely not. He's just a guy who needs a good lawyer. He's up on murder charges."

"A state court murder case?" Anna asked incredulously.

"That's right. He needs a lawyer, and I'm his man. His mother has $10,000 as a retainer. That's all. When Irma and Kathy had me talk to this guy's mom, I finally figured it out. I've gone from being a highly paid advocate to being a businessman. But you know what? I didn't go to law school to be a businessman. I'm going to try the hell out of John Kennedy Watkins's case. He's going to get the best representation I can give him."

"Good for you. I admire that."

"Then come work for me. I'll make you a name partner," he said.

"That's right, you will. And hey, I could try a state murder case. I've never done a state case."

Darcy smiled. "I'm hearing nasty rumors that you may get the nomination to be the U.S. attorney."

"Hmm, me too," she said. "And you know, I thought that's what I wanted. But now I'm thinking I might want to join a firm run by a crazy old man who wants to do cases for free. You're going to need me to protect the firm."

"Is that a yes?" Darcy asked.

Anna leaned over and kissed him on the cheek. "It's a maybe."

About the Author

Larry Axelrood practices law in Chicago and is a former prosecutor in the State's Attorney's office in Cook County. A member of the National Association of Criminal Defense Lawyers, he is a graduate of Indiana State University and the Chicago Kent College of Law. A native Chicagoan, Axelrood and his family live in Evanston, Illinois. *The Advocate* is his first novel.